JAN - 2010

THE
731
LEGACY

THE 731 LEGACY

LEGACY

A COTTEN STONE MYSTERY

LYNN
SHOLES **&** JOE
MOORE

MIDNIGHT INK
WOODBURY, MINNESOTA

First Edition
First Printing, 2008

Book design and format by Donna Burch
Cover design by Kevin R. Brown
Editing by Connie Hill

Midnight Ink, an imprint of Llewellyn Publications

Library of Congress Cataloging-in-Publication Data
Sholes, Lynn.
  The 731 legacy : a Cotten Stone mystery / Lynn Sholes & Joe Moore. —
1st ed.
      p.   cm. — (Cotten Stone mystery ; 4)
  ISBN 978-0-7387-1317-5
  1. Stone, Cotten (Fictitious character)—Fiction. 2. Women journalists—
Fiction. 3. Bioterrorism—United States—Fiction. 4. Korea (North)—Foreign
relations—United states—Fiction. I. Moore, Joe, 1948–. II. Title.
III. Title: Seven hundred thirty-one legacy.
  PS3619.H646A615 2008
  813'.6—dc22

                                                            2008020054

Midnight Ink
Llewellyn Publications
2143 Wooddale Drive, Dept. 978-0-7387-1317-5
Woodbury, MN 55125-2989 USA
www.midnightinkbooks.com

Printed in the United States of America

ACKNOWLEDGMENTS

The authors wish to thank the following for their assistance in adding a sense of realism to this work of fiction:

Brian W. J. Mahy, MA, PhD, ScD, DSc
Senior Scientific Advisor
Coordinating Center for Infectious Diseases
Centers for Disease Control

CDR James P. Cody, USN
Commanding Officer
USS *Robert G. Bradley* (FFG 49)

Dr. Nelson Erlick, DPM
Author of *The Xeno Solution* and *GermLine*

Special thanks to Nancy Barba, Leon Clinch, Nancy Cohen, Carol Moore, Denise Pack, Tommy Sholes, and Mark Terry, and to our agent, Susan Ann Protter, and editor, Barbara Moore.

NOTES FROM THE HISTORICAL RECORD

#1. In 1941, a division of the Imperial Japanese Army was formed and called the *Epidemic Prevention and Water Purification Department.* Disguised under the innocent-sounding title, the group's real purpose was to promote the belief in Japanese racial superiority.

The EPWP conducted horrific medical experiments, causing the deaths of tens of thousands of civilians and military personnel from China, Korea, Mongolia, and Russia. An ultra secret unit of the EPWP experimented with biological weapons research, resulting in an estimated 200,000 additional deaths. Untold numbers of atrocities were committed in the name of science by the group known as Unit 731.

#2. In 2006, researchers in France recreated a five-million-year-old virus whose remains are scattered across the human genome. This ancient retrovirus inserted copies of its genetic material into our DNA. The remnants of those copies in our DNA, human endogenous retroviruses, or HERVs, make up about 8 percent of our genetic code. Most of the copies have mutated over the millennia to the point that they are obsolete. However, scientists have found one that can still alter itself into new, infectious virus particles. Scientists at the Gustave Roussy Institute in Villejuif, France successfully resurrected one of the retroviruses, calling it Phoenix after the mythical bird reborn from its own ashes. This group of scientists also found indications that some of the other HERVs in our genomes might still be infectious.

"Most dangerous is that temptation that doth goad us on to sin in loving virtue."
—William Shakespeare
Measure for Measure, Act II, Scene II

SUBWAY

CALDERON KNEW HE WAS dying as he shoved the token in the slot before stumbling through the turnstile and down the steps to the subway platform. The rumble of the train, even though muffled by the clotted blood in his ears, sent a spear of searing pain shooting through his skull.

Calderon braced his head with both hands until the train finally came to a stop, its doors sliding open with a hiss. He wasn't sure how long his legs would hold him. The raging 105-degree fever seemed to be melting his bones into what felt like a slurry of molten marrow. He snatched a gulp of air, and it howled through his airways like wind in a chimney.

Get on the train. Move. Get on the train.

Laboring, Calderon trapped himself in the flow of boarding passengers, their bodies pushing him along.

There were no seats available, only a spot for his hand to grip a pole. Just as he wrapped his fingers around it, a deep croupy cough clutched up in his chest. With his free hand, he covered his lips with a handkerchief, and the coppery taste of blood-streaked mucous sprayed the inside of his mouth. The flecks of phlegm bloomed like miniature scarlet geraniums, seeping through the threads of the white cloth.

The train lurched, and Calderon rocked sideways, bumping a young man with an earphone crammed in his ear and an iPod clipped to his belt.

"What the—" The young guy stared at the handkerchief. He let go of the pole and stepped back. "What's the matter with you, man?"

Like dominos, the passengers' attentions turned to focus on Calderon. They retreated from him, crowding into the opposite ends of the subway car.

"Oh, my God," a woman said, using her hands like a surgical mask.

Calderon wiped his face, breaking loose the crusts of dried blood and spittle from the corners of his mouth. He didn't blame the passengers for staring or for feeling disgust alongside their horror. They had good reason.

His eyes burned and his skin hurt to touch. The five ibuprofen tablets he choked down an hour ago hadn't seemed to dent the pain or the fever. Probably made the bleeding worse. He felt a warm, thick trickle drip from his nose and again heard gasps. He wiped away the blood with the back of his hand, smearing it across his cheek.

The train pulled into the next station, and all the passengers except Calderon fought their way through the open doors.

The first incoming passenger froze in the doorway before backing out and stretching his arms like a gate. "Stop!" he yelled. "Nobody get on the train."

"What's going on?" a man said, forcing his way past. "Get outta my way." But then, as his eyes landed on the sole occupant of the car, he bolted back. "Holy shit."

The doors slid closed, and Calderon watched the faces staring at him through the window. In a moment the train was in the darkness of the tunnel, and he closed his eyes. He wheezed a shallow breath and again was overcome by a strangling cough. He tried to stifle it. Over the last twenty-four hours he had learned that each time he coughed it irritated his airways even more, bringing about a fit of uncontrollable spasmodic hacking. He kept his mouth closed, coughing as if in a theater and not wanting to disturb anyone. His cheeks flared with the gush of air from his lungs, but the force behind the cough burst through. A jet of blood and mucous spewed out, splattering the pole, and a fine pink cloud floated in the air. After several minutes his lungs rested. Time was running out.

The next stop would be his last. He was almost there. This time when the doors opened, Calderon nearly fell out onto the platform. He saw the expressions of those who looked at him in total revulsion. He lowered his head and kept his eyes cast on the concrete. Halfway up the stairs, he grabbed the railing, doubting he could go on. He stopped and propped his side against the wall for a moment before continuing to the sidewalk.

The fever had him shivering, and he thought about what a paradox that was. His body was burning up and what he felt, except for the scorching in his eyes, was a bottomless chill.

Only half a block to go.

He approached the front entrance to his final destination.

The crowd on the street seemed to part like the Red Sea when God divided it to save the Israelites from the Egyptians. But he knew this was not the work of God. It was the result of the terror that took hold of the pedestrians at the sight of a nearly fleshless skeleton of a man whose eye sockets were soot black and every orifice leaked blood and body fluids.

Calderon pushed through the revolving doors into the lobby of the Satellite News Network. Then all his remaining strength caved in and his knees buckled. He collapsed face down on the marble floor.

An SNN security officer was first at his side. Squatting, he pressed the button on his shoulder-mounted mic and said, "Code red. Dial nine-one-one." Slowly, he maneuvered Calderon onto his side. "Jesus Christ!" He reared back at the sight.

Calderon opened one eye. He felt the strings of mucous that glued his lips together, stretch as he spoke.

"Cotten Stone. I must speak to Cotten Stone."

MOON RISE

Chung Moon Jung tried to calculate how many people she was going to kill as she stood on the sidewalk under the lone streetlamp. Most of the city lights were turned off, causing details to be lost in darkness. Only a scattering of lights reflected off the Taedong River. Across the water, stark government buildings and apartment complexes formed a harsh skyline.

Moon's gaze took in the shadowy shapes of the two ships moored at the river's edge: the USS *Pueblo*, the armed spy ship seized in 1968 from the U.S. imperialist aggression forces, and the Oceanautics research vessel *Pitcairn*, taken only a year ago after it drifted into North Korean waters. They were two examples of North Korea's ability to thumb its nose at the West. The *Pueblo* had brought the Communist nation a bargaining chip on the world stage while the *Pitcairn* had delivered a means to dominate the stage.

Moon pulled a photograph from the inside pocket of her coat. In the soft glow of the streetlight, she looked upon the fading black and white image of her parents. The sting of recalling their fates still twisted inside her, the pain never letting up.

As she touched the photograph, her finger lightly hovered on her mother's face. A lifetime ago. Moon was now more than twice the age of her mother at the time the picture was taken. She looked at the photograph often, never wanting to forget.

"Dr. Chung?" Her driver held up a cell phone as he stood beside her sleek black limo parked a dozen yards away.

She slipped the photo back into her pocket. Turning from the river and the two ships, she said, "Yes?"

"He is ready to see you."

———

Moon watched the General Secretary savor the last sip of green tea before placing his cup on the small, cherrywood table. He leaned back in his chair; a signal the meal was finished. Instantly, a servant rushed forward, removing the dishes. A second servant brought a porcelain pot of fresh tea, filling the General Secretary's cup. The servant offered more to Moon, but she held her hand up in refusal. When the table was cleared and the two were alone in the small private dining room, the General Secretary said, "I dreamed of your father last night."

"Dear Leader," Moon said with a slight head bow, "he would be most honored to know that. For only those who have the highest love and devotion for you are worthy of a place in your dreams. I, too, often dream of him. He was a great man." She raised her cup to her lips as she admired the row of two-thousand-year-old vases along one wall.

"They're from the *Baekje* Kingdom."

"Beautiful, Dear Leader. We have such a rich heritage. It is contemptible that savages divided our beloved land with such an arbitrary border."

"You are correct in referring to them as savages."

"And they will soon feel our wrath," Moon said. "The Americans and all their allies will be paid back for the death and destruction they have spread across the globe."

"You have made amazing progress, Dr. Chung, in the year since the *Pitcairn* death ship was found. We are most fortunate that it fell into our hands before the United States could retrieve it."

"I considered it an omen, Dear Leader. A sign that we were meant to achieve our revenge. That which we are about to execute is guided by the hand of fate."

"The satellite medical labs are all in place?"

"And fully functional. We have borrowed a term from the computer industry and are calling each field test a *ping*."

The General Secretary shrugged. "I don't understand the term."

"When a technician wants to confirm that his computer can communicate with another computer, he pings it."

"Oh," he said with an expression of revelation. "Like our submarine fleet pings other vessels?"

"Exactly. With each ping, we see the results of the virus and how it reacts to the genes of various races. At this point, we are down to a handful of groups. So far, all are perfect recipients."

"And how are those *pings* being delivered?"

"Aerosols, throat sprays. Whatever is appropriate and we think will work for the target."

"Ahh, and while the imperialists wring their hands over our so-called nuclear weapons program, they have no idea we are really planning their demise in a most unexpected manner."

Moon smiled with self-satisfaction as she brushed a strand of silver hair from her face.

"Debts must be paid, Dr. Chung. We were betrayed many times in the past. There will be no more betrayals because there are no more negotiations. No more deals. No more talk. The days of the imperialists and the corrupt communists are about to end. We will watch as our enemies all begin to die. Soon their citizens will become paralyzed by fear. They will be afraid to leave their homes, afraid to go to their jobs or send their children to school, afraid to come in contact with one another. There will be no safe place. And as each country falls into chaos and anarchy, world dominance will come to us like a sparrow upon the breeze. We will win by the simple process of elimination. You are about to unleash Hell, Dr. Chung, and cause our enemies to feel the wrath of Black Needles."

LAST WORDS

"How long will you be in New York?" Cotten Stone asked before taking a sip of coffee. She sat in a booth of her favorite deli on Broadway, a few blocks south of the world headquarters and studios of the Satellite News Network. Across from her was John Tyler, her closest friend, confidant, and the unfulfilled love of her life. In the eyes of the world, Cardinal John Tyler was the prelate of the Pontifical Commission for Sacred Archeology. To a select few in the world of international espionage and security, John was the director of the Venatori, the ultra covert intelligence agency of the Vatican. To her, he was the man she could never have.

"Just a few days," he answered. "Once I finish with the meetings here, I'm taking a quick side trip to Washington to visit with the President. I'll fly back to Rome from there. Did I ever tell you how far back he and I go? Way before he became a politician, Steve Brennan actually entertained the idea of becoming a priest. We were pretty good friends in our early twenties."

"You mentioned knowing him, but I didn't realize your friendship let you drop in on the White House whenever you want."

"It's a lot easier as director of the Venatori than before."

Cotten watched a group of French-speaking tourists wander in, looking for a table. "Then while you're here we might be able to squeeze in some time to catch up. I mean I don't want to interrupt your schedule or anything. I just thought ... "

"There's no way you could be interrupting. I've looked forward to this trip especially because I thought we could spend a little time together. You're good for me, Cotten Stone."

She closed her eyes and shook her head. "How do you always do that—make me feel like I'm the first thing on your mind?" She set her cup down. "Wait, don't answer. I don't want an explanation. It might take the magic out of it."

"Magic, huh? Is that what it is?"

"Yep. Nobody else in my entire life has ever made me feel that I was special like you do."

"Well, maybe I make you feel that way because you *are* a special lady."

"Damn," she said, wrapping her hands around the cup.

"What?" John said.

"You know exactly what. The priest thing."

He reached across and took her hands in his. "But we've learned to deal with it."

He was right. But it didn't stop her wishing. She tilted her head. "Know what else?"

"No. What?" he said.

"Those red robes cardinals wear aren't all that flattering. I like you better like this, in a polo shirt and jeans."

"It's casual Friday at the Vatican," John said with a chuckle. "I've got a meeting later this afternoon, but I thought we could have dinner—"

Cotten's cell rang. *Bad timing.* "Hold that thought." Groping in her purse, she dug the phone out and flipped it open. "Cotten Stone."

She listened for a minute before snapping the phone closed. Plowing her fingers though her hair, she said, "Never fails. It just doesn't work out for us, does it? I've been called back to SNN. Some guy just staggered into the lobby and collapsed. Says he needs to talk to me." She gathered up her purse, and as she slipped out of the booth, she said, "John, I'm so sorry. I told them to only call me in an emergency. They said I'd better get there right away, the guy's in pretty bad shape."

"No problem. I'll settle up here and give you a call later. So, maybe dinner?"

"That would be perfect." Cotten paused next to him. "It's so good to be with you, John Tyler. But it wasn't long enough. You promise to call me later?"

"You bet," he said.

"Now let me go find out why some guy's dying to see me."

———

Cotten barreled through the Satellite News Network's revolving doors. A crowd of SNN employees had gathered around a man lying on the floor.

News director, Ted Casselman, Cotten's boss, mentor, and friend, ushered her through the group.

"Who is he?" she asked, catching the first glimpse of the man.

"No idea," Ted said. "Security says he's got no ID."

"Has he said anything?"

"Not a word since he asked for you. Ambulance is on its way."

Cotten glared down at the man sprawled on the floor. "What's the matter with him? Jesus, he looks so—"

"Stone." The raspy voice was barely heard over the commotion in the lobby.

Cotten started to kneel, but Ted tugged on her arm. "Don't get too close. We have no idea what's wrong with him."

An SNN cameraman suddenly appeared. "Okay?" he asked Ted.

Ted gave his consent with a nod. "I'm going to get this on tape," he told Cotten.

The cameraman moved closer, flipped on the camera-mounted floodlight, and focused.

The man muttered a few words, followed by a flow of frothy blood foaming from his mouth.

"I didn't understand you," Cotten said, ignoring Ted and going to her knees.

The fast-approaching sound of sirens heralded the arrival of NYC Fire and Rescue.

The man tried to speak, with no success. Cotten lifted his head. He coughed, and crimson-lined bubbles swelled and burst out his nostrils. A thin thread of glistening red mucous dangled from his bottom lip.

She heard the sirens build to a crescendo before suddenly going quiet on the street outside. "What did you say?" she asked him.

"Step aside! Move back!" shouted security from the direction of the lobby doors as the paramedics rushed toward her.

Cotten bent close to the man's face. His glazed-over eyes finally found their target and latched on to hers.

"Tell me," Cotten said.

"Black Needles," he barely mumbled before closing his eyes.

DOA

AFTER THE EXCITEMENT SETTLED down, employees began filing out of the SNN lobby to return to work. Through the glass doors, Cotten and Ted watched the medics load the sick man into the ambulance.

"What did he say to you?" Ted asked.

Cotten threaded her tea-colored hair behind one ear and shrugged. "He was delirious. Mumbled something about dirty needles, I think. Probably a junkie."

"We need to reevaluate our building's security procedures," Ted said, looking over his shoulder at maintenance cleaning up the area where the man had collapsed. He and Cotten walked across the marble floor inlaid with the gold satellite dish and SNN world globe logo. Entering the elevators, Ted pushed the eighth-floor button. "How's John?"

"He's great. In town for meetings with some people from the FBI and the State Department." She watched the digital floor indicator click off the levels as the elevator climbed to the eighth floor where the network had its news department, video edit suites, and archives.

Cotten shifted her gaze to Ted's reflection in the polished bronze walls of the elevator, thinking how much she appreciated and respected him. The gray around his temples was becoming more pronounced, and she knew a great deal of it was her doing. He was a handsome black man, with a face etched with strength and eyes filled with a sparkle that always inspired her and the rest of his staff. He was a constant source of unequivocal support—in the best and worst times of her career. And she'd had her share of major screwups. But when she did, Ted was there to remind her that it was okay to make mistakes, just not to make them again. His recent second heart attack forced him to slow down his work schedule and Cotten worried about him, but Ted didn't like anyone fussing over him. Even with the health issues, he still made a strong, commanding figure as news director.

"It's hard for you, isn't it?" he said to her reflection in the bronze.

"What?"

"John coming in and out of your life."

"It's that obvious?" Cotten looked away.

"Want my typical fatherly advice?"

"Do I have a choice?"

"Enjoy the time you have together. After my close calls with the Grim Reaper, I've learned to live in the moment, not in the next one. Everything else is a waste of time."

The elevator came to a stop and the doors opened.

Ted put his arm around Cotten's shoulders and gave a comforting hug. "Live in the moment," he said, then let her exit first. "We've had enough excitement for one day, kiddo."

"You're right. That guy was pretty sick. Hope he makes it." She glanced around the newsroom at the reporters and editors moving like bees in a hive. "Talk to you later, Ted."

He waved as they parted, and Cotten headed for her office. But something kept nagging like an unscratchable itch; why had the guy in the lobby asked for her?

———

Late that afternoon, a young intern fresh out of journalism school came to Cotten's door. "Here's the first draft of the Shroud of Turin piece, Ms. Stone."

"Thanks." She motioned the girl in. "Do me a favor."

"Sure. I'd be glad to."

"You heard about the commotion in the lobby earlier?"

"Yeah. Poor guy."

"See if you can find out which hospital they transported him to and the status of his condition."

"Do you have his name?"

Cotten shook her head. "He had no ID."

"Okay, I'll see what I can come up with." She spun on her heels and scurried away.

Cotten glanced at her phone for the umpteenth time, just in case the message light was blinking and John had called while she was on the line. She swiveled her chair and peered out her window at Central Park West. This was her favorite time of year, particularly with the leaves turning and the brisk air she enjoyed during her walk to work each morning. Only when the elements would become unbearable later in the season did she give up her sidewalk commute and take a cab.

She scanned the Shroud story—a report of a new test on pollen traces found in the Shroud of Turin. The pollen was identified as a type of thistle plant called *Gundelia tournefortii* which was thought to have been used to fashion the Crown of Thorns worn by Jesus Christ at the Crucifixion. The plant is found primarily in Israel, around Jerusalem.

After reading the script, Cotten wrote *possible second segment* across the top. She hosted a weekly science- and religion-based program called *Relics* that explored the facts and myths of ancient objects. This might make a good filler piece, she thought. Her prime story for the next show was the debunking of the bones thought to belong to Joan of Arc.

She did some line edits on the Shroud story, then a little more research on the Internet. But no matter what she tried to do to distract herself, two things remained on her mind for the rest of the afternoon—John Tyler and the man in the lobby.

She assumed John's meeting had run long, and was about to pack it in for the day when there came a knock. The new intern stood in her doorway. "Come in. Have a seat."

The girl smiled broadly.

"What's up?" Cotten asked.

After hesitating, she said, "I don't want this to come off sounding like a major suck-up, Ms. Stone, but I just needed to say what an honor it is to be able to work with you."

"Well, thank you," Cotten said. "You just made my day. And please, call me Cotten."

The girl smiled again and dropped into a chair. "Did you know we studied you in broadcasting? There's an elective on how ancient religious objects have changed our lives. It's a lot about the impact of your reporting work. When I found out SNN had accepted me into the internship program, I hoped I would just get to meet you, much less work with you."

"You're awfully sweet, and I appreciate the kind words. We work as a team at SNN, and it's only with everyone giving their all that we make those worthy accomplishments happen."

"Well, I'm just proud to be a part of it."

"So, what did you find out about our mystery man?"

The intern stared at the paper in her hand. "I followed the story right up to a dead end. I can't believe it's the first assignment you give me, and I couldn't ..." She looked at Cotten. "I hope you won't be too disappointed in me."

"Give me what you've got."

She unfolded the paper and handed it to Cotten. "He died en route to the hospital. The name of the ER physician I spoke to is on there."

"Did they determine cause of death?"

"The doctor said that they brought the guy in, but there was some kind of mix-up. Somebody released the body to a mortuary before the coroner picked it up to do the autopsy."

Cotten rolled her eyes. "How does this happen? Typical of the right hand not knowing, blah, blah, blah. Incompetence at its best. I guess they'll get it straight in the end. So, where did they take the body? You can follow up with the mortuary."

"That's just it. Nobody could find the documentation identifying the funeral home."

DEVIL'S DEATH PING

LUTHER SUTTON STARED OUT the farmhouse window at the grave markers where generations of Suttons rested atop a distant crest. Two hundred fifty-five acres of land in the middle of West Virginia had been in the family for over a hundred years. At the age of sixty-three, he was the eldest of Big Thelma's brood. And as such, he had ambled up to the graveyard yesterday morning and checked out her spot. A long time ago, she'd laid claim to the space beside Hubert, her husband for over forty years.

"All the good plots is taken," she said to Luther when they put Hubert in the ground. "Them first Suttons was buried under the trees when the roots was small. Can't dig under 'em now. Oh well, Hubert liked the sun. Hated the winter, he did. Sweat didn't bother him like it does me."

The thought of laying his mother to rest without benefit of shade made his bottom lip quiver. *Gotta plant a goddamn tree,* he thought. It wouldn't be right for her to suffer eternally just because

Papa tolerated the heat. Course in the winter, it would be a different story. And they had some mean West Virginia winters.

Turning away from the window and memories of his father's passing, Luther's stare returned to the front room where twelve other Suttons had gathered at his request. His step-daddy, Daniel, sat in the corner whittling. Daniel was a good man, but had lost his mind over the last few years. Dementia, the doctors called it. Sometimes Daniel knew where he was and who his family members were, but most often he was no different than a stranger.

Luther sat on a chair near the window and stroked his gray beard before taking out his watch from the pocket of his flannel shirt. He dangled it by the chain before palming it to see the time. "Guess Mary couldn't make it," he said, referring to one of his sisters. "She's been feeling down in her back lately."

He returned the watch to his pocket, rested both hands on top of his cane, and propped it between his legs. He took another visual assessment of all those present before rapping the cane on the wood floor. The sound had the effect of a courtroom gavel.

"I've called this meeting cause of being the oldest child of Big Thelma. Mother is tired now and says she wants to go home to her Maker. I know it makes us all full of sorrow, but she's a good woman and has led a long life. She'll be rewarded in Heaven. She's wanting to say her goodbyes and—"

"Luther, why aren't you taking her to the hospital over in—"

Luther slammed the cane on the floor and glared at the interrupter. "Quiet, Everett Roy. I'm not finished yet." He cleared his throat. "Mother said Grandpa Calvin came to her last night in a vision and said he was coming to take her home. She said she's ready to go."

"But Luther," cousin Belle said. "Why—"

Luther's eyes darted to her. He lifted his cane shoulder height, like it was an extension of his arm, and pointed it at her. "I said I ain't finished yet." His voice, harsh with anger, filled the parlor.

Everyone lowered their eyes, staring at the worn plank floor. Then Luther spoke again. "Mother said she don't want us taking her back to that new Oriental doctor she saw last week. And she definitely don't want to go to no hospital. Says that's why she didn't let nobody know she was sick. If I hadn't picked up Daniel from his sister's last Sunday and brought him home from his visit, we wouldn't have found out Mother was in a bad way. Guess one of us would have checked on her sooner or later. No mind all that, she says her time is come and she wants us to let her go. And she wants to be in the comforts of her own home, not tied up to some machine, surrounded by folks she don't know. Says that's the peaceful way. If you are wanting to speak your piece with Big Thelma, then you'll get your turn, one at a time. But I'm thinking today might be the last day she'll be speaking to any of us. She's real weak and the fever's spiked."

There was silence in the room for a moment. Then Harlan, Luther's nephew, looked around before speaking up. "I don't think it right that you aren't going to take her to the hospital. It's not just about Big Thelma. What about the rest of us? We need to know what kind of sickness she's got. Maybe there's shots or something that could keep the rest of the family from getting it." Harlan's face reddened and the vein in the center of his forehead bulged. "It ain't right, Luther. From what you told us, Big Thelma's in an awful way.

And I'm not at all sure any of us should go in there. We could get sick with her fever and take it home to the rest of our families."

"Nobody's saying you got to," Luther said. "Your choice."

Thelma's youngest son, Ellis, stood. "I'm going to say my farewells. I ain't scared of catching nothing."

Luther shot a glare to each face. "While you be making up your minds, I'm going in to tell Mother she has company."

Luther pushed down on the cane to help him to his feet. Before he turned his back on the Sutton family, he glanced at his stepfather sitting in the corner, a small mound of wood shavings between his mud-caked boots. "Somebody's got to tell Daniel his wife is going to meet her Maker." Then he shuffled to Big Thelma's room and cracked open the door. The sourness stung his nostrils. He slipped in and closed the door, hoping to contain the sickness from getting out.

At her bedside he took the wet cloth from the basin on the night table, wrung it, and swabbed away the slime of bloody mucous that had dribbled out the side of her mouth and pooled on the pillowcase. He rinsed the rag, wrung it again, and wiped away the crust from her nose and the wine-colored clots from her ears. As soon as he loosened them, a trickle of fresh blood oozed out.

He didn't blame Harlan for being afraid. Luther had never seen a sickness like this. But he figured if he was to get it, he'd already have it.

"Mother," he whispered. "Can you hear me?"

"Luther?" she said, sounding the most lucid she had in the last two days. Swallowed by the black sockets, her eyes were cast over with a gray film, but she seemed to focus. "Luther?"

"I'm here, Mother."

"Don't let nobody but the family see me like this," she whispered. "Just put me in the ground yourself. It's the devil's death."

KEEP SAFE

"IT'S NOT OFTEN THAT *SNN is the subject of the news, but today it walked in our front door. Now we're asking your help in identifying this man who wandered into the lobby of our Manhattan headquarters. Please be warned that the photograph we are about to show is graphic. Viewer discretion is advised.*"

A close-up of a face appeared. Though SNN technicians had tried to choose a video frame that was not too detailed, it still had to be good enough to make identification possible. The blood on his lips, chin, neck, and corners of his eyes, couldn't be missed.

"*The unidentified man asked to speak to Cotten Stone, our own senior investigative correspondent. Appearing to be gravely ill, he collapsed and later died en route to the hospital. But not before delivering a two-word message to Ms. Stone which she told Headline News was 'Black Needles'.*

"*Stone stated that although he seemed delirious and barely conscious, the words were clear. If you know the identity of this man or the meaning of his strange message, please contact the Satellite News*

Network at the toll-free number on your screen or online at w-w-w-dot-satellitenews-dot-org."

Sitting on her living room couch, Cotten pressed the pause button on the TiVo remote and froze the image of the sick man's face. "It was the craziest thing, John," she said into the speaker phone. "At first, I thought he was a drug addict who wandered into the building after overdosing, but that didn't explain the blood. I figured he wanted help, and my name was the first one that popped into his head from seeing me on the news, and that's why he asked for me. And I just assumed he was talking about hypodermic needles."

"What was the phrase again?" John asked.

"You can clearly hear it on the video playback. It was Black Needles." There was a soft clinking sound as she sipped her Absolut over ice.

"My first impression is the same as yours—a junkie on his last trip. But like you say, that doesn't explain the blood. He may have had some other health issues."

"Yes, but then you add in the whole issue of his body being taken from the hospital by an unidentified mortuary before the CDC could be alerted and the medical examiner could conduct an autopsy—well, it just struck me as highly suspicious."

"What if it's nothing more than what the ER doctor suggested, a foul-up in the paperwork?"

"Maybe. But for the heck of it, I had Headline News run the story, asking for the public to help identify the guy." She drained the glass. "I just finished watching it."

"Maybe something will come of it."

"These kinds of things always come as a mixed bag. We'll still have to sift out the wackos from the real leads."

There was a pause before John spoke again. "I'm really sorry about tonight. I was looking forward to us having dinner together, but when the United States ambassador to the U.N. requested a private meeting, I had no choice."

Cotten sighed. "It would have been nice." She finger-combed her hair away from her face. "Any idea what the State Department wants?"

"There are some serious negotiations going on behind the scenes in the Eastern European Republic of Moldova. It involves a border conflict with a narrow breakaway strip of land called Transnistria. The violence is escalating while the formal talks have stalled. My guess is that they want a neutral party involved. Maybe pull the Vatican's foreign minister into the fray. Right now, your crystal ball is as good as mine."

"And you fly back to Rome tomorrow?"

"Hey, stop trying to hustle me out of the country. I was hoping to at least take you to breakfast. What do you think? Seven-thirty? My flight is at ten."

"Sounds like a perfect way to start my day."

"Hang on a second."

She heard him cover the receiver, followed by muted voices.

"The Secret Service is here," John said. "I'll give you a call later."

"Have fun playing diplomat."

———

At breakfast the next morning, Cotten toyed with her soft-boiled egg. Her appetite dwindled as they talked of John's leaving and when he might come back to the States.

"The Grand Hyatt menu is great, but I still think I prefer good old Cracker Barrel," John said.

"You know there's not one anywhere near Manhattan. I guess New Yorkers aren't into grits, hash browns, buttermilk biscuits, and gravy."

"No matter. The company doesn't get any better," John said, winking.

"What was all the hush-hush about last night?"

He looked at her over the rim of his coffee cup. "Off the record?"

Cotten nodded.

He rested the cup with a clink on the saucer. "I'm hand-carrying a letter back to the Holy Father. Although I haven't read it, I'm guessing it's a request to get the Holy See involved in the negotiations to stop the Moldovan conflict before it worsens. Officially, everything is completely behind the scenes."

"Why would they call upon the Vatican?"

"That was my first question," John said. "Truth is, once the Russians finally pulled their Fourteenth Army out, the Transnistrians feel as strongly as ever that they should be independent from Moldova. The hostility is fueled by a burning desire to establish an independent state. This is nothing new to those people, it's been going on at some level since they were part of the Kingdom of Lithuania in the fifteenth century. Trouble is, the Transnistrians are sitting on a massive stockpile of arms left behind by the Russians, and they're willing to fight to the last man in order to establish their breakaway republic. The level of frustration is so intense in the region that all parties are grasping at anything that will bring peace, including the obscure fact that the pope's grandmother was Eastern Orthodox— so is the majority of both Transnistria and Moldova."

27

"Will you be going there if the Vatican gets involved?"

"Yes."

"What's your cover story this time?"

"An archaeological dig site in Romania that was originally un-covered back in 1971 is turning up some new finds. Mainly the remains of two martyrs who died during the repressions of Emperor Decius. So for all intents and purposes, I'll be tagging along with the diplomatic contingency before heading off to the dig site. Shouldn't raise any suspicions as to why I'm there."

"Would there be much risk?"

"Know what?" John smiled and cocked his head. "You're going to ruin that pretty face with premature wrinkles if you don't stop worrying so much." He patted the top of her hand.

"Then promise me you'll keep safe."

———

"How was your breakfast with John?" Ted asked as he sat across from Cotten in her office that afternoon.

"Too short," she said. "He had to rush to Kennedy for his flight."

"Did he tell you what the big meeting was all about?"

"Only in general terms." She stared out her window at Central Park. "Off the record."

"Then we have to respect that," Ted said. "Of course, I expect him to give you the exclusive when it's time to talk."

Cotten nodded reluctantly. "I worry about him, Ted. I wish he just did the priest thing. But his job with the Venatori puts him in danger. There are a lot of people who want to harm him."

"Let it go, kiddo. You can't change anything."

"I know, but if something happened to John, I don't think I could bear it."

"He'll be fine. You just hate to see him leave."

"I guess so." Cotten leaned back in her chair. "So what's your hot news?"

"The name of our mystery man is Jeff Calderon," Ted said. "His aunt called this morning after seeing the story."

Cotten turned to look at her boss. "How did he wind up in our lobby?"

"Mr. Calderon was a pharmaceutical salesman for the last ten years. Apparently he started using more of his samples than his clients did. According to his dear old aunt, he was fired a couple of months back, before dropping off her radar screen about six weeks ago. She hasn't heard from him since. But she did give us his last known address—a low-rent apartment in Bed Stuy."

"I thought that area of Brooklyn was getting cleaned up?"

"Still some seedy sections," Ted said. "But it's a thousand times better than just a few years ago."

"Let me see the address."

Ted handed her a sheet of paper.

"This isn't too far from Tompkins Park."

"You know the area?"

"Only in passing. I went over there one Sunday last summer to attend a baseball game for a charity I was covering."

"Let me guess," Ted said. "Now you want to go back and see where Calderon lived?"

Cotten shrugged. "It'll give me something to do this weekend. I need to get out anyway."

"Take a walk through Central Park. Go shopping at Bloomies. It's safer." Ted rose to leave.

Cotten smiled as she gathered up her things to go home. "You worry too much."

SHATTER

The ribbon of the four-lane motorway flowing into Pyongyang was virtually deserted as Moon watched the rolling hills slip past. Like all the motorways around the North Korean capital, this one was beautifully tended by the peasants living nearby. In the mornings on her way to the lab, she would see them dusting out the gutters and pruning the shrubs along the sides of the road. They would bow respectfully as her black limousine raced past on its way to the high security government compound north of the city.

Tonight, she was exhausted as she absentmindedly watched the farmland sweep by. The long days at the genetics facility wore away at her frail 105-pound frame. And at sixty-four, her body was starting to show its age with an assortment of ailments creeping into her life. Arthritis and hypertension were the latest. But it was the tremor in her hands that reminded her of the Parkinson's disease that was continually and progressively taking its toll. The *substantia nigra*, the dopamine cells in her brain, were dying. Without them the messages from the brain telling her body how and when to move were delayed. Parkinson's wouldn't kill her, but at some point she would become debilitated. Moon knew that time worked against her. The rigors of aging and the disease would soon make it too hard to maintain her schedule, her stamina, and her drive.

But she was so close to the final climactic act in the drama of her life's work. Soon there would be no more awakening in the middle of the night bathed in a sweat of fear and doubt. No more wondering if such a small, frail woman in an obscure, closed society could reach out and strike down so many of her hated enemy.

Again she pulled the photograph from the pocket of her coat. As she gazed at her mother and father, she trembled with excitement at the thought of what she was about to do. And when her task would finally be over—when she had accomplished her mission to punish those who brought pain and suffering to her parents, her friends, her people—she planned to retire in her adopted homeland with all the benefits and privileges of a native-born North Korean high official. Protected from the retaliation that was sure to come, and secure from the ruthless imperialist aggressors, she would be well taken care of in her final years.

Moon's parents had been studying medicine at Kyoto Imperial University during the Sino-Japanese War when they were recruited by the head of the secret Japanese biological warfare center named by Emperor Hirohito as Unit 731.

Her parents were honorable and noble people who dedicated their lives to defending Japan, but after the war they became outraged as they watched their country get in bed with the Americans. Unlike the Japanese government, which seemed to ignore the catastrophic destruction of Hiroshima and Nagasaki, and the generations that would suffer later, her parents could not forgive America and its allies, nor could they excuse Japanese leaders from such a betrayal. Before many of their colleagues were brought to trial by an Allied war crimes tribunal, Moon's mother and father escaped to Korea, renouncing their Japanese heritage, even discarding their Japanese surname of Nakamura, and taking on the Korean name of Chung. They were determined to carry on what Unit 731 had started. Shortly after their arrival in Pyongyang, Moon was born.

At age six, during the last days of the Korean War, Moon witnessed the rape and murder of her mother by the imperialist aggressors. Time had not dimmed that vivid memory, nor did she want it to. That memory was what fed her, what drove her, what gave her purpose. Moon squeezed her eyes shut to ward off the tears as the hatred for the Americans bloomed on her face. She focused on the photograph again—this time studying the face of her beloved father—a brilliant man, loyal husband, loving father. She bit hard on the inside of her cheek to relocate the pain in her heart and squelch the urge to sob aloud. *So young then. So vibrant.* This was the photograph she preferred to carry with her—when her parents were young, with bright eyes and promise in their smiles.

Moon's father was the one who made her understand the importance of her parents' work and why it was done in secret. Her father had once said, "After all, if germ warfare was so terrible that it had to be banned by the Geneva Protocol, then it had to be a very good weapon. And in war, you must win." It had not only been biological warfare her parents studied, but also methods to best treat injured soldiers and civilians.

Small sacrifices were imperative for the validity of the experiments. Most people appreciated the results, but preferred not to know how those results were attained. So few understood how much good had come from their work, like the discovery of how to best treat frostbite, which had saved thousands around the world from amputations.

It had taken Moon a long time to recover from her father's death eleven years ago. Staring up from his deathbed, he asked her to look into his eyes. "Do you see, there is no more fire left inside?" he said. "It must now burn within you, Daughter." Those were his last words. She held his hand until it grew cold, and promised she would avenge her parents. Moon would use the secrets her father revealed to her to punish the imperialist aggressors and their lap-dogs, bring them to their knees, and watch them scream in agony as they died a terrible death.

As Moon put away the photograph, she caught a glimpse of her tired eyes and runaway silver strands of hair in the limousine window's reflection. She smiled at how ironic it was that those whom she was about to kill already carried the manner of their death inside themselves.

———

"What did they just say?" Moon froze as she stood in the kitchen of her high-rise apartment in the official Communist Party residence section of Pyongyang. Ready for bed, she had just emptied the remaining tea from a china cup into the sink and was about to rinse it.

Her housekeeper, a tiny woman in her seventies, had stopped wiping the counter to watch a flat-screen plasma TV mounted underneath a cabinet. It was connected to only a handful of government sanctioned satellite dishes and was tuned to an American news broadcast with Korean subtitles. She turned to Moon. "What did *who* say, Dr. Chung?"

Moon motioned to the TV. "That person. What did she just say?"

"Oh. She spoke of a man who died suddenly after walking into the news organization's New York offices."

Moon glared at the image of a woman with light brown hair and dark eyes filling the screen. The woman was being interviewed, and across the bottom of the frame was her title: Cotten Stone, SNN Senior Correspondent.

As she listened, Moon's hands clenched, and heat surged up her neck to her face. She felt as if an invisible fist had just struck her in the gut, and she didn't notice the cup slip from her grasp until she heard it shatter on the floor.

There was no mistake. Moon had heard the woman utter two words that cut through the air like a blast of winter wind. Two simple words.

Black Needles.

DEADBOLTS

COTTEN STARTED UP THE third flight of steps in the Bedford Stuyvesant tenement, last known residence of Jeff Calderon. The pungent smells of simmering Jamaican jerk spiced meat mixed with the faint odors of urine and mildew hung heavily in the air. A skin of dark-green paint covered the walls, giving the surroundings a feeling of anonymity—a place to hide secrets and identities, Cotten thought. Scars of a slightly darker green revealed where someone had painted over graffiti. The audio of a Saturday morning cartoon seemed out of place.

Moving along the hallway, she noticed that the cooking odors were stronger on this floor. So was the cartoon soundtrack. Cotten stopped in front of an apartment door and checked the number written on the note Ted gave to her. She knocked, wondering if Calderon had lived alone.

"You ain't gonna get an answer knocking like that, lady."

She turned to see a mountain of a black man approaching—easily three hundred pounds and over six feet tall. He wore a long-sleeved shirt under blue coveralls and a hardhat, and carried a lunch pail.

As he passed, he said, "Stoned most of the time. Won't hear you unless you pound."

"Are you referring to Mr. Calderon?" Cotten asked, feeling slightly on edge by the sheer bulk of the man.

He stopped and stared at her. "Do I know you?"

"I'm with SNN," she said. "You might have seen me on the news."

"Thought so."

As he turned to leave, Cotten said, "Do you know Mr. Calderon?"

"Don't know nobody, news lady."

She heard his heavy footfalls fading down the stairs and took the Hulk's advice, rapping hard on the door. Thirty seconds later, she was about to give up when there came a faint sound from inside the apartment.

"I ain't got the rent, okay?" a voice said. "I'm just getting my shit, and I'll be out of here."

"I'm not here to collect rent. I'm Cotten Stone from SNN. May I talk to you?"

No response, as if the person on the other side of the door was weighing options. Then Cotten heard the clicking of multiple deadbolts. The door opened a few inches, still tethered by a rusty chain. Half a face peered through—one squinting eye and pinched brow, and a turned-down corner of the mouth.

"You a cop?" the man whispered.

"No, like I said, I'm from SNN, the cable news channel." She watched as he opened the door enough to reveal more of his face and a short, scrawny frame. Ruts and pockmarks, evidence of rough mileage over the years, she supposed, crisscrossed his features, making it hard for Cotten to accurately judge his age. But she guessed late forties. The whisker stubble had to be a week's worth.

"What you want?" His eyes nervously scanned the hall behind her.

"Do you know Jeff Calderon?"

"Shit. I knew it. I friggin' knew it."

He started to close the door, but Cotten caught it with her hand. "You're not in any trouble, I promise. I'm just looking for some information on Mr. Calderon."

"I told him we were screwed. That they'd come looking." He pushed on the door to close it.

"Please, sir, I only want to talk. You have nothing to fear from me, I assure you. Please. Just want to ask you a few simple questions. That's all. Then I'll leave."

The door closed, but then the chain rattled.

"You better not be lying," he said as the door opened. Stepping away with obvious reluctance, he let her enter.

"Thank you, Mr...." Cotten walked into the apartment and heard the click of the door behind her. The foul smell of a landfill greeted her nostrils. Trash littered the floor, the sparse furniture, and the kitchen. Food wrappers, heaps of clothes, a mountain of dishes and plastic food containers encrusted with moldy remains—layer upon rancid layer contributed to the odor causing her to cover her mouth and nose. Her eyes focused on a bloody rag that had dried to a deep brownish rust color wadded in the corner of the sofa.

"Franks," he said.

"Pardon?"

"I'm Franks. Jimmy Franks."

"Nice to meet you, Mr. Franks." Cotten didn't extend her hand, and Franks didn't offer his.

He brushed back his straw-like hair that appeared combed with a Weed Eater and then stuffed his jittery hands in his pockets. Still, he couldn't hide having the shakes. Small facial tics and eye twitches combined with repeated sniffling were dead-on clues as to his malady.

Cotten had the feeling that Jimmy Franks was about to short circuit. "Are you all right?"

He gave a nervous laugh. "What the fuck do you want, anyway?" He looked around the room with the same anxious glances as when she stood in the doorway.

Cotten knew this conversation was going to be short-lived and limited to single-syllable words. "What happened to Jeff Calderon?"

"They fuckin' gave him some shit. Sick fucks. They gave him something that fucked him up."

"Who, Mr. Franks? Who made him sick?"

"All we wanted was to get in there and score some shit. We just wanted to get high and maybe pinch something we could pawn. Sick bastards. They fucked him up."

"Do you know who *they* are?"

"Yeah, a bunch of sick fucks."

"Okay, how about a location? Where did this all happen?"

He shook his head. "Some warehouse. I don't know. Over near the expressway."

"Queens Expressway?"

"Maybe." Franks rubbed his head. "I don't know—I was messed up." He clasped his hands on the crown of his head and bent his elbows in close to his face. "Oh, God, they're gonna come get me." Franks danced from one foot to the other, his hands dropping off his head to massage the back of his neck. "Off Furman or Doughty, maybe. Near the bridge. Called T-Kup."

"Teacup?"

"Yeah, that's right. I think. Shit, I was so fucked up."

"You and Mr. Calderon went there to buy drugs?"

Franks laughed, then sniffed and wiped his nose on his shirt sleeve. "We broke into the place—Jeff did, I kept watch outside. He never came out. Fucking sick bastards. He was in there forever. I left. Said fuck it. He finally showed up five or six days ago. Said he got away and had been sleeping in a dumpster for a couple of days. No sooner gets here and he starts getting really sick, man. Blood and shit coming out his nose and ears and everywhere." Franks turned his head and grimaced. "I never seen nothing like that kinda shit. Scared the hell out of me. I tried to get him to go to the clinic, but he was afraid they'd find out about what we done and he'd end up in jail. At first he thought he was going to get better, but he was fuckin' dying, man. Finally, he could barely open his eyes. Just laid there."

Franks motioned toward the couch and the bloody rag. "Watched TV sometimes. In and out of it, like a really bad trip. Got to where he didn't make good sense. Confused, you know, really mixed up. Once he thought I was his friggin' mother for Christ's sake. Freaked me out. Then he saw some bitch on TV and said he was gonna go find her. Tell her what happened. Like he could just get up, get dressed, and head into the city all perky like. I told him his ass wasn't going nowhere, not the way he was, but he swore he was gonna try—had to see her about what those bastards done to him."

Franks' eyes widened as if he noticed Cotten for the first time. He studied her for a minute. "Fuckin' A," he said, running his hands over his face, obviously making the connection. "It was you. Is this gonna be on the news?" Franks tugged at his hair. "No TV, lady. Oh, sweet Jesus, they'll see it and come for me."

"No, Mr. Franks. No TV. You don't have to worry about that." Cotten tried to calm him. "Just tell me what happened."

"I took off a couple of days ago—didn't want to catch whatever Jeff got. Put my stuff in a plastic bag and bailed, man. Was sleeping on the street—anything's better than being around whatever the fuck got him so sick. Then I hear that Jeff's picture is all over the news and that he's dead. So I come back here this morning to get the rest of my shit." Franks started to pace, turning his back to Cotten, his hands on top of his head again. He seemed to forget she was there. "God damn."

"Mr. Franks, did Mr. Calderon say what happened to him?"

Suddenly, Franks became even more agitated. "Jeff said he didn't tell them about me being outside keeping watch, but I don't know." He wiped the sweat from his hands on the front of his shirt. "I don't fucking know. They're gonna come get me. Give me the same shit." He swabbed the perspiration from his face on his sleeve. "Oh shit, I'm fucked. That's it. No more talk. Get out." He started for the door.

Following him, Cotten asked, "Was there anything else he said? Anything at all?"

He nudged her into the hall and slammed the door. As Cotten heard the clunking of the deadbolts, Franks yelled, "Said they used him like a fuckin' lab rat."

T-KUP

COTTEN STARED AT THE New York City business directory on her computer monitor and the results of her search for businesses called *tea cup* and any derivative of the words. There was a knick-knack store selling miniature dragon and wizard fantasy figures, an Asian tea parlor specializing in exotic imported tea and coffee, a Persian rug dealer, a high-end china and crystal specialty store, a pet shop selling tiny dogs, and a few others, none of which were located in the area described by Jimmy Franks.

"We'll be ready for you in ten minutes," the assistant director said as he stuck his head in her office door.

"Thanks," Cotten said, looking up. The weekly taping of her *Relics* show was about to begin and she had to get to makeup. Maybe this whole Calderon thing was a waste of time anyway, she thought. What was she dealing with here? A couple of guys strung out on drugs, breaking into a business of some sort to steal narcotics. One got sick and died—the other so paranoid that he may be beyond help. She felt sorry for both, but she wondered if she had invested too much time in it already.

Still, there was something nagging at her gut. Why had he chosen her? The reasoning that she was a familiar face on TV made some sense. But he could have given his two-word message to anyone and requested they tell her. Even more than his efforts to find her, the thing that kept nudging her mind was the message itself.

Black Needles.

He didn't say, bad needles, as in contaminated or dirty hypos. He didn't say I'm sick, get me to a doctor. With his last breath he said, Black Needles.

Then there was Jimmy Franks. Obviously on drugs and out of touch with reality as he rambled on. He kept referring to *they*. Who were *they*? Why did *they* make Calderon sick?

"Cotten?"

She looked up. The assistant director again. Waving, she said, "Sorry—on my way."

Cotten picked up her copy of the *Relics* script and headed out of her office to the studio and makeup.

Four minutes later, and with only seconds to spare, she dropped down into a forest-green wingback chair on the *Relics* set, smoothed her skirt and blouse, gave the sound engineer a voice level, and took in a deep breath. Her guest, a French forensic scientist from the University of Paris, sat on a matching couch to her right. Behind her was a backdrop graphic displaying a dark, mysterious-looking composite photograph showing ghostly tunnels and partially excavated tombs with the word *Relics* scrawled on what looked like ancient parchment. As the stage manager counted down, Cotten smiled and gazed into the camera, its lens hidden behind the teleprompter. The script rolled from the bottom to the top of the teleprompter screen and she read, "Good evening and welcome to *Relics*, the weekly SNN investigation into ancient man and myth, folklore, and legend. Pieces of our past that just might shed new rays of light on our future."

Electronically superimposed over her shoulder, an image of a small bone appeared.

"Is this the rib of Saint Joan of Arc or a fake, what some think is actually a bone from an Egyptian mummy? Tonight we attempt to answer that by traveling back in time to the small town of Rouen, France. The year was 1431, and a young girl was about to be burned at the stake.

"And we'll also discuss new test results on recently discovered pollen samples taken from the famous Shroud of Turin. Could the samples be from a rare thistle plant thought to have been used to fashion the Crown of Thorns worn by Jesus Christ at the Crucifixion? All this and more on *Relics*."

Cotten leaned back in her chair. "We'd like to welcome a new sponsor tonight—Blaze PCs and their new generation of wireless notebooks. Blaze notebooks bring you blazing speed with their exclusive octo-core processors from—"

The scrolling script paused, waiting for Cotten to continue. She stared at the words. Composing herself, she continued, "Their exclusive octo-core processors from T-Kup Technologies."

———

"Blaze doesn't make T-Kup processors," said the SNN international sales manager. "They just use the technology. You know, like Intel or AMD."

Cotten sat in the sales manager's office. "Where is the Blaze corporate office?"

"Singapore."

"And T-Kup?"

"Seoul, South Korea. A bunch of engineers from Samsung decided to put together their own chip manufacturing company. In business for a couple of years—claim to have the fastest processing chips around—eight cores, whatever that means."

"So does T-Kup have any manufacturing facilities in New York City?" Cotten asked.

"Seems like the marketing manager at Blaze mentioned that they have a service center here and one out on the West Coast in Los Angeles. No manufacturing, just replacement parts and repairs." He turned to his keyboard and typed. A moment later, a sheet of paper slipped from his laser printer. "Here's the info. The facility here is located in Brooklyn."

"Thanks, you've been a big help." She stood and took the paper.

"Hey, anytime," he said. "So why the interest?"

Cotten smiled. "I'm thinking about buying a new laptop."

CAGES

THE SIGN OVER THE door read *T-Kup Technologies, Factory Service and Support*. The building, one of three in a row along Doughty Street, was a windowless, three-story brick structure. As Cotten watched the taxi that brought her pull away, she began to have second thoughts of coming alone. The new intern had offered to accompany her, but canceled at the last moment, saying something had come up. So with determination and a glance in both directions, Cotten pulled on the handle to the front door of T-Kup Technologies, but found it was locked. She pushed the button on the security entrance speaker. No response. She pulled out her cell phone and dialed the number on the sheet given to her by the SNN sales manager. A recording stated the number had been disconnected.

Next, she walked down the sidewalk to an alley running along the side of the building. She glanced over her shoulder at Fulton Ferry Landing and the hundreds of tourists snapping pictures of the New York City skyline across the East River. The constant thunder of traffic from the Brooklyn Bridge and Expressway in the distance never let up.

She headed into the alley. A hundred feet later, she passed a dumpster and came to a loading dock. Beside two large metal roll-up doors was a back entrance. Climbing the steps, she knocked on the rear door. A sign read: *T-Kup deliveries*. No answer. She tried the knob. Locked. But pushing on the door caused it to give. Someone had used duct tape to keep the lock in the open position. With a rusty screech, the door swung open.

A large empty room, probably the shipping department, stretched before her—shiny floor, scarred white walls, a few scraps of paper. The place reeked, not unlike the rancid odor inside Jeff Calderon's apartment.

She pulled out her small LCD Maglite and a handful of tissues from her purse. Covering her nose with the tissues, Cotten aimed the light as she wandered through the semi-darkness of the vacant warehouse. The place had been stripped bare. She shone the light in a sweeping arc, suddenly coming to a stop on the only objects left behind. Jimmy Franks' story started to make sense.

———

"Cages?" Ted Casselman said.

"Yeah." Cotten and her boss sat on a bench just inside Central Park across the street from SNN headquarters.

"You mean like security cages for parts or supplies?"

"That's what I thought at first. There were twenty in all—ten stacked on top of ten."

"Okay, so?"

"How many storage cages have you ever seen with a mattress in each?"

Ted glanced at the traffic on Columbus Circle. "Well, you got me there."

"They were just big enough for someone to lie down in. Not much more. Like cages in the back of a vet's office for boarding pets, but imagine them large enough for humans instead." Cotten watched a double-decker tour bus swing into the Circle. She could almost hear the camera shutters clicking. "Calderon told his buddy that whoever made him sick used him like a lab rat."

"So you think he was kept in one of those cages?"

She nodded.

"What did you find out about the building?"

"Owned by a consortium of Asian investors called Rising Moon. Based out of Hong Kong. Privately held. The warehouse in Brooklyn is their only property in New York. But they also own a building in Los Angeles. Their sole tenant in each location is T-Kup Technologies. Then I expanded the search to other countries. Wait until you hear this list. They span the globe, owning property in the UK, Russia, Poland, France, Greece, Belgium, Canada, Denmark, Japan, and Australia. And that's not all. They have holdings in Brazil, China, New Zealand, Norway, South Africa, and the Netherlands."

Ted turned from the traffic and gave her a sly smile. "Let me guess. Their only tenant in each country is T-Kup Tech."

"Correct. This whole Calderon thing smells bad, Ted. Literally and figuratively. I can't tell you what it is or why I feel that way other than my gut says something ain't right in T-Kup land."

"Could be nothing more than a coincidence?"

"You really believe that?"

He rubbed his forehead. "Read me that list of countries again."

She did.

He smacked his lips then nodded. "Sounds like a list of the U.S. allies in World War Two. Except for Japan. That's the only one that doesn't fit."

"Interesting. I'm going to make a mental note. It might mean something to us later."

"Maybe. Anyway, right now you don't have much to grab on to. Don't make it your life's work, but dig some more. Shake a few bushes and see what falls out. Maybe it's time for us to take a look at T-Kup Technologies in the cold light of dawn."

As they crossed Central Park West heading back to SNN, Ted said, "Where did John wind up going?"

"Some out-of-the-way strip of land between Moldova and the Ukraine called Transnistria."

"Never heard of it."

THE PATH

Moon walked alongside the General Secretary as they wandered through the gardens of his palace near Wonsan on the Sea of Japan coast. She had traveled to the east coast by rail that afternoon at his request—the subject of the meeting not disclosed to her in advance, only that it was important.

The night breeze chilled her as it swept in off the ocean. Even the heavy *durumagi* she wore over her clothes didn't keep the frosty air at bay. Hidden in the foothills of Mt. Kumgang, the replica of the Loire Valley *Chateau de Blois* was surrounded by 8,000 acres of heavily patrolled forest. From the path below the mansion, she saw the Wonsan city lights in the distance.

"We have closed the satellite lab in New York City, Dear Leader," Moon said. "We moved it to a new location in a neighboring state. I ordered there be nothing left behind that could lead the authorities to believe it was anything more than an electronics manufacturer's warehouse."

"We will trust your orders were followed." He did not look at her, and that caused a hairline fracture in her normally granite confidence. She had been warned many times over the years that if he chose not to make eye contact, he harbored resentment or anger. She hoped that he was simply preoccupied with other matters of state.

They came to a bend in the path. A waist-high wall protected them from a rocky precipice that dropped into the darkness.

"No plan is immune to failure, Dr. Chung," he said as he gazed out over the wall toward the distant city. "Even one as exquisitely planned and meticulously executed as yours."

"Dear Leader, I fully realize—"

He held his hand up. "I know you do, Dr. Chung." His voice was almost a whisper. "We sympathize with your tremendous task and marvel daily how you manage to accomplish so much. It is a mountain of an undertaking for anyone—even someone of your unquestionable talents and abilities."

Moon sighed silently, thankful that he was not upset. "Thank you, Dear—"

"But from time to time, we all must come to the realization that we require a little extra help."

"I don't understand. My team is working without regard to their own needs to make this a reality. I can't imagine who I could add to my staff that would increase our chances of success anymore than those whom I have handpicked over the last year."

A bead of sweat ran down the spillway of her spine at the threat of losing control of the project. "My scientists bring with them years of unquestionable knowledge in the field of genetics and viral research, not to mention the thousand warriors we have assembled who have taken an oath to arm themselves with our deadly weapon, walk right into the midst of our enemies, and execute them. Although it is small, there is no finer, more dedicated army on the face of the earth. What we have experienced with this minor glitch in New York is a momentary setback." Her palms dampened, and her hands shook more from nerves than the Parkinson's. "This news reporter—this Stone woman—is no danger to us. She will soon realize that there is nothing to pursue, nothing to report, nothing—"

The General Secretary turned to face Moon. "Dr. Chung, I am sure that you are completely correct. I have not one second of doubt about you or your team of scientists and soldiers. You have done an outstanding job of conceptualizing and developing a plan that goes beyond even the most extreme boundaries of my own imagination. And that in itself is an accomplishment. For that, you have my admiration and blessing. But like any wise investor, it is my resources that underwrite your efforts, and I must protect my interests. And that is why I have asked an acquaintance to come and lend a hand."

Moon felt as if she had taken a blow to her chest. For a moment she seemed to teeter, and wondered if she could maintain her balance. Her breathing was labored. The words of the General Secretary washed over her like glacial runoff, sending a frozen blade of fear to the core of her being. This was her life-work being threatened. No one could take that from her. She would not allow it.

From behind her, Moon heard footsteps on the gravel path. She turned to see a man approach, but in the darkness, few details were visible. In fact, he seemed to be a part of the darkness itself—his features as indistinguishable as the deep forest shadows surrounding her.

When he was only a few paces away, Moon saw that he appeared to be in his late sixties or early seventies, with hair the color of ash and skin the texture of leather. His shirt, pants, and long coat, all the shade of coal, hung like an extension of his skin. There was a general darkness about him, except for his eyes, which glinted in the reflected starlight like smoldering embers.

"Good evening, my dear friend," the General Secretary said as the Old Man approached. "I am most grateful that you have come."

"How could I not accept such a compelling invitation?"

Moon realized this was the first time she had ever heard anyone address the General Secretary without referring to him as Dear Leader. There was something about this stranger that took command of her attention as absolutely as gravity took control of a falling object. His presence affected her like the sudden heaviness one senses when emerging from a pool. A shudder coursed through her, and a bitter taste rose in her throat.

The General Secretary motioned toward Moon. "It is my pleasure to introduce Dr. Chung Moon Jung."

Moon respectfully and briefly bowed her head. She expected the General Secretary to in turn name the visitor, but he did not.

"My compliments, Dr. Chung," the Old Man said. "Your ability to bring about such a work of genius has exceeded even my expectations."

Who was this man who knew of her work and had placed his expectations upon her? How dare he be so presumptuous!

"You were about to ask my name?" he said. He turned to the General Secretary. "A logical question, don't you think?" Before the

Communist leader spoke, the Old Man reached out and touched Moon's arm. "For now, consider me a special advisor. And don't be concerned, Dr. Chung. I have no intention of interfering with your work or your authority. I am here at the request of my friend to assist you in guaranteeing the success of your project."

"Guarantee?" Moon said. "How is that possible?" She glanced at the General Secretary. "I don't understand."

The Old Man took his hand away. "We share common goals, you and I, Dr. Chung. You seek revenge. For a different set of reasons, so do I. As does your Dear Leader and so many others who have experienced the atrocities committed by your enemies and their allies. All you have to understand is that I am willing to assist you. For me, this is just a stop along the way to my ultimate goal. At the end of all this, I must bring a dear family member home again. You and your project are a rung in the ladder that will lead to my success. So, I have chosen to help your endeavor. I have the ability to create a diversion that will take away the unwanted attention you are now getting and allow you to proceed with your project unhindered."

"A diversion?" Moon said. "From what?"

"Not what, but who."

WOLF CASTLE

THE SOVIET-ERA ZIL LIMOUSINE carrying its six passengers glided along the two-lane highway fifty miles east of Chisinau, Moldova. John watched the farms and woodlands roll by—a mixture of hornbeam, oaks, linden, maple, and beech. Most had already shed the last of their autumn leaves as their sap retreated into the protection of the earth before the onslaught of winter. At one point, the limo was waved through a border checkpoint and crossed a bridge over the Dniester River into Transnistria.

Soon, they turned off the main highway onto a hard surface country road. The terrain became hilly and finally transformed into a range of low but rugged mountains.

"Reminds me of the Great Smokey Mountains," John said to Archbishop Luigi Roberti, the Vatican Foreign Minister sitting next to him. "My family had a summer cabin in North Carolina. I spent a lot of time there as a kid."

"Simpler times, yes?" Roberti said.

"Much." John had grown up in a suburb of Boston but spent vacations and summers at the family cabin. His life had been a journey of faith—faith in his calling to serve God and his passion to find the secrets that man left buried in antiquity. It was after he and Cotten had destroyed a diabolical plot to clone Christ from blood residue found in the Holy Grail that he was called to Rome to take on the position of Prelate of the Pontifical Commission for Sacred Archeology. His immediate elevation to the rank of bishop, and later archbishop, along with the secret recruitment into the Venatori put him on the fast track to leadership in the clandestine organization. Within five years he moved into the position of director of the Venatori, an office that came with the rank of cardinal. Now as the chief advisor to the pope on matters of intelligence and security, John was considered by a select few in the spy communities of the Western world as the second-most powerful man at the Vatican.

After arriving in Moldova from Rome the previous day, he and the small Vatican delegation had stayed the night at the LeoGrand Hotel in the capital city of Chisinau before departing the following morning for a remote location near the Transnistrian border—a last-minute change of location, they were told. John knew it was not uncommon when dealing with fragile diplomatic issues for arrangements to change at the last moment. Their schedule called for meetings with representatives of the Moldova state department and their counterparts from Transnistria and the Ukraine.

Major General Nikolai Borodin of the Republic of Transnistria sat opposite John in the limo. The officer appeared to be nodding off. John stared at him, thinking it peculiar that the general himself was their escort rather than some military attaché. But he supposed their resources were limited. One of the last Communist bastions, the Transnistrian Parliament was not recognized by any government in the world. The general's uniform seemed a little tattered, and the man wearing it was on the brink of being unkempt, which John thought was a sure indicator of the disastrous economy.

He also noticed that the driver's appearance was just as ragged. Even the limo was old and worn—parts of the headliner sagged, and the paint flaked in places.

The ZIL made another turn onto a narrow country road leading into the shadows of the mountains. They approached a security fence and passed through a gate guarded by a half-dozen heavily armed soldiers. John saw a sign written in Russian and English that said: *No Unauthorized Vehicles or Personnel beyond this point.*

A bump in the road stirred the general and he looked out the window. "We're getting close, gentlemen," he said, with the faintest of accents. "I predict you will be impressed with our destination. It's called Wolf Castle and was built in the mid-1400s by Vlad Tepes III, known as The Impaler, Prince of Wallachia. He was the son of Vlad Drucul and came to be known as Dracula. So you will be spending your first day in Dracula's Castle. Dracul, by the way, is Romanian for devil."

John smiled as he listened. *One way or another, I'm always fighting the same enemy.*

Borodin continued, "Many years ago, Comrade Brezhnev would visit here during the summer months to get away from the political heat of the Kremlin. He called it his Russian Camp David, like the Maryland retreat of the American presidents."

The ZIL wound its way along an ever-increasing incline as the road snaked up the side of a particularly steep mountain. Thinning forest turned to rocky terrain and finally to sheer cliffs. Leveling off, the ZIL rounded a bend and John saw a medieval structure loom out of the mountaintop as if it had grown from the very granite. He heard the deep rumble as the heavy limousine rolled over the thick wooden drawbridge and entered the courtyard.

"We have arrived," Borodin said as he waited for the driver to get out and open the side door. Stepping from the limo first, the general waited for the others.

John and Archbishop Roberti got out next, followed by Father Michael Burns, a young priest who traveled with the group as Roberti's new assistant. The last to exit the ZIL were two plain-clothes members of the Swiss Guard assigned as a diplomatic security unit.

"Welcome to Wolf Castle," Borodin said, motioning the entourage past him and toward the steps leading to the front entrance of the central building.

John looked up at the great walls that rose to challenge any medieval invasion. Their colossal battlements were imposing, and numerous conical roofs resembled giant missiles ready for launch.

A sudden muffled *POP – POP* made him stop and spin around.

The two Swiss Guards sprawled prostrate on the ground, blood pooling at their heads. General Borodin stood over them, a smoking automatic pistol in his hand.

CASTLE KEEP

"Sweet Jesus, what have you done?" John stared at the two bodies on the ground. He took a step toward them.

"Don't be foolish," Borodin said, aiming the pistol.

"Have you lost your mind?" Archbishop Roberti's voice shook—his whole body shook.

Borodin waved the gun. "Shut up!" He spoke to his driver in Romanian, then ordered the priests to hand over their cell phones. After the driver collected the phones, Borodin commanded them to move inside.

John turned away from the bloody scene, sickened by what he had just witnessed. Obviously they had walked into a trap. The last-minute change of pickup time and meeting location, the tattered appearance of the soldiers and the car—it was a setup, and it had cost two good men their lives.

With the driver in the lead, they passed through a set of thick wooden doors into the largest of the buildings inside the walled fortress. Entering what John assumed was once a ceremonial great hall, their footfalls echoed off the ancient riverstone floor. Except for a handful of wooden benches and a few metal folding chairs, the room was bare. He saw a spotting of mounted antler racks, and a couple of ragged tapestries hung on the walls. Overall, the fortress appeared neglected and in need of maintenance and repairs.

The priests were taken to a wing of the castle that contained a number of small bedrooms. They passed a handful of armed soldiers along the way.

"To use the toilet facilities, knock on your door for the guard," Borodin told them. "Otherwise, you will remain in your rooms. If you leave your room without one of my men as an escort, you will be shot. Remember your dead friends outside? That will be you if you disobey."

One of the soldiers shoved John into the bedroom. The door closed. He waited a moment before confirming it was locked.

The room was sparsely furnished with a straight-back chair and wood-frame bed with carvings of winged demons in the headboard. The mattress was thin and without linens, and the air heavy with the smell of mold and damp stone.

John sat on the bed and said a prayer for the two men murdered in the courtyard below. They had been his friends, serving him faithfully for years. He knew their families. It was such a waste of life, such a tragedy. He reached to hold the small cross hanging on a chain at his neck and whispered a plea for guidance.

———

As evening fell, the priests were taken from their rooms to a small chamber adjacent to the castle's kitchen. They were provided hard bread and what John assumed was the equivalent of beef jerky. But he was certain it wasn't beef. They washed the food down with water from metal cups. An armed soldier stood guard by the kitchen exit.

"They must come to their senses," Roberti said, sitting next to Father Burns and across from John at the rough-hewn wood table. His Roman nose pointed like the tip of a sword and his thick, dark hair seemed as unruly as his increasingly nervous manner. "Murdering two innocent men is beyond belief." He wheezed as he spoke. "We came here at the request of their country."

John shook his head. "Luigi, they are impostors."

"Then who are they?" Roberti asked.

"Terrorists," Father Burns said. He bore a round face with short blond hair and dark, brown eyes.

"That would be my assessment, as well," John said. "They have kidnapped us. Probably for ransom."

"*Liniste!*" the guard shouted from his position by the door.

"I think he wants us to be quiet," John said.

They sat in silence for a few moments. Roberti, whose back was to the guard, whispered, "Do they really expect the Vatican to negotiate with terrorists?"

"Perhaps they're tempted by the perceived wealth of the Church, Luigi," John said, covering his mouth with the metal cup as he pretended to drink.

Father Burns whispered, "And they are probably counting on the fact that, unlike most countries, we have no real army to come and rescue us. They have little to fear in reprisal."

"The Church won't negotiate," John said, taking a bite of bread. "Think what that would mean. Every priest, every church official, would become an instant target."

"They won't strike a deal," Burns said. "They can't. And if they refuse to negotiate, as I'm sure they will, there's only one choice left."

"Are you saying you think they would shoot us, too?" Roberti said.

John gave Burns a look of disapproval. The archbishop was already on edge. There was no reason to put him over. "Without us," John said, looking at Roberti, "there is no chance their demands will be met. Besides, it's too early to make predictions. As irrational as these men are, they know that we must be kept alive to collect."

"But the Holy See will never pay a ransom," Burns said.

Roberti glared at Burns, then John. "We will never leave here alive."

MISSING

COTTEN STOOD IN THE middle of the dark room, the glow of video monitors washing her face with soft pastels. "Advance the source video by three frames then back-time the theme music into the bumper."

"You haven't lost your touch," the editor said as he programmed the change into the computer. "Here's a preview." A moment later, the new edit appeared in the program monitor.

"Perfect," Cotten said. It was rare that she made an appearance at the edit of her weekly *Relics* program. Having done so many shows, the editor usually assembled the whole program alone, then sent a DVD to Cotten for weekend review. The show aired on Monday night. But since she was still at the office doing research into T-Kup, she decided to visit the Friday night edit session.

"So you didn't tell me, what brings you into the cave of Edit C?" the editor asked as he instructed the computer to continue assembling the show from the offline edit decision list.

"Just here to make sure you're not goofing off."

"Yeah, right." He clicked the mouse and looked up at the program monitor. "Okay, here we go from a ten-second pre-roll."

Cotten watched the change she had requested. "I like it." She heard the door open behind her. Turning, she saw Ted enter the room.

"How's it going?" he asked.

"Another masterpiece," the editor said as he crossed his arms, leaned back, and watched the computer continue to build the show from the footage stored on the hard disks.

"You got a minute?" Ted said, placing his hand on Cotten's back.

She turned to face him. "Sure."

He motioned toward the door. "Let's leave Michelangelo to his work while we chat outside."

"Finally, someone recognizes artistic genius when they see it," the editor said.

"Time to ask for a raise," she said as she patted him on the head and followed Ted out of the edit suite.

Across the hall was a break room with vending machines. "Over there," Ted said.

Cotten felt an unnatural chill course through her. *Something was up. Ted was acting squirrelly.*

Once they were alone in the break room, Ted put his hands in his trouser pockets and faced Cotten. "Want to sit down?" he asked, cocking his head toward the sofa.

Over the years she'd learned to read Ted pretty well, and his stance and tone were clear. "This isn't going to be good, is it?"

Ted shook his head. "John is missing."

For a moment, Cotten couldn't say anything for the jumble of thoughts and emotions that exploded inside. Finally she said, "Define missing."

"He and the Vatican's foreign minister, along with a couple of security guards and a priest, flew from Rome to Moldova to meet with delegations from neighboring countries. They stayed overnight in the capital. When their local hosts came to pick them up the next morning, the hotel said that the Vatican group had already left."

"When was this?" she asked.

"We just got word. The Vatican assumed that the meetings were being held in a secret location for security reasons. There's a lot of unrest in the region. Now the Holy See confirmed that they have lost contact with John, the foreign minister, and the others in the party."

"So what are they doing about it?"

"We don't know."

Cotten paced in front of the drink machine. "They have to be doing something. They can't just ignore it." An angry thought spewed its way into her head and out her mouth. "Don't tell me they're doing what they usually do and leave it all up to God." Cotten clasped her hands over her face. "Damn," she muttered, then looked at Ted. "I didn't mean it the way it sounded."

"You don't have to explain to me. I know about those love-hate feelings you have for the Catholic Church."

Cotten shoved her hair back from her face. "Can we at least send someone to cover it and bring attention to what's going on?" She glared at her boss. "We've got to do something."

Ted rested his hand on her shoulder. "I'm way ahead of you, kiddo. Our Moscow office has a truck with a three-man crew headed to Moldova. They'll be there in the morning."

"Then I'm going, too."

"There's no reason for you to get all worked up, yet. We have a reporter en route right now. As far as we know, this could all be unsubstantiated information. I understand how this is more than a news story to you. But let's wait and see what we find out first."

"Have we tried to contact John or the foreign minister?"

"Of course."

"And?"

"No luck."

"That doesn't seem strange to you?"

"Just like the flow of news, cell technology in parts of the former Soviet Union is dicey as well."

"This stinks, Ted."

"Or it could be perfectly innocent."

"You really believe that?"

Ted looked away.

Cotten crossed her arms. "I'm going."

"So you fly to Moldova. Then what? Wander around the countryside asking if anyone has seen a bunch of priests? You don't even speak the language. It would be a total waste of time."

She stared at the ceiling, her mind sorting through the limited choices. Ted was right. But she couldn't stand by and wait helplessly.

"You're correct, Ted," she said, "going to Moldova would be a waste."

"Finally you're making sense."

"I'm going to Rome."

ISLE ROYALE PING

AMARUG CROUCHED BENEATH A paper birch tree in Isle Royale National Park, an island separated from the rest of the world by more than fifteen miles of frigid Lake Superior waters. She lifted the binoculars to her eyes to get a closer look at number 17, the Alpha male of the wolf pack. Inbreeding had brought about genetic weaknesses and placed the wolves' survival in jeopardy. That, and the decline in the moose population, had taken its toll. The numbers were down from twenty-five wolves the previous year to only nineteen today.

Amarug was part of a multi-grant-funded study group doing research on the Isle Royale wolves. When the other researchers left in October as the park closed for the season, Amarug volunteered to stay behind wanting to gather additional data until the rest of the group returned in January. The winter was harsh, but being Inuit and having grown up in a cold, inhospitable environment, she had no fear of toughing it out. And if things got particularly rough, she had the radio to call for help.

At the sound of the seaplane, she lowered the binoculars and got to her feet. The plane brought her supplies each month, but why was it a week early? She would have hung closer to the base camp in anticipation of its arrival if she'd known it was coming today. It wasn't the harshest of the season yet, by any means, but the days were going to get harder and she wanted to check the supply list before the seaplane took off again.

Running through the forest, Amarug dodged firs and white spruce until finally emerging on the shoreline. The seaplane was beached two hundred yards in the distance.

"Eric," she shouted and waved, seeing him carrying boxes from the plane toward her yurt—the round, single-story structure that served as her home. He didn't appear to hear her. She picked up her speed, sprinting along the narrow beach, and at last found herself winded as she approached the yurt. He was bent over stacking some boxes on the front deck.

"Eric," she sputtered, hands on her knees catching her breath. "What are you doing here today?"

When he turned to face her, Amarug realized it wasn't the regular pilot who always flew in their provisions. This man was younger than Eric, mid-twenties, black hair, and noticeably Asian facial features. "Where's Eric?" she asked, still huffing.

The man cocked his head back toward the mainland. "Vacation—two weeks off." He smiled at her. "Use it or lose it."

"Lucky dog," she said. "Oh, I'm sorry, I'm Sialuk, but everybody calls me Amarug—means wolf."

She stuck out her hand and he shook it.

"But aren't you early?" she asked, swinging open the door to the yurt for him.

"Yeah, when they're shorthanded the schedule gets crazy. Figured you'd rather we be early than late." He lifted one of the boxes, carried it inside to her small kitchen area and set it on the counter.

"But I could have missed you," she said, moving her stuff out of the way for him, while thinking someone should have contacted her about the change. "Well, it doesn't matter I guess." She swept her bangs off her forehead with the back of her arm. After he set the box down, Amarug opened the lid and glanced inside. While she inspected the contents, he brought in another two boxes.

"Can I see the manifest?"

He took a folded paper from his pocket and handed it over before retrieving the final two cartons.

Amarug pulled her ballpoint from her pocket and went down the list, checking off each item.

"Any chance I could use your radio?" he asked. "I'm supposed to check in. The unit on the plane is acting up."

"It's over there." She pointed toward the equipment on the desk in her living area before continuing to check off the supplies.

"Get everything you wanted?" he asked, returning to the kitchen a few moments later.

"What's this?" She held up a bottle of antiseptic throat spray.

"Didn't have the brand you wanted. That's supposed to be better."

She stared at the label. "I'll give it a try. Chronic sore throat is killing me this time of year."

"All right then. Been a pleasure meeting you. I'll tell Eric you said hi."

She accompanied him to the door. "I didn't catch your name."

"Hiu," he called over his shoulder as he headed for the seaplane.

———

Falling snow covered the retreating wolves' footprints near the yurt. The thinning moose population had altered the predator's behavior—the struggle to survive could do that to any animal. The last kill the pack made, they ate the entire carcass, including the teeth and skull, something wolves with normal diets hardly ever did.

The pack's last kill was weeks ago.

Tonight they smelled blood and death—maybe it was a kill by another pack. The scent came from inside the yurt. They circled the structure, paced the deck, pawing at the doorway and windows, trying to find a way in to stop the stabbing hunger in their bellies. Then by sheer accident, as the animals howled and scratched in a frenzy at the door, one managed to climb over another desperately trying to get at its prey. The fury of fur and flesh turned the knob just enough for the lock to slip free of the strike plate, and the door eased open.

———

The droning came from the east as the seaplane banked and glided in for a landing on the surface of the sheltered inlet. A few moments later, the front edge of the pontoons crunched up onto the beach. Hiu switched off the engine, opened the door, maneuvered along the float, and jumped onto the beach. He knew the regular supply plane was scheduled for a delivery the next day, so he had only the rest of today to clean everything up.

"Damn, it's cold." He pulled his collar around his neck, still not understanding who would be dumb enough to stick it out in this weather just to watch wolves fuck each other and eat moose. The researchers weren't going to do anything to save the animals, anyway. Just let nature take its course. Waste of time.

As he approached the yurt, Hiu noticed the open door. His first thought was that perhaps the *ping* had failed, that her Inuit genetics had interfered with the trigger virus, and that Amarug was out and about somewhere in the woods tracking her wolf pack. In which case, he would have a lot of explaining to do, starting with why he was there for no apparent reason.

There was nothing surprising about the door being open. The last time he was there, it hadn't been locked. She'd just turned the knob and poof. He supposed there was no reason to keep it secured during the winter months. There were no visitors to the island. Virtually abandoned except for the Inuit wolf woman.

What if she had found where he disabled her radio and she somehow fixed it? But there had been no distress call. That was a good sign.

As he stepped through the doorway into the yurt, he was almost knocked over by the stench. "Shit," he said. "She's dead, no doubt about it."

As his eyes adjusted to the darkness inside the yurt and he was about to take a step forward, he noticed the overturned table, the bloody rug, and the ripped sheets hanging off the single bed. Hiu knew immediately what he was looking at, and the hair on the back of his neck stood on end—like a cat's when startled—or a wolf's ruff. A few small white splinters of bone resembling fragile toothpicks poked out of the rug's nap.

"Jesus," he whispered and stared at the hank of matted black hair—the only thing left of Amarug, the wolf woman.

RANSOM DEMAND

COTTEN STOPPED IN FRONT of John's office on the way to the upper floor of the Government Palace where the department of the Vatican Secretariat of State was located. She turned to the Venatori agent escorting her. "Do you mind if I just take a quick look inside?"

He hesitated. "Normally, it wouldn't be allowed, but knowing what you're probably going through right now, I don't see any harm. Just for a moment."

"Thank you." She gave him a grateful smile before pressing her palm to the dark wood of the door as if she might glean a sense of John's presence.

Cotten opened the door, stepped inside and drank in a heavy breath. She heard the door softly close behind her. Her escort had allowed her a moment of privacy. Cotten's throat pinched at the thought that something had happened to John. She fought back, thinking of all the possibilities. Her fingertips feathered over the books on his shelf, then slid across the surface of his polished desk.

She wanted to touch the things he touched, soak up whatever sense of him there was. Clutching the top of John's high-back desk chair, she closed her eyes and rested her cheek on the leather, wrapping her arms about the backrest of the chair. She envisioned his face, his eyes—those eyes—those deep-blue-ocean eyes. "Come home to me," she whispered. John was the only person in her life who had never asked anything of her, except to believe in herself. There had never been any man she had cared about the way she cared about this man—a man she could never have. And maybe there was safety in that. *I can't lose what I never had in the first place.*

The door opened. "I'm sorry, Ms. Stone, but we really have to be going."

"I know," she said, straightening and sweeping back her hair. Just before leaving she peered over her shoulder one last time.

———

Cotten sat in the reception area of the Vatican Secretariat of State's office and watched a steady parade coming and going from the diplomat's office. Most were priests, a few were laymen in suits. None looked happy.

She had arrived on a flight from New York that morning and came straight to Vatican City. Numerous calls from Ted to the Vatican had produced tentative promises of a meeting with the chief diplomat of the Holy See. Although the Church played down the news of the missing priests, it was obvious to Cotten that within the walls of the Government Palace, everyone seemed to take the situation seriously.

After half an hour of waiting, she was about to pull her cell phone from her purse and leave Ted an update message when the door from the main hallway opened and a priest entered. He wore a black suit and Roman collar, and carried a briefcase. As he passed, he glanced in her direction and they recognized one another.

"Cotten!" he said, even as she got to her feet and moved toward him. "What a wonderful surprise."

"Your Excellency. So good to see you again." They shook hands. A feeling of comfort came over her, seeing the friendly, familiar face of Archbishop Felipe Montiagro, the Vatican Apostolic Nuncio to the United States. Montiagro was the Holy See's equivalent of an ambassador and they had met years ago during what the press dubbed the Grail conspiracy and her finding of the Holy Grail.

"I would ask what brings you here," he said, "but I can guess that it's this matter of John's disappearance."

"Can I assume that's why you're here, too?"

He gestured to a couple of chairs. "Wait just one minute. Let me check in with the receptionist."

After he had signed in on the visitor's log, he sat in the chair next to Cotten. "Again, let me say how good it is to see you, but sorry it is under these circumstances. Unfortunately, I was one of the principles who helped arrange for John and Archbishop Roberti to get involved in the negotiations between the three disputing parties. So you can imagine how much this has upset me."

"Has there been any word? Please tell me he's safe."

"At this point we don't have much information, but we have nothing to indicate that he is not."

"Thank God."

"Yes. Thank God. As you can imagine, this is not something the Holy See deals with every day. We are proceeding cautiously."

"So what *can* you tell me?"

"The official release of information to the press is virtually cut off at this point. I can't discuss any of the details. But believe me, I fully understand the personal relationship you have with John and I sympathize. I realize you are here both because of that relationship and in the role of a network correspondent. This must be painful for you, not knowing anything more than the crumbs of information already in the press. To be honest, I don't know much more myself."

"But you believe John is all right?"

"We are keeping the faith," Montiagro said.

"I understand you can't talk to me on the record. But, Excellency, I'm here to help any way I can. Perhaps there's something I can do to assist. I'm willing to try anything."

The archbishop seemed to consider her offer. Then he said, "There are few organizations in the world more secretive and downright paranoid than the Holy See. The reasons go back centuries. But suffice it to say, bringing an outsider like you into the middle of this would be unprecedented." He smiled. "But not impossible. After all, you do have a reputation around here for getting things done."

"Archbishop," the receptionist said as she placed the phone down, "the cardinal will see you now."

Montiagro stood and gave the woman an acknowledging wave. As he picked up his briefcase, he said to Cotten, "Give me a few moments. Let me respectfully remind His Eminence that he's kept you waiting too long."

When Cotten was ushered into the inner office, she was greeted by a man she guessed to be in his mid-seventies—tall with a long, narrow face, and short-cropped gray hair. His eyelids sagged and dark puffy pockets underscored his eyes. Unlike Montiagro whose appearance, except for the Roman collar, was basic black business suit, the prelate was dressed in the traditional attire of his office—a *simar* which resembled a regular black cassock but with a short shoulder cape attached that reminded Cotten of Sherlock Homes. There was also a wide sash called a *fascia* that he wore high up on his sternum, and a skullcap called a *zucchetto*. The sash and skullcap had a kind of moiré pattern that gave the material a 3-D effect. John had once explained to Cotten all about the traditional garb of the clergy and told her the unusual material was called watered silk. A simple pectoral cross hung on a gold chain around the man's neck. The buttons and piping on the cassock along with the sash and skullcap were scarlet, designating the rank of cardinal.

"Your Eminence, may I present Cotten Stone," Archbishop Montiagro said as she walked across the sprawling Oriental rug and came to stand before a massive, ornately carved desk.

The cardinal came around the desk with an outstretched hand.

Montiagro continued, looking at Cotten. "May I introduce Cardinal Giovanni Fazio, the Secretary of State to His Holiness."

"It's an honor," Cotten said shaking his hand.

"My dear Ms. Stone," Fazio said. "I was privileged to be in attendance in the Great Hall of Constantine on that glorious day when you presented the Cup of Christ to the Universal Church. I know what you did in order to rescue our most precious relic from the grasp of darkness. In my seventy-three years of service to God, I have never come face-to-face with pure evil as you did. I am sincerely blessed to be in your presence."

For a moment, Cotten was speechless. It was incredible anyone, much less a man of this stature in the Church, would feel *blessed* to be in her presence. "Thank you," she finally managed to say.

"Please," Cardinal Fazio said, motioning to a grouping of chairs off to the side of his desk. He indicated to Montiagro to join her. When they were all seated, the cardinal gave a heavy sigh and interlocked his fingers, resting them in his lap. "These are trying times, my dear friends. Our Lord tests us each moment, but in these past days, he has outdone himself."

"Can you tell me the latest news?" Cotten asked.

"It goes without saying, Ms. Stone," the cardinal said, "that what we discuss is to remain in this room. My words are spoken with total anonymity."

"I understand. For now, I am here as John Tyler's friend, not as a reporter."

"Cardinal Tyler, Archbishop Roberti, and Father Michael Burns, Roberti's assistant, are being held for one hundred million dollars ransom."

"So the Church will pay it, and we'll get them back safe?" Cotten said. "Right?"

Fazio looked away for a moment as if fighting an inner turmoil. Then he said, "Ms. Stone, the Vatican does not negotiate with kidnappers and terrorists. I'm afraid there will be no payment."

NIGHT VISITOR

THERE WAS A SMALL fireplace in John's room that gave off a minimum amount of heat, but the night was bitter cold despite the fire. Even though the walls were extremely thick, the wind seemed to find its way inside.

His bare mattress was uncomfortable, but at least they had provided a wool blanket, musty as it was. With the bedside lamp out, he lay watching the fire cast undulating shadows across the ceiling.

As he listened to the creaks and moans of the aging fortress, he wondered what it must have been like when Count Dracula walked the halls of the castle. Bram Stoker and Hollywood had done a great job of glorifying the legendary figure.

John reviewed all the day's events in his head but nothing seemed to make sense. These men were bold and reckless in kidnapping diplomats. It was as if they didn't care about the political ramifications. If nothing else, this would bring condemnation from most other nations. One of the oldest and most honored practices between countries, even those at war, was the exchange of diplomats and the assurance of their safety. The sanctity of diplomats had been observed for centuries, going back to the standards set by Genghis Khan who strongly insisted on the rights of diplomats and would take horrific vengeance against any states violating the codes of honor. Diplomatic immunity was understood and accepted by virtually every nation on earth—agreed upon and ratified according to the Vienna Convention of Diplomatic Relations. What was happening here was against every code of diplomacy.

The constantly moving patterns shimmering across the ceiling became hypnotic. Even when John closed his eyes, he still saw them. The howl of the wind mixed with the crackle and pop of the fire produced an eerie, uncomfortable feeling as John fought to try to fall asleep.

Soon, the fire died and the room fell dark—only the soft glow of embers cast off a faint light. Finally, he relaxed and drifted off.

He hadn't been asleep long when a noise—a creaking footstep on the wooden floor—roused him. Confused about where he was at first, John tried to get his bearings. When he caught the low light of the burning embers, he remembered his room in the castle. That's when he saw a shadow move in front of the fireplace's glow. Silently, it swept across the room, coming toward him.

John sat up. "Who's there? Who is it?"

Still groggy from sleep, he felt icy fingers upon his skin as if the grip of winter rode the wind into his room and wrapped around his neck.

THE PHOTO

"What do you mean you won't meet the demands and pay the ransom?" Cotten said. "You're risking their lives if you don't."

Cardinal Fazio leaned forward. "First, the Church doesn't have that kind of—"

Cotten rose and paced. "Spare me." She turned in a circle and waved her hand at the grandeur of the room. "Don't even start with *you don't have the money*. Give me a break."

"Ms. Stone, I understand your frustration," Cardinal Fazio said. "The main assets of the Church are in art treasures, antiquities, and property holdings. Liquid assets—cash—that is a different matter. Please calm yourself and be rational. If we negotiate with these men, we set precedence for an endless stream of the same. You know why El Al is never hijacked and why there aren't thousands of Israelis being kidnapped every year? Because Israel refuses to negotiate with terrorists under any circumstances. The Vatican must take the same stance."

Cotten felt her breathing come hard and fast. She understood the principle, but this was John. *How different it is when something like this hits home—when someone you love is in jeopardy*. Intellectually, she understood the cardinal's point, but in her heart...

"I'm trying to be rational," she said. "Really I am. But these are priests, for heaven's sake. Good men. They have dedicated their lives to God. Can't God give a little back?"

She dropped into the chair. "Damn."

"We will do what we can, but negotiations are out of the question," Fazio said.

Montiagro reached to touch her shoulder. "I know you understand our position, but that doesn't take the sting out of it."

"No, it doesn't." Cotten wiped the budding tears from her eyes. "But didn't I hear there were security men with them. Members of the Swiss Guard? Why weren't they able to stop this from happening?"

Fazio glanced at his hands. "There were two bodyguards with them, that is correct, but ..."

"But what?" Cotten shoved her hair away from her face.

"They were executed," Montiagro said.

"Executed? How do you know that? What are you keeping from me? Please, tell me everything."

Fazio rose and walked to his desk. He opened a drawer, took out a brown envelope, and removed its contents. "We received these digital images. Nothing you would want to see. Just take my word for it."

"Trust me, as a network journalist, I've seen just about everything. Show me what you have." She held out her hand.

"Be warned, this one is graphic," the cardinal said. "Actually, barbaric. Are you sure?"

Cotten's throat felt closed, and so instead of speaking she nodded.

The cardinal handed her the first photo.

The image almost sucked her breath from her. The heads of two men she assumed were the guards were impaled on metal stakes sticking up from the ground, a stark winter forest their backdrop.

Cotten studied the picture. "And you are sure these are the men who accompanied John and the others?"

"Yes," Fazio said.

She slumped in the chair. "But you don't have pictures like this of John?" She didn't want to ask that question, because she wasn't sure she wanted to hear the answer. Cotten held her breath waiting for the response.

"No, not like those," Fazio said.

Cotten picked up on his hesitation. "But you do have a picture of John?"

"Yes," Fazio said.

She stared into his dark brown eyes, her hand outstretched.

The cardinal handed her the other photo.

A huge, deep sigh involuntarily escaped her as she looked at the photograph. "John is alive," she said, tears choking her. She studied the color laser printout of John along with two other priests.

"He was alive when the photo was taken. That's all that we know," Fazio said.

The photo was of John and the other two standing in front of a stone wall. Snow covered the ground. Other than the wall and the snow, there were no details to help identify their location.

"What do you make of the wall?" she asked.

Fazio shrugged. "It could be anywhere."

"But there's snow," she said. "Where is it snowing right now?"

The cardinal shook his head. "Most of the mountains of Eastern Europe are under an early winter blizzard. The area covers massive amounts of land."

"So we know they're in the mountains?"

"Perhaps."

"The wall looks old," she said. "Maybe a fort or castle?"

Fazio spread his hands apart. "All of Europe is old."

Montiagro spoke up. "The point is, Cotten, we really have little to go on. It's obvious the kidnappers chose a location for the photo that offered no concrete information. Same thing as in terrorist's videos, like those of Bin Laden. Very generic."

"What about the other photo? The one of the dead guards?" she asked. "Did you notice any clues?"

"Even less information," Fazio said. "You saw it. Just the winter forest backdrop—a bit of snow on the ground."

Cotten scrutinized the picture of the three priests again. The shortest of the trio stood with his hands buried in his overcoat pockets, his gaze was away from the camera. In the middle, the other priest appeared uncomfortable with his arms folded against his chest as he looked at the ground. Beside him, John stared into the camera. One hand was in the pocket of his coat, the other resting on the side of his neck. He seemed a bit awkward. Something about it niggled at her. Finally she broke her gaze away from the photo. "Would you make me a copy? I'd like to study it again later. There's just something … Actually," she said, "I'd like a copy of both."

"The Swiss Guards?" Montiagro asked.

"There might be some clue—something we haven't seen yet."

Montiagro looked at Fazio. The cardinal finally gave his approval by handing the images to the archbishop. "Felipe, please go to my secretary's office and make color photocopies for Ms. Stone. Make sure no one else sees them."

Montiagro took the images and left the room.

"Thank you," Cotten said.

"But they are for your eyes only," Fazio said. "We are agreed? If they suddenly appeared on broadcast news or in the newspaper it might be cause for great harm to come to Cardinal Tyler and the others."

"My eyes only," she said.

As the archbishop's footsteps echoed away, Cotten asked, "So what do you intend to do, Eminence? And more importantly, how can I help?"

"We are working with the governments of Moldova and the Ukraine to try to locate the three men. But those countries are embroiled in this escalating border conflict with Transnistria and have little time or resources to assist us. To be honest with you, Ms. Stone, I'm not sure they even care. They want our help when they need it, but are reluctant to return the favor."

"What about the Transnistrian government? Can't you get them to do anything?"

Montiagro returned, handing Cotten an envelope. "Your copies," he said.

"Thank you."

"Transnistria is just barely a government," Cardinal Fazio said. "Technically, Transnistria is a breakaway territory within the established borders of Moldova. But they're not officially recognized by any state or international organization. We're having little luck in communicating with them or gaining their cooperation."

Cotten's face flushed, and she made a conscious effort to keep her voice from trembling. "So basically, you're just giving up? That's what I'm hearing. You won't negotiate. You have no idea where they are, and you aren't going to do anything about it because you fear more kidnappings, more ransoms. What about the value of a single God-given life? Why isn't that at the top of your agenda? I can't believe you are just going to sit back and risk their lives. And you call yourself a man of God?"

Cardinal Fazio rocked back in his chair, and Montiagro grasped Cotten's forearm as if wanting to still her. But it was to no avail.

"You aren't going to do anything … nothing? You might be able to live with yourself if John dies, but I can't. I can't justify in my heart or my head sacrificing even one single life even if it might save thousands. I don't think it is about the numbers. And to tell you the truth, I don't think God thinks in terms of numbers either. God is a father, the Father, and I can't imagine Him abandoning any one of his children. There is no Grace shining on the Church right now. So, if you're not going to do anything to save John, then you leave me only one choice. I'll have to do it."

DESERT HEAT
AND SANDSTORMS

COTTEN COULD STILL FEEL the anger burning inside her as she left Cardinal Fazio's office.

Felipe Montiagro followed her. "Cotten, wait up."

She didn't look back, but heard his footsteps as he trotted down the hall until he was beside her.

"I'm sorry you didn't hear what you wanted to hear. But it is the only stance the Holy See can take. You understand that. I know you must."

Cotten stopped. "No. That's the position that politicians and governments take. And what about the Venatori? Why doesn't the Church send in a team?" She waved the envelope containing the photos in the air. "If this super secret spy agency is so freaking powerful, why aren't they saving one of their own?"

"The Venatori is an intelligence gathering organization, not a combat or SWAT team. It's made up almost entirely of priests, not commandos."

Cotten resumed her course down the hall, the archbishop beside her. "Well, maybe it's something they should consider. What good is the intelligence if you don't have any way of—"

"You're wasting your energy. It is what it is, and that's where we are. You can't change that."

She stopped again and looked him straight in the eye. "Then just where do you suggest I focus my energy? In prayer? That's your job. Yours and the cardinal's. I'm no good at that." Cotten pinched the bridge of her nose. "Listen, I appreciate you being my friend and trying to make me feel better, but I'm not going to rest until John is safe and home again." She paused a moment then said, "I've gotta go." She turned away from Montiagro.

"Don't do anything foolish," he called. "John wouldn't want it."

———

Moon leaned over a microscope in her lab and peered through it one last time before shutting down the diagnostic systems and preparing to lock up. The past few days had been difficult physically, the tremors often interfering with her work. Her doctor advised her to rest, but that was not an option. Not at this point. She was so close to completing her work, a work that would bring the Americans and their allies to their knees, as helpless as flopping fish in the bottom of a boat. At first they would not understand, just as they had not understood the *pings*. But when the day came that they did...

It was late and the wind outside made the building moan. The night sounds of creaking and snapping were different from those during the day. In the sunlight she never noticed the noises. But at night the howl of the wind made her edgy.

As she switched the last of the computers off, she heard the door to the lab whine open. Moon turned around, clutching her chest as she saw a figure in the doorway.

"Good evening," the Old Man said. "You are working late, Dr. Chung."

Moon let out a long breath. "I am sorry. You startled me."

"Then I am the one to apologize." He walked into the room. "How is your work progressing?"

"Good," she answered, wondering why the late-night visit. "Everything is in its place."

"How much more time do you need?"

Moon shifted her weight to her other foot. She wasn't sure exactly how to answer how many more days it would take to confirm the virus would work as she had engineered it. So far all tests were positive. None of the different ethnic groups tested appeared to harbor primitive genes or mutations that would interfere. All the *pings* had been successful. There was still one left to complete, one that would test a group of people who had the same genetic make-up of primitive man 8,000 years ago—and that would mean that whatever genes they had were probably from the dawn of man and shared at some level by billions. If that one proved positive, then nothing would stand in her way.

Still there was the final work to be done in the medical labs, preparing the new generation of zealots who would give their lives for the cause. And that was going to be testy. They would probably lose a few. But she didn't want to reveal too many details to the Old Man. Not now. Soon she would present her final report to Dear Leader, and with his blessing they would launch the three waves of attacks. For now, all the Old Man needed to know was that they were progressing as expected, perhaps even a little ahead of the predicted schedule.

"A day?" he asked. "A week, a month?"

"Two weeks at the most. There is a strong likelihood we may be ready before that."

"Good," he said with a wide smile. "That is what I like to hear. The distraction I have designed is working. No one will be following up on Calderon or T-Kup for a while."

"Not even that woman reporter?" Moon asked.

"No."

"Has she been eliminated?"

The Old Man laughed. "I am afraid not. That would be a complicated endeavor. But I have arranged to divert her attention."

"You can be certain? If there is an investigation into T-Kup it will lead directly to us."

"Don't worry, Dr. Chung. I promised you additional time, and you have it. I know the Stone woman well and the way she thinks. She is strong-willed. That is precisely what will keep her from investigating T-Kup and the Calderon debacle—at least for a while. I have thrown her off track. But that doesn't mean you have extra time to squander."

She watched his eyes turn even darker, like a deep abyss spiraling into a world of desert heat and sandstorms.

In that instant, Moon was certain who she dealt with. But she dared not utter his name.

GRAY DAWN

JOHN OPENED HIS EYES. A predawn gray filtered in from the small window set high up the wall over his bed.

With a sudden jolt, he remembered the night visitor, or at least he thought he did. It had been a dark form against the blackness of the room. No words, no sound—just a presence. And then the sudden cold grip on his neck, the choking that must have caused him to black out.

Had it been real? Or just a reaction to the stress and fatigue of the hostage situation? Perhaps the heaviness of the dust, mildew, and musty bedding had made it hard for him to breathe.

He sat on the edge of the bed trying to recall exactly what had happened. He felt a slight tenderness on his neck. That wasn't his imagination or the result of stress. And it wasn't the remnants of a nightmare still hanging on.

He had no idea who or what had come to stand beside his bed last night. And if he was choked, why hadn't they finished the job? Why just enough to have him black out? Or had the intruder thought he was dead? That was a frightening thought. The last thing John remembered before losing consciousness was a strange alien squeaking sound coming from his throat as the pressure of the grip intensified, closing off his windpipe and carotids. And in what seemed almost the next moment, he was awake, staring at the pale glow of the approaching dawn. The night had ended. At this point, if not for the tenderness that encircled his neck, he could not be sure anything had happened at all.

———

A guard accompanied John to the small dining chamber just off the castle's kitchen. Archbishop Roberti and Father Burns were already seated at the table, eating what looked like stale biscuits stacked on a plate. A pitcher of water sat in the middle of the table.

"John," Roberti said, looking up. He slumped in his chair, a woolen blanket wrapped around his shoulders.

"Luigi," John said. "Michael. Were you both able to sleep?"

"Are you kidding?" Roberti said. "I could not sleep for the sound of my teeth chattering. We might as well be sleeping outside in the snow. It would be only slightly colder."

"I slept fine, Eminence," Father Burns said. "Had to get up and stoke the fire a few times."

John lifted a biscuit from the plate and examined it before returning it to the pile. "Hockey pucks." He poured himself some water, and sipped. In a whisper, he said, "Did either of you hear or see anything unusual last night?"

Roberti glanced up. "Like what?"

"I'm not sure," John said. "But I think someone may have come in my room sometime after midnight."

John didn't want to say that someone choked him and maybe left him for dead. There was no sense in adding more tension to the situation. He was alive. So he chose to leave it alone.

Father Burns said, "You mean one of the guards or General Borodin?"

John shrugged. "I don't know."

"This *is* Dracula's castle," Roberti said with a huff. "Check your neck for bite marks."

John humored Roberti and ran his fingers up and down the sides of his neck. He hadn't looked in a mirror to see if he was bruised. As a matter of fact, it occurred to John that there were no mirrors in his room. How fitting for the legend of Dracula. "No bite—"

As his hand took a final pass over his neck, he suddenly paused, then spread his palm across the hollow of his throat. That's when he made the discovery.

THE IMPALER

COTTEN BUMPED THE DOOR closed with her hip and kicked one shoe off inside her room at the *Residenza Del Roselli* Hotel. She hadn't calmed down from the meeting with Cardinal Fazio and Archbishop Montiagro. And she was wrestling with the thought that she had come all this way for nothing. At least Ted gave her the time away from her job, even if the expenses weren't on SNN's dime.

She stood lopsided, one bare foot flat on the floor and the other ramped up in a mid-size heel. The damn room was costing her over two hundred bucks a night and it was only a three-star hotel. And for what? To find that the Church wasn't going to lift a frigging finger to get John back. Plus, to further depress her, Cotten knew she had made an ass of herself, saying she was going to go find John on her own. The cardinal must have had a good laugh when she left, or even worse, felt sorry for her, and her friend Montiagro had to be embarrassed for her. But she was going to do it, going to find John no matter what it took. If no one else would help, she would do it alone. She didn't know how yet, but she would find a way.

Cotten plopped down on the bed, then fell back, her legs still dangling over the edge. *Yes, I understand why you can't negotiate with terrorists, but still... Priests, men of God, should think differently. To them every single life should be important.*

Cotten still gripped the envelope containing the two photos. She raised it above her head and stared up at it. There had to be some clue she could follow. *Come on Cotten, you're a reporter. You're good at tracking down leads, good at solving mysteries. What are you missing here?*

She turned on the bedside light, opened up the envelope, and removed the pictures. First, she studied the image of the two Swiss Guards. *Such gore. Heads impaled on metal stakes. It made her stomach turn. These were barbarians who did this. Animals.*

The decapitations didn't look like they had been clean and swift. She prayed the two men were already dead before their heads were hacked off. The photos were clear enough to see that the skin at the separation was ragged with fibrous tissue and filaments of muscle dangling.

Cotten studied the background. Barren trees. Forest. A few evergreens. Snow on the ground. Nothing distinctive or remarkable.

She slipped the picture behind the one of John, Roberti, and Burns. Lightly, she touched her finger to John's face. Her heart sank.

Why was he posing so oddly? *What are you trying to tell me, John?* There was something bothering her about the picture. It was John and his body language. Particularly the placement of his hand. Not the one out of sight in his coat pocket, but the one he had purposefully posed at his neck. Actually, it was his fingers that bothered her. His right hand was at his neck with his index and middle fingers forming a victory sign. But he wasn't making the traditional V for victory gesture. Instead his two fingers formed a hooking curve, sort of like a claw or talon. The tips of his finger-talons touched the side of his neck as if he were covering two spots. Or was he indicating two spots?

It had to mean something. He wouldn't do that unless he had a reason. Was he attempting to identify his abductors? Was it a letter or phrase in sign language? Maybe that was it: sign language. Or maybe it had something to do with where he was being held. Crooked something, maybe? But it would be crooked in a different language, one he knew she would not understand or speak. No, it was a simple clue from a simple gesture. She was certain. But what?

She threw the pictures on the bed beside her, shaking her head. His damn fingers looked more like a snake's fangs than anything. *Okay, think, Cotten.* John had to be within driving distance of Chisinau, Moldova. The cardinal said they received the ransom demand the same day as the abduction. She would call down to the front desk and ask if they had maps of Eastern Europe. Specifically Moldova or Transnistria. Maybe there was a place with the word *crooked* in its name, or someplace named after a snake.

"Transnistria," she repeated aloud. *Almost sounds like Transylvania.* Wasn't Transylvania in the same general area? No, it was a region of western Romania. That much she remembered from European history class. The famous home of vampires and Dracula.

Cotten bolted upright and sat on the edge of the bed. Could it be that simple? John had a split second to think of a way to send a message, to give a clue. He knew the Vatican would see the photo. Did he think that maybe she would, too?

Cotten held the picture under the light again. *Maybe his fingers are posed like fangs, but not snake fangs. Like vampire fangs. Like Dracula's bite.*

No. That was nuts. No one would buy it. But what else could it mean? Simple clue, simple answer. Wherever they were being held had something to do with vampires or Dracula.

She checked her watch. 3:15 PM. That meant it was 9:15 AM in New York. Ted should be in his office by now.

She placed the call.

"Cotten, you okay?" Ted said as soon as he picked up.

"I'm fine," she said.

"Any news? We've all been keeping our fingers crossed. Absolutely nothing is coming over the wires about the situation. Our crew is just arriving in Moldova, but they're getting hit with a ton of government red tape and runaround. You got anything?"

"I met with Cardinal Fazio. Archbishop Felipe Montiagro was there, too. He was called to the Vatican because of what has happened to John and the foreign minister."

She switched the receiver to the other ear and swallowed hard knowing she had promised the cardinal not to divulge anything from their meeting. But because they didn't seem to be taking action to save John, she had little choice. "Ted, anything I tell you has to be kept between us for now. Things are fragile, and I don't want to do anything that would risk John's safety. Is that a deal?"

"Whatever you say, kiddo."

"The cardinal confirmed that John and his group have been kidnapped and are being held somewhere in or near Chisinau,

Moldova, or perhaps across the border in Transnistria. The kidnappers are demanding one hundred million dollars in ransom. So far, no one knows for sure exactly who the kidnappers are. There are so many factions there."

"Are they going to pay?"

"No. The Vatican has emphatically refused to negotiate. I have conflicted emotions about that."

"I can imagine."

"The thing is, Ted, John is in real danger. There were two Swiss Guards who accompanied the group. The kidnappers murdered them. Decapitated. Their heads were impaled on stakes. They wanted it to be a message to the Vatican to pay up or else. These men are thugs with no conscience. They sent pictures of the decapitated heads to the Vatican." Cotten's voice clutched up. "I'm really afraid for John. The powers that be in the Vatican are sitting on their hands, Ted. I have to do something."

"You're just one person. This is an international incident. I think you should leave it to the experts. The negotiators. You stick your nose in the wrong place over there and you'll end up being snatched, too. You want your head to be the next one impaled? I understand how you must be feeling, but—"

"Stop. I don't need a lecture. I need your help. I may have something. But it's a long shot. Just give me a chance, okay? Be my friend."

She heard a long frustrated groan from Ted.

"I am being your friend. I don't want to see anything happen to you." He paused, then said. "Guess I should know by now I can never talk you out of something once you get it in that bull head of yours. Okay, what have you got?"

"Before I tell you, I need you to promise that you won't think I've lost my senses. What I'm about to say is deadly serious, no matter how farfetched it sounds. Okay?"

"Let's hear it."

"In addition to the photo of the two impaled heads, the kidnappers sent a picture of John and the other two priests."

"So they're alive."

"Yes. Well, at least when the photo was taken. You can't tell much from their location except that it's probably someplace old. There's a stone wall behind them that I think is a building. Reminds me of a fort or castle or something like that. Anyway, Roberti and Burns look normal, but it appears to me that John is deliberately posing. I think he is trying to send a clue to his location. What he's doing is too strange, too awkward to be natural. He has one hand at his neck, and his fingers are curved, crooked. My first thought was it looked like he was imitating snake fangs. But then—" She knew this was going to sound ridiculous, but she had to go for it. "I think he's trying to indicate bite marks on his neck."

"Bite marks. I don't get it. You mean like insect bites?"

"No ... more like vampire bites."

"Vampire bites?"

She heard him smother a laugh. "Ted, you promised to take me seriously. I think John is sending a clue that he's being held at some location that has something to do with vampires. Maybe with Dracula."

"Know what I think? You're under so much stress with this that you're seeing things that aren't there. Cotten, it's just plain crazy. There's no such thing as vampires. What if John was just scratching his neck?"

"Or trying to send us a message. Ted, can you please just humor me for a second?"

"I've got a general staff meeting in five minutes. Whatever you've got left, make it quick. I don't mean to minimize this, but if you were on this end of the conversation, you'd be skeptical, too."

"This will only take a minute more, I promise. I think John is possibly being held in Dracula's Castle. But I don't have Internet access here so I can't research to find out where that might be. Are you at your computer?"

"Yes."

"Google Dracula's castle for me. Don't argue that it's a stupid idea, just do it, and then I'll leave you alone and you can go to your meeting."

"Okay, hang on. I'm indulging you as a friend, but I think you are grasping at wisps of smoke." There was a pause and then Ted came back on. "I'm putting you on speaker, but there's nobody else in my office, and the door is closed. God knows if anyone overheard this conversation, they would have us both committed."

She heard the clicking of his keyboard. "What have you found?"

"Bran Castle in the Carpathian Mountains is the famous Dracula castle. It's a major tourist attraction. I don't think that would be practical for the kidnapper's purposes. No better than holding the hostages in the middle of the Acropolis. And it would be a long drive from Moldova."

Cotten's shoulders sagged. Maybe Ted was right about her grasping smoke. "All right. You win. Sorry to have bothered, I was so hoping …"

"Cotten, I understand. I'm on your side. I want to get John back safely, too. You're doing the best you can."

"Will you indulge me, as you put it, a little longer? Just dig a little deeper. Maybe there was more than one castle or Bran Castle has secret dungeons or something."

"Well, now, wait a minute. Here's another one. It's in Romania. Poienari Castle in the Fagaras Mountains. But it's in complete ruins and virtually inaccessible."

"Anything else? Anything at all?"

The line was silent for a few moments. Finally, Ted said, "Cotten, you still there?"

"I'm here."

"Hang on, kiddo. You might have actually come up with something in that pretty little head of yours. Listen to this. There's a third castle. It's called Wolf Castle, located in the mountains of Transnistria, just across the border with Moldova. It was built by Vlad Tepes III, aka Dracula. Seems that Vlad would torture his enemies, cut off their heads, and then he would ..."

"Would what?" she asked.

"He got his surname, *Tepes*, from his favorite method of killing. *Tepes* means *The Impaler*."

THE CROSS

JOHN REALIZED THAT HIS crucifix and chain were missing as he rubbed his neck—the same crucifix given to him by his grandfather on the day of John's ordination into the priesthood. He never took the crucifix off.

"No bite marks?" Father Burns whispered, staring at John from across the table.

"Apparently not," John answered, "but it appears I've lost something." He stood and called to the guard to take him back to his room.

———

On his hands and knees, John searched under the bed in his room for his cross and chain. He had already thrown off the blanket and mattress.

"Lose something?"

John looked up to see General Borodin standing in the doorway. He had been so preoccupied with searching for the cross that he hadn't heard the man enter.

"Yes," John said as he stood and brushed off his hands. "I've misplaced my crucifix and chain. I hoped it might have come off during the night and fallen to the floor."

The General glanced around the room. "It's said that strange things happen when darkness falls upon this place."

He moved about the room as if he were a hotel manager checking to see if housekeeping had done a good job. He touched the chair and slid his hand across the headboard carvings of winged demons. "How can you sleep beneath such grotesque images?"

John returned the mattress to the bed frame and decided to take advantage of Borodin's visit. "I don't believe you fully understand the position you're in with our abduction. We are diplomats protected by international protocol. Holding us against our will is a violation of—"

"I'm well aware of the situation." Borodin folded his arms. "The international condemnation of our actions is of no importance to me. We are opportunists, here to collect a large sum of money in exchange for your freedom. If your pope decides not to pay, you will be executed like your friends."

"Killing those men accomplished nothing."

"It sent a clear message that if our demands are not met, the same thing will happen to you and the others. The Vatican has received a photo of the two dead men. A picture is worth a thousand words, wouldn't you say? Everyone needs motivating, Cardinal Tyler. Without proper incentive, there is hesitation, doubt, and miscalculation. We want to expedite this exchange as quickly as possible. Giving them good reason to meet our demands lowers the chances of any kind of interference or foolhardy rescue mission—although I would find it hard to believe there would be such an attempt."

"Have they responded to your demands?"

"It is only a matter of time." He walked to the door, paused, and turned back to John. "Legend says that Count Dracula was not fond of the Christian cross. Perhaps it was his ghost who took your crucifix."

LOBBY MEETING

"Hello, Ms. Stone."

Cotten looked up to see a tall, well-dressed man in a business suit approach her table. She sat on an L-shaped couch in the lobby of the LeoGrand Hotel near the business center of Chisinau, having arrived from Rome on Air Moldova that morning. It was the same hotel where John, Roberti, and the others stayed before disappearing. "Ambassador Russell?" Cotten stood and extended her hand.

"Sorry I'm late."

The U.S. Ambassador to Moldova was well over six feet tall, with a slender face and pale complexion, mud-colored hair with an extreme comb-over, and horn-rimmed glasses. Cotten estimated he was in his late forties.

"Please join me," she said, sitting up straight and pointing to a wingback chair opposite the couch. "I really appreciate you taking the time to meet with me."

"It's the least I can do for such an important member of the international press," Russell said. "And such a beautiful one, I might add."

"Thank you." She settled back into the thick cushion. "Care for something to drink?"

"Just had lunch," he said, taking his seat. "What brings you to Moldova?"

"I'm hoping you can shed some light on the disappearance of the Vatican delegation. Anything would be helpful. What do you know?"

"Not much, I'm afraid. At the request of the Holy See, I've made some inquiries with the local government, but they seem reluctant to get too involved. I was told by their chief of national security that the delegation came here at their own risk and may have fallen into the hands of the extremist breakaway group who are fueling this nasty border dispute. To be honest with you, it's getting more and more dangerous to travel to the outlying areas."

"I was under the impression that the State Department helped arrange for the Vatican to get involved, and that they did so at the request of the Moldovian government."

"Well, there is some truth to that." Russell scratched his head and hand brushed his comb-over. "But this is a crazy part of the world, Ms. Stone. For starters, the self-declared republic of Transnistria is an enigma to everyone. Because of the rising political and economic turmoil, traveling across the border can be very dangerous. The few times I've done so, I felt like I was being watched every moment."

"Yes, but you're a high-profile American diplomat. Wouldn't that be expected?"

He shrugged. "I hear reports of people being detained just for speaking English in public or taking a picture of a government building. It's like the old Soviet mentality of paranoia and fear hanging on by its nails for one last breath. The Ministry of State Security, which is nothing more than a modern-day KGB, has all-encompassing, extensive powers. Most of the citizens live in dread. There's widespread corruption at all levels of government. And there is no middleclass to speak of. You're either dirt poor or rich beyond most of the world's standards."

"That's all fine, ambassador, but it still doesn't explain what happened to Cardinal Tyler, Archbishop Roberti, and Father Burns." Cotten glanced around the hotel lobby. There was a scattering of guests moving about. The closest was an older man sitting in a chair nearby reading a newspaper. She lowered her voice. "Are you aware that two Vatican security guards were murdered—executed?"

"Yes, I read about it in my security briefing this morning. It's so tragic." Russell shook his head. "I was shocked, but not entirely surprised."

"What happened to the legitimate representatives of the three countries that were to take part in the meetings and negotiations?"

"Once the news got out that the Vatican delegation was missing, perhaps kidnapped, the entire agenda for the meetings vaporized. Until there is some definite news of what really happened, I'm told there will be no further negotiations."

Cotten knew she was getting nowhere with Russell. He had completely ignored her question. But she had to play out her requests before deciding what to do next. "What are you doing to locate the missing men?"

"At this point, there's really nothing I can do." He brushed his hair again. "I have no authority here. All I can try to do is encourage the local government to take action and attempt to find the men. But so far, they've been preoccupied with counterpositioning themselves against their rivals across the border. I'm afraid my hands are tied."

Cotten leaned toward Russell, deciding to get to the heart of the issue. "Are you familiar with a medieval structure called Wolf Castle?"

He seemed to consider the question first. "It's an old castle in the mountains northeast of here, just across the border into Transnistria. I'm afraid it's not open to the public. Are you thinking of doing some sightseeing, Ms. Stone?"

"Can you arrange transportation for me to go to Wolf Castle?"

"Out of the question. First of all, they would never let you cross the border without an invitation from the Transnistrian government. And second, it used to be heavily guarded and may still be. I don't know. It once serve as a secret getaway for Soviet government officials and foreign communist dignitaries."

Russell glanced at his watch. "I hate to break our visit short, Ms. Stone, but I have a pressing engagement and really have to run." He stood. "Is there anything else I can assist you with while you're in Moldova?"

Cotten shook his hand. "I wish there were, Mr. Ambassador. Thank you, anyway."

"Don't hesitate to call me if you think of anything." Before she could answer, he spun on his heels and headed across the lobby to the front entrance.

Dropping back onto the couch, Cotten felt the heat rise in her face. Anger made her grit her teeth. What a waste. Russell was no help whatsoever. Either he was hiding something or he simply didn't give a shit. Whatever the case, she couldn't count on him for any assistance. She was going to have to do this on her own.

"Excuse, please."

Cotten looked up to see a man standing over her. He appeared to be in his sixties, had small, dark eyes and a wide, bulbous nose billowing out over a bushy mustache. His skin was pasty white and his brown-stained teeth were probably the result of years of smoking the popular Sobranie Black Russian cigarettes. In his hand was a folded newspaper. She recognized him as the man who had been sitting nearby reading.

"Yes?" she said, hoping he wasn't one of the scam artists that targeted tourists and foreigners.

"May I join you?"

Cotten motioned to the ambassador's vacant chair. "Help yourself."

He eased himself down and seemed to take a moment to get comfortable. His smile was gentle and warm as he silently gazed at her.

"What can I do for you, Mr…?"

"Please forgive me, but I couldn't help overhearing that you desire to visit Wolf Castle?"

"Yes," Cotten said with a bit of hesitation.

"Perhaps I can be of assistance."

YANOMAMO PING

THE DARK SHADOWS OF the Amazon rainforest fluttered across the ground, surfing on beams of moonlight that sliced through the thick canopy. This was the time for *ayahuasca*, the ritual drink that took one to an altered state of consciousness—another dimension—a place where one learned who he was and came to connect with all the elements on earth and in the universe.

Pierre Charles swallowed the bitter brew made from the *banisteriopsis cappi* vine, knowing that the purging would soon follow in all its violence. The bowl for his vomiting rested between his knees, and moments later was put into use. But the healing, the transformation of his soul was worth the twenty-five minutes of misery.

Afterward, his body's reaction to the concoction would calm, and the vomiting cease. Pierre reclined on a straw mat in the hut. The village shaman continued his constant beat of bundled leaves, a repetitious swishing that blotted out other sounds, a white noise and monotonous rhythm, a vibration that helped set Pierre's brain free.

Soon the psychedelic flashing and geometric patterns superimposed on serpents filled his mind, and he was immersed in the visions.

———

When the sun burned off the early mist, Pierre reflected on his visionary journey the previous night. He was convinced there really were other dimensions and universes that existed on alternative, vibrational levels. This morning, as always after such an experience, he felt refreshed and self-assured. Initially, he hadn't come here to discover or experiment with native drugs and hallucinogens, but rather he came as part of his doctoral program to study the horrific practice of infanticide amongst the Yanomamo and other primitive tribes of the Amazon. But his curiosity and his yearning to find the meaning of his life had led him to *ayahuasca*. And he was thankful.

After spending more than two years with these people, he finally had no desire to return to the University of Florida to present his dissertation. Here in the jungle he had found peace. He hoped no one would ever seek to intervene and subject these people, this spectacular culture, to modernization. Instead, every effort should be made to protect their right to maintain their culture at all costs.

Just a week ago, an Asian anthropologist traveling along the Amazon River had spent a day with the tribe. Something had bothered Pierre about the man. Call it an inner sense, a gut feeling that he should drive the man away. He suspected that the Asian viewed these people as subhuman and had no interest in their survival as a culture, but might find a way to exploit them. To his relief, the man quickly departed.

Pierre stretched and decided to go for a refreshing swim in the creek that ran from the river. The cold water would further invigorate him.

He had long given up his clothing, but still had not freed himself enough to throw away his boxer shorts. Beside the creek he pulled the threadbare Hanes shorts past his ankles and left them on the bank, then stepped into the clear water. It wasn't blue like the ocean, but a crystal clear that made him feel he was swimming through glass.

Pierre sunk beneath the water, letting it wash over him. He swam below the surface, basking in its pristine cleanness when suddenly he thought he heard someone calling. Springing to the top, he wiped away the sheet of water from his face.

"Ven! Ven!"

He had learned some of the basic language, enough to get by, but understood more than he could speak. However he did speak Spanish, and so did many of the tribe members.

Pierre scrambled out of the water and pulled on his boxers. "What is it?" he called in Spanish to a tribesmen standing on the bank. "What is wrong?"

The man answered, "You must come quickly. Hurry."

Pierre sprinted through the brush. When he arrived at the *shabano*, a round communal hut with individual living quarters, he saw the shaman ministering to a woman who was curled up in a hammock. Pierre knew that this woman had been sick for several days, and over the course of her illness he had watched the Indian prepare medicines, blow special smoke on her, and try to suck the evil from her mouth.

The shaman motioned for Pierre to come close.

Approaching the woman in the hammock, Pierre got a good look at her. Fear resonated through him as if his nerves had been plucked like a guitar string.

Blood seeped from her eyes, leaked from her nose, trickled from her ears, from every orifice.

"My God," Pierre said. It looked like Ebola or Marburg hemorrhagic fever. He'd seen detailed photos of the outbreak in Angola in 2005. Slowly, he backed away.

The shaman stared at him, his face filled with anger. The cords in his neck stood out and his mouth grimaced. "This sickness comes from your world!"

KGB

COTTEN WALKED THROUGH THE glass and chrome revolving door of the LeoGrand Hotel's Varlaam Street entrance, turned left and headed for the Central Park a block away. Crossing busy Puskin Street, she entered the expansive park situated in the heart of the city. A few fluttering leaves were still on the trees while most formed a soggy brown carpet of decay preparing for the bitter cold that was only weeks away. The wind chilled Cotten as she pulled her coat collar tightly around her neck.

A large, round fountain dominated the center of the park. The powerful water jets were turned off, and the pool drained for the winter. Rather than coins, a collection of twigs and rubbish covered the bottom.

Cotten wandered over to a bench beneath a statue of Stephen the Great, the fifteenth-century ruler of Moldova. It was a workday and the nasty weather caused the park to be virtually deserted—a few individuals moved in anonymity on their paths to other places. Sitting on the bench, she waited.

Ten minutes passed before she heard footsteps approaching. Moving toward her was the man from the hotel lobby. He had instructed her to meet him in the park. He motioned toward the bench before getting a nod from Cotten to sit.

He joined her in silence as his eyes scanned the park, almost as if he were taking inventory of every plant and object.

Finally, he turned to Cotten. "I am Colonel Vladimir Ivanov, former KGB, now retired."

"Cotten Stone, Satellite News Network."

"Yes," he said, shaking her hand. "I recognize you in lobby. I have seen you many times on American television."

"You speak good English, Colonel."

"Many of my comrades learn your language. Part of job. I still use English working as part-time tour guide at Museum of History in the Old City."

"Tell me what you know of Wolf Castle."

He smiled. "Dracula's Castle is scary place."

"Because of the vampire legend?"

Ivanov chuckled. "No, Ms. Stone, vampires are only in movies."

"How do you know about Wolf Castle?"

"Place has been used for many years as location to detain and question those suspected to be danger to old Soviet Union. I conducted interrogation sessions there that were ... productive. And when special persons like Comrades Andropov or Chernenko visit, I would be in charge of security unit during stay in castle."

"Are you aware of the recent abduction of the Vatican delegation?"

"Yes. Although I am retired, I still keep fingers in pie."

"Then do you believe that could be where the kidnappers are holding them?"

"Odds are good. It is perfect place."

"What else have you heard?"

"Two men shot."

"What about the others?"

"They were alive this morning."

Cotten leaned back against the bench. "Thank God." She felt a swelling of relief rush through her. "You're certain?"

He shrugged. "Nothing is for certain in this life. But I would stick neck out and say they are still alive. Men who took them want money. Without proof of life, they get spit."

"The people at the hotel told me that the priests were picked up by the Moldovian military. One was an army general. Is that true?"

Ivanov laughed again. "They are gangsters from across border. Everyone there is either gangster or victim."

"Why isn't the Moldovian government doing anything to help get the delegation back?"

"Wolf Castle is in Transnistria. Border war already on verge of blowing up again. This would set fuse to explode. Moldovian officials turn away. Say it is not their problem. Priests came at own risk. Very tragic. Too bad. Have nice day."

"And the Transnistrian officials won't help, either?"

He smiled at her. "You are not listening to Vladimir. You do not deal with gangsters."

She stared at the fountain for a few moments. "You could get me into Wolf Castle?"

"You don't want to go there."

"I have to help my friend and his colleagues. If the government won't do anything, I will."

"You are brave soul. I admire your backbone and stupidity."

"Excuse me?"

"Not meant to insult, Ms. Stone. But there is nothing you can do against armed gangsters. You would quickly become hostage and your American TV company would get ransom demand."

"So why are we having this conversation, Colonel? If you're not going to help me, then we're wasting each other's time."

"Didn't say I would not help you." He reached to pat her leg. "Only that you would be stupid to go alone."

"What other choice do I have?"

"Perhaps some of my old comrades and I help you get friends back."

"What do you mean? Who are your comrades? And why would they want to get involved?"

"So many questions." He paused as a woman pushing a baby stroller walked by. When she was out of earshot, he said, "Many reasons why comrades and I would like to embarrass criminals who take your friends. Despite fact that this is no longer Soviet country, we still have to survive. We had good times before fall of Moscow. After that, life went to shit. But now things are better. We enjoy pretty good life. Plenty food and work, and we rarely have to shoot anyone." He smiled broadly. "Joke."

"I still don't understand."

"New Moldova is partner with West. They do not want to have blemish on record with NATO. Want to join European Union. Be big shots. This thing with Vatican priests is best left to others. Out of their hands. But gangsters make fools of my country. Good

117

times may go away. Have to start shooting people again." Another big smile. "Must maintain sense of humor, Ms. Stone."

As quirky as he was, she began to see him as her only hope to get anything accomplished. And somewhere deep inside, she knew he probably was not joking about shooting people.

"What do you have in mind, Colonel?"

"My comrades go to castle and rescue your friends. Simple plan."

"I thought it was heavily guarded. How will you get in?"

"There are many ways in and out of Wolf Castle. Some only known to Vladimir."

"What do you want in return?"

"I want to be big hero on American television news. Then maybe I run for office here and become mayor of great former Soviet city of Chisinau."

"That's it?"

He shrugged. "Better than part-time guide at museum."

"You have to take me along."

"Impossible," he said.

"No, Colonel, that's the deal. Take me or forget becoming the new mayor."

He stared at her for a long time. Then with a big smile, he said, "You have bulletproof vest?"

THE RIVER

THE LATE 1960S VOLKSWAGEN panel minibus rumbled along the
back country road past endless miles of farmland. Cotten sat on
the floor in the back, feeling every bump and rut. Colonel Ivanov
had given her an old boat cushion to use, but it was of little help.
She felt her spine vibrating with every pothole and crack in the
pavement.

Ivanov and three of his former KGB friends had picked her up
a few blocks from her hotel just before sunset. Earlier that afternoon, she had taken a taxi to a store that sold hunting gear and
Soviet-era army surplus clothing. There she bought a pair of rugged hunting pants, a heavy woolen sweater, ski mask, and a thick
mountain jacket with a sheep's wool collar. The salesman couldn't
find boots small enough to fit her, so she bought additional pairs
of extra thick socks to fill up the space. A few hours later, dressed
in the heavy clothing with her gloved hands jammed deep into her
coat pockets, she tried to keep warm in the back of the VW.

Sitting across from her was Krystof, a skinny little man with sad eyes and a week-old growth of stubble. He had fallen asleep soon after leaving the city and didn't seem bothered by the bumpy ride.

To his left was Victor, a white-haired grandfatherly man with thick glasses and crooked teeth. She had learned that he and Krystof were both former officers in the Russian navy before being recruited by the KGB many years ago. His eyebrows were the bushiest Cotten had ever seen, and he spent the time listening to a small radio in his coat pocket, using a single earplug.

In the front passenger's seat was Alexei. He had a dark, full beard and small black eyes. Cotten estimated he weighed at least 250 pounds, and despite the chilly weather, his forehead had a permanent sheen of sweat. He constantly hummed a nameless tune.

Colonel Ivanov drove the minibus.

All the men wore side arms under their long coats, and Cotten assumed they probably had additional weapons hidden elsewhere on their bodies. When she had asked Ivanov if she needed a weapon, he laughed out loud. Then he patted her arm. "You might accidentally shoot someone." With a wide grin, he pointed to the other three. "Perhaps one of us."

As the minibus rolled through the dark farmland of eastern Moldova, she wondered if this was really the route she needed to take to help get John back? Instead, should she be camped out on the steps of the Moldovian Parliament building demanding that the government conduct a search and rescue mission?

She had left the SNN Moscow reporter and crew trying to do just that. So far, they had little success. But with other international press starting to hear the news and converge on the capital, perhaps the world would take notice and react with outrage to the reports of the missing Vatican diplomats. Was Cotten's place back in Chisinau instead of somewhere in the backcountry with a bunch of old, burned-out KGB losers from a country that no longer existed? As every mile passed by, she became less convinced that she was doing the right thing.

Colonel Ivanov turned the minibus off the pavement onto a dirt farm road. Although there were no windows in the panel van, Cotten could raise up enough to get a glimpse of the terrain in the headlights. The farmland had transformed into forest, and the road snaked its way through an ever-thickening wooded countryside. Soon, the forest became so dense that branches scraped against the sides of the van.

Finally, they descended a gentle slope and ground to a halt. Ivanov switched off the engine and headlights. A heavy silence surrounded the minivan. Krystof awoke. Cotten noticed that he was looking at her. With a toothy grin, he whispered, "River."

After a full five minutes, the colonel slowly and quietly opened his door. Alexei did the same on the passenger's side. Cotten started to rise, but Krystof motioned her to remain seated. She could hear the low conversation of the two men outside. Then another lengthy wait.

She wondered if Krystof had dozed off again. Then Ivanov quietly slid the side door open.

"Everyone out," he whispered.

"Where are we?" Cotten asked as she stepped down onto the crunchy dirt.

"Dniester River," Ivanov said. "We go for boat ride."

Krystof reached inside the van and pulled back a thick sheet of canvas, revealing a stash of weapons. "Kalashnikov," he said to Cotten as he lifted an AK-47 from the pile. "Best in world."

Ivanov chose a similar rifle from the pile. Alexei lifted a slim Dragunov sniper rifle from the stash along with a bag the size of an attaché case. Victor finished his selection by taking a compact machine pistol with an extra long magazine clip. When all were satisfied with their choices, Ivanov carefully slid the door to the minibus closed. He led the group down a hillside past an old cabin and onto a wooden pier running about twenty feet out over the water.

Cotten saw the starlight reflecting off the slow-moving water. It was hard to tell, but in the dim light, she estimated the river to be about a quarter of a mile across.

Tied to the end of the dock was a rowboat about twelve feet long. In the bow rested what looked like a pile of fish netting. Two large oars lay across a pair of wooden benches. Ivanov placed his index finger over his lips and then motioned for everyone to get into the boat. Cotten sat in the stern beside Victor. Ivanov removed the ropes that moored the boat to the dock and pitched them in the boat before positioning himself in the bow on top of the netting. Appearing to move in slow motion, Alexei and Krystof took the fat-shafted oars and eased them into the gunwale guides. Ivanov and Victor gently shoved the boat away from the dock. With an almost unperceivable effort, the other two men lowered their oars into the water and started rowing.

Silently, the boat rocked away from the dock and headed across the black water. Cotten glanced over her shoulder. The minibus, dock, and cabin faded into the darkness of the riverbank. She wrapped her arms around herself, not from the bitter cold and first flakes of snow that fell, but from the fear that John might already be dead. This was the only way, she told herself. No one else would come to his aid. This was his only chance for survival.

Her fragile confidence was suddenly shattered as a powerful spotlight swept across the surface of the river and lit up the rowboat like daylight.

THE ISLAND

MOON SAT ALONE IN her living room, her housekeeper gone for the day. Tired, exhausted, the work was taking its toll on her frail frame. But she was so close. Close enough to count the days, perhaps even the hours until the first wave of attacks.

Soon.

She had turned out all the lights. Only the soft glow of the television lit the room. She was about to watch the videocassettes—again.

Moon had memorized every word. She could close her eyes and recall every scene in amazing detail. To her, it was a living being—a direct connection to the past, to her father, to his work. In the tapes were images of the place where he unknowingly gave birth to the virus that would become Black Needles.

Aiming the remote, she pressed play.

The video from the handheld camera was shaky at first as the landmass emerged from the Gaussian blur of the fog bank. It was early morning, but the sun had not yet burned off the blanket of mist over the ocean. Slowly, the pieces of a dark, rocky beach came together to form a wide expanse of headland stretching across the bow of the boat.

There were three young ethno-botanists aboard the launch—Gina, a brunette with dark-eyes and olive-skin; Stefen, a lanky fellow with hair the color of oatmeal and fair skin who was shooting the video; and Lesley, a tall pecan-skinned girl who drove the boat.

Moon fast-forwarded the tape until the boat's bow knifed into the sandy bottom as they put ashore on the island.

After disembarking, Stefen aimed the camera at himself, holding it at arm's length. Feigning a British accent he said, "Welcome to Pleasure Island. I will be your host for the day." Stefen gave a theatrical grin, then twisted around and aimed the camera toward the sea, zooming in on the hulky silhouette of the *Pitcairn* anchored in the distance. The Oceanautics research vessel had served as home for the three botanists along with other graduate student-scientists.

Moon paused the tape and stared at the *Pitcairn*. The ship was only a part of her prize. For three months they had kept the ship in quarantine while it was decontaminated. Today it was moored along the banks of the Taedong River in the middle of the North Korean capital alongside the USS *Pueblo*—two shining jewels in the General Secretary's political treasury.

When Moon and her bio-hazmat medical team had first boarded the *Pitcairn*, among the dead they found Stefen's videotape collection, eleven in all, but two of them were what captured her attention. Those two tapes and the ship's log revealed that the research vessel had found the island by accident when a violent electrical storm caused an onboard fire and knocked out the navigation and communication systems. The ship strayed off course for a day until it came across one of the thousands of islands in the vast Korea Bay. With the possible chance of discovering new plant life, the three botanists had set off to explore the desolate volcanic island while the ship's crew worked on repairing the damaged electronics. The repair took longer than expected, giving the botanists a number of opportunities to visit the island over the next few days. Each time, they explored a different section of the twenty-square-mile landmass.

Moon fast-forwarded through the videotape until she saw Lesley holding a digital SLR camera. She let the recording resume normal play. Stefen was again the videographer.

"Look," Lesley whispered and pointed. "There's an amur falcon in that tree." Then she refocused her telephoto lens. "How strange." Lowering the camera, she stepped a few paces forward, sweeping back the tall grass with her hand. "Check it out. About forty yards straight out."

"What the hell?" Stefen said, pointing the video camera and zooming.

Gina said, "What do you think it is … or was?"

"Looks like an old building," Lesley said. "At least what's left of it."

"But out here in the middle of nowhere?" Lesley used her hand like a sun visor. "You guys want to have a look?"

"Definitely," Stefen said. Before following the two girls, he panned the camera in a circle, capturing their surroundings. "For posterity, on Pleasure Island we have your basic craggy-faced cliffs, a lot of dark, spooky forest, and thick undergrowth, probably filled with venomous snakes and deadly scorpions."

The video jiggled as Stefen continued to tape while walking to the building.

Moon watched the three students stare at a lone concrete wall. It was hard to judge from the image, but the wall appeared to be about two hundred feet long and thirty feet high. The rest of the building was nothing more than heaps of rubble with chunks of concrete and iron rods occasionally poking through the under-brush. Openings in the wall that had once been windows were now only gaping wounds.

Moon's parents had worked there for many years during the Japanese occupation. In the video, the ultra-secret lab of the Japa-nese Army's Unit 731 was now nothing but rubble and weeds. Her father had no idea what he had left behind—something so inno-cent at the time—but that had all changed now. Her discovery was more than serendipity. It was as if it were meant to be there, just waiting for her.

Her eyes focused on the video. It showed two tall cylindrical stacks, reaching a good ten feet higher than the rest of the struc-ture, rising behind the wall, standing like sentries over the ruins.

"Incinerators of some kind, maybe?" Lesley motioned toward the stacks. "And look at that." She pointed at a faint image painted above an entrance doorway—a weather-worn red circle with six-teen rays on a nearly vanished white field.

"Hinomaru," Gina said. "The Japanese war flag. Maybe this was a World War II military facility."

"Let's see what else we can find." Lesley led the way around to the other side of the wall. The rubble and tangle of brush and vines made it difficult to walk.

Gina said, "My guess is there was an explosion or the place was bombed. Either way, it was a long time ago."

"And something more recent," Lesley said. "Maybe an earth-quake? Some of the damage appears recent."

"Wait!" Stefen pointed as he aimed the camera at a piece of rusted machinery.

Lesley froze and glanced down. Sticking out of the ground was a protruding metal spike. "Damn, I didn't even see it." She blew out her breath. "Thanks. That would have been nasty."

"Hey, take a look." Stefen handed the camera to Gina. With a grunt, he bent and pulled back a piece of rusted sheet metal the size of a car hood.

The video showed a narrow set of concrete steps leading into the ground.

"This is wild," Stefen said. "Who wants to go first?"

He took the camera back and focused on Gina as she declined and sat on a nearby chunk of wall. "Jesus, Stefen, do you have to tape every little thing? You're obsessive about that damn video camera."

He laughed, but kept the camera pointed at Gina. "Coming?"

"You guys have at it," Gina said. "Think I'm catching the flu." She rubbed her arms as if chilled, then shivered.

"Too much cheap wine last night," Stefen said.

"Get the freakin' camera off me, would you! Christ, you're a pain in the ass," Gina said.

"Testy today, aren't we?" Stefen panned toward Lesley.

"We'll just take a quick look," Lesley said to Gina. "Be right back."

Stefen dug into his backpack and pulled out his flashlight. Lesley located hers. With Stefen in the lead, still videotaping everything, they started down the steps.

At the bottom was a tunnel littered with debris, but passable. Lesley shined her light into the darkness. Ten paces ahead was a much larger tunnel running perpendicular to the smaller one.

With great care, they maneuvered over pieces of fallen lumber and chunks of concrete until they stood in the wider passage. It was smooth-surfaced and large enough to drive a car through. Pitch-blackness lay ahead. They shined their beams in both directions before Stefen motioned to the right.

"Let's see where this leads."

"You first," Lesley said.

The tunnel cut into the volcanic rock for about fifty feet before widening into a large room housing what appeared to be two power generators.

"They remind me of locomotive engines," Lesley said as they moved past the hulks of rusted metal.

Moon pressed the fast-forward button again, speeding through the parts where Lesley and Stefen found a chamber with bunk beds, all in various states of collapse and dry rot. They backtracked and followed another tunnel, passing toilets and a kitchen and then into a storage room. That's when Moon returned the video to normal play.

This was the part she cherished.

Stefen flashed his light on the back wall of the storage room. "Check it out."

The video revealed a sizeable hole in the wall—chunks of concrete crumbled on the floor below it.

Stefen approached the hole and examined its rough edges. "Looks like it collapsed recently, probably from the earthquake." He aimed his beam into the hole and the space beyond. "What do you make of that?"

Lesley came closer. "A store room? Or maybe a safe room in case of attack?"

What the video showed was a concrete-walled room about the size of a modest walk-in closet. In the center was a wooden pallet. Neatly stacked on top were cylinders that looked to be about three inches in diameter and ten inches long. Lesley counted. "Twenty-five."

Squeezing through the opening, Stefen stood beside the pallet. He lifted one of the cylinders. "Not metal. Feels more like ceramic." Replacing it, he shined his light around the small room. At the corner of the pallet, a single canister had dropped off and rolled over against the wall. "Oh shit, that one sprang a leak." He aimed the light at the floor illuminating a dark smudged stain beside the canister. "No telling what that crap was. Want to take one back? We might get a pretty penny for war memorabilia."

"Forget it. Could be toxic." The alarm on Lesley's watch beeped. "We need to report back to the ship." She silenced the alarm and maneuvered through the hole in the wall. "Remember the captain said to use the walkie-talkie to radio in every hour in case they get the equipment repaired."

"He's worse than a mother hen." Stefen said.

Lesley pulled the small, handheld radio from her backpack and pressed the transmit button. "Hello, *Pitcairn*?"

Static.

"It's never going to work down here," she said. "We need to get above ground."

"Go ahead. I've gotta take a piss. I'll catch up."

As Lesley walked away, Stefen pointed the camera at himself. "Never pass up an opportunity, Stealthy Stefen says. This shit will be on eBay as soon as I can get back online." The camera bobbled as Stefen lowered it to the ground. Moon saw him pick up a canister and stuff it into his backpack. He lifted the camera again. Focusing it on his face, he raised and lowered his eyebrows like Groucho Marx. "No one the wiser."

With the camera still recording, Stefen maneuvered through the passageways until he caught up to Lesley.

As they passed the rusty hulks of the power generators, Lesley said, "I see the sunlight coming from the entrance." A moment later, they were up the steps and into the brightness of the clear-sky day.

Stefen aimed the camera at Gina, who sat propped against the wall, her eyes closed. "Sleeping on the job," he said.

Moon leaned in closer to the television, not wanting to miss anything.

Gina picked her head up.

"Hey, are you all right?" Stefen asked.

"You don't look so good, girl," Lesley said.

"Definitely need to pay a visit to sickbay," Gina said. "Probably just picked up a bug or something."

Stefen said, "Couple of shots of José Cuervo should kill it."

"Maybe not," Lesley said. She scored her bottom lip and looked at Gina.

"What?" Gina said. Obviously noting her friend's stare and responding to it, she touched her cheek, then felt across her jaw line. She took her hand away and looked at her fingertips.

Stefen peered closer before recoiling. "Holy crap, Gina, there's blood coming out your ear."

Moon paused the image, savoring what the monster virus could do—and so quickly. The three botanists had first set foot on the island only a few days before this video was made. And already, one of them showed symptoms. She smiled as images of hundreds of thousands would soon show those same first signs of the deadly Black Needles. The girl from the ship was already dying. Soon the others would follow.

Moon stood and went to the videocassette player. She extracted the tape and loaded the second.

It started abruptly with Stefen in his cabin, obviously drunk. He had propped the camera on a nearby shelf and talked to it as if it were a person in the room. "So here is my treasure find for the day." His speech was slurred from too much beer. "A fucking jug of Jap juice. Who knows what was in it, or what it still has in it. Only The Shadow knows for sure. Maybe it is a midget alien, or maybe, yeah, maybe, a secret love potion that turns women into horny, sex-craved whores with no inhibitions and thousands of fantasies." Stefen started dancing with the canister as he sang *I Could Have Danced All Night.* His image moved in and out of view—the auto focus trying to keep up with him as he swayed around the room. Finally he stumbled backward and flopped onto his bunk. As he did he lost his grip on the canister and it flipped from his hands hitting the metal railing of the bed. Stefen laughed at his drunken clumsiness. "Fucking A," he said. "The bitch just knocked me on my ass." He bent forward, trying to keep his body somewhat steady, but still swaying. He glared down. "Son-of-a-bitch. Look at that. The goddamn thing cracked. Who'd of thunk it?"

Moon watched as Stefen grappled his way off the bunk and re-trieved the canister from the floor.

"Probably ain't worth a shit, now," he said, back-pedaling to his bunk. Stefen fell onto his bunk, the canister beside him. "Asshole," he said to himself. "Damn it, Stefen, you could screw up a wet dream." His eyes closed.

Moon froze the image. "Thank you, Stefen," she whispered.

MONSTER

VICTOR LET OUT A rant of profanity as the spotlight lingered on the rowboat. Cotten tried to slump down, but there was no room to hide. They were completely exposed. Within seconds, she heard the low thumping of a large, powerful engine. A quick burst of an air horn cut through the night and rolled across the river like a charging herd as it echoed off both shores.

"Shit!" Victor said. He leaned forward. "Row faster, you bastards!"

Krystof and Alexei responded by doubling their efforts. Cotten heard their grunts as they pulled the oars through the water.

"Son-of-bitch," Ivanov said from the bow. "Bastard is going to run us over!"

"What is it?" Cotten asked Victor.

"River barge."

Cotten focused in the darkness and suddenly saw the monster bearing down on them. At least sixty feet wide, the barge plowed through the water, pushing white churning foam ahead of the flat bow. Its cargo, probably coal, was piled high in peaked mounds.

Then she saw the lights of the tug behind the barge. Millions of tons were about to roll over their tiny rowboat and crush it with no more effort than if it were a fallen tree branch.

"Oh, my God," Cotten said, covering her mouth with her palm. "Don't they see us? I mean, they'll stop won't they?"

"Would take miles to stop barge," Victor said. He turned back to Alexei and Krystof. "Put backs into it, you fucking pussies."

The thumping of the tug's diesel engine was drowned out by a hissing sound. Cotten saw it was the wave of frothing water being pushed ahead of the barge's bow as it curled over and broke onto the surface of the river. The hulk filled her vision, blocking out all else. The hiss turned into a roar.

The monster was upon them.

With one tremendous effort, Krystof and Alexei pulled on the oars, sending the rowboat past the front corner of the barge's bow. The steel vertical surface of the monster nearly scraped the side of their boat—so close, Cotten thought she could reach out and touch it.

She felt the boat rise up and lean to her right as it rode over the crest of the bow's wake. Just as she was about to be thrown over the side into the water, the rowboat slipped down the back of the wave and was shoved forward. While the two men continued to pull on the oars, taking the small boat away from the barge, Cotten looked to see the giant black mass pass by, followed by the thumping and grinding of the tug's engine. She spotted the pilot standing in the wheelhouse sweeping the river up ahead with his spotlight.

"Hang on," Ivanov shouted.

A second later, the tug's wake hit the rowboat, raising it up and over the crest. Cotten grabbed the wooden bench, this time almost certain that she would be thrown into the cold, black water. But as quickly as the wave came, it passed beneath them, and the small vessel settled back onto the river.

Krystof and Alexei were panting like long-distance runners while Victor continued his endless cursing. Colonel Ivanov stood in the bow surveying the river in all directions.

"Are you fucking blind?" Victor whispered in Ivanov's direction. "How could you miss something big as god-damn tugboat?"

"Shut mouth," Krystof said, still panting heavily. "Idiot drive tub boat as bad as you drive Russian destroyer."

"Air horn probably woke up everyone for miles," Alexei said.

Ivanov huffed. "Ship horn is common all times of day and night. No big deal."

"I say, get hell out of this place," Krystof said. Pulling on the oars, the two men returned to rowing.

Cotten watched the red and green lights of the tug grow small and finally disappear around a bend in the river. Soon, the water flattened, erasing all traces of the monster's passing.

BACK DOOR

"WE ARE ABOUT FIVE miles from castle," Ivanov said as he secured the bowline of the rowboat to a tree.

"That's not so bad," Cotten said. "I jog five miles through Central Park on the weekends."

"This will be the worst five miles of your life," Victor said with a chuckle. He and Alexei pulled the net over the boat.

Cotten noticed in the beam of one of their flashlights that it wasn't fishnet at all, but military camouflage netting.

"Why will it be the worst?" she asked.

Krystof raised his arm like a Nazi salute. "All uphill."

"Alexei will lose twenty kilos by end of climb," Ivanov said, patting his overweight friend's belly.

"Who wants to be skinny prick like you?" Alexei slung his sniper rifle over his shoulder. Carrying his supply bag in his left hand, he said, "Let's go before I sit on your tiny head."

As they formed a line with Ivanov in the lead, Cotten realized that despite the rough language and harsh outer skins, these old men seemed to have a tight friendship and respect for each other. She wondered what it had been like when they were in their prime and possessed the undisputed power of the Soviet KGB. And she hoped they still had enough left in them to accomplish this mission. Every moment that passed could be John's last.

Climbing a steep embankment, the five followed a hunting trail through thick forest for a few hundred yards before it turned away from the river. Immediately, the grade increased and their pace slowed. It was obvious to Cotten that the men had made this trip before—at least Ivanov had. Even in the dim light of the overcast sky, they moved forward with confidence.

As light snow fell, the rocky path led constantly upward. In the darkness, Cotten tried to be extra careful. Her footing in the oversized boots was anything but sure. A number of times, Victor grabbed her arm as he climbed behind her to keep Cotten from losing balance and falling.

After a half hour, they paused to rest. Cotten looked at her watch—just past nine.

"How do you know this path so well?" she asked the colonel.

"Old route," Ivanov said, sitting on a rock next to her.

"But if it's old and you know about it, won't the men holding the hostages know of it, too?"

"Maybe," he said. "But they are not expecting four old KGB to come in through back door. They are in for big surprise." He turned to face her. "They are already dead, just don't know it."

His words sent a chill through her. These men looked weathered and had that mellow appearance that comes with old age. And yet, their profession had been all about brutality and death.

She wondered how many had fallen at their hands, and she was thankful not to be on the receiving end of their *talents*.

With a grunt, Victor stood and pointed to Alexei. "Come on lazy bastard. We go rescue lady's friends. Get off fat ass."

The trail wound through thick woods and rocky terrain. They moved up switchbacks, climbing ever higher into the mountains. Soon, the trees thinned, giving way to rocky crevices and sheer drop-offs. In the dark, with only small flashlights to find their way, the trail was treacherous and slippery. At another short resting point she glanced at her watch: 10:44 PM.

When Ivanov saw her check the time, he said, "Hopefully, men in castle are sleeping. Better to die in sleep."

His comment brought muted chuckles from the others. Once again, Cotten was thankful that they were on her side. She had to keep telling herself that this was the only way to get John back. If blood was shed, then it was justified for what they did to the two Swiss Guards. An eye for an eye. That was in the Bible somewhere.

"We are almost there," Ivanov said to Cotten. "Soon you will see friends."

The group got to their feet and moved on through the snow, climbing higher into the clouds.

The wind became fiercer. It was hard for Cotten to stay on her feet as she hugged the rocky face of the cliffs on one side, while avoiding a glance down in the other direction. It was too dark to see how high they were, and she considered that a blessing. If she could see how far she might fall, it would prove impossible to go on.

Cotten was bone tired. Her feet cramped, and her legs ached from lifting the large shoes. The wind bit through her heavy clothes. The tip of her nose, sticking through the triangular hole in the ski mask, was numb when she touched it. They had to be getting close.

Suddenly, just as they maneuvered around an outcrop of granite, Ivanov brought them to a halt. As the wind battered her, she saw him point upward. Straining to see through the blowing snow, Cotten stared in awe at the looming structure towering over them. Its dark silhouette formed a foreboding mass against the snow-laden clouds.

Wolf Castle rose up from the mountain, as ominous and menacing to her as it must have been throughout the centuries to all would-be invaders. In the howl of the wind that raced up the face of the cliffs, she could imagine the castle laughing at her.

The task of carrying out an assault suddenly seemed impossible. But she had come this far. When no one believed she could do it, she was now so close to John that she might call out to him. There was no turning back.

"First time I see Wolf, I piss in pants," Victor said from behind her.

"I see why," she said, still staring at the imposing fortress.

Krystof turned and asked, "Ready?"

"Yes," Cotten said.

He signaled Ivanov, and the group started forward again.

When she dared, Cotten glanced up again. The rock was a sheer vertical wall at this point, hundreds of feet high. She assumed that if anyone was standing on the castle ramparts, they would be unable to see the path. At least at one time it had been a path or trail, but there was not much left to identify it as that today. Still, it was well concealed among the rocks and outcroppings below the castle, a perfect route to enter or flee from the fortress. It would be impossible to get an entire army into the fortress this way, but a few individuals could do it easily.

The group moved behind a large boulder and stopped. Cotten saw a metal grate covering an opening cut into the rock. It was barely three feet high and not quite as wide.

Ivanov knelt and pulled on the iron grate. It held firm. "Bastard," he said. He looked up at Alexei. "Well, don't just stand around yankin' pecker. Help me."

The big man squatted beside the colonel and together they took a strong grip on the grate. With a mighty heave, it gave and pulled open.

"You okay in tiny spaces?" Ivanov asked Cotten.

"Do I have a choice?" she said.

"It is back door," he said. "Let's go."

The colonel tightened the strap to his AK-47 securing it to his back. Then he crawled into the hole. When his feet had disappeared, Krystof secured his rifle in the same manner and followed. Alexei went third, pushing his supply bag in front of him.

Cotten and Victor stood on the rocky ledge as the snow swirled around them. She looked at him, but could see only his eyes through his ski mask.

"First time I crawl through hole, I shit in pants." Then he laughed out loud and patted her on the shoulder. "You do fine as long as not afraid of rats."

Not sure whether to laugh or cry, Cotten dropped to her knees and entered the back door.

TORTURE CHAMBER

THE TUNNEL THAT IVANOV called the back door was small and cramped. Crawling on her hands and knees, Cotten found the floor coated with slime and patches of ice. She heard Alexei in front of her grunting and breathing heavily as he squeezed his bulky frame through the passage. From behind, the beam of Victor's flashlight jumped around erratically, proving to be little help in revealing their surroundings.

The passage was obviously man-made—Cotten figured it could be hundreds of years old. About forty feet into the mountain, it opened into a natural gap in the rock. The space was not much wider than the tunnel, but was high enough to stand. The floor of the V-shaped cavern was littered with stones forming a crude, uneven floor. Cotten looked up, but in the darkness she couldn't determine the height of the ceiling.

The group moved along the upward-pitched rock path as it zigzagged farther into the mountain. Sometimes it widened, while other times the fissure became narrow, causing everyone to turn sideways and squeeze through. It was particularly hard for Alexei.

Cotten heard the sound of water dripping all around her. The flashlight beams reflected off moisture seeping out of a thousand cracks.

After ten minutes of climbing, the gap opened into a small cavern allowing all five to stand together. An enormous flat rock formed the floor. On the opposite side were steps carved into the wall leading into darkness.

"From here on, we must be like ghosts," Ivanov said. "No noise, no talking."

"How much farther?" Cotten whispered.

"Not far. We come up through storm drain in basement. Basement nasty place. Many men die there. Next, we follow stairs through wall to tower. From top of tower, Alexei will go to work." He shined his flashlight on each of their faces then at his watch. "Midnight. Time for Dracula and KGB to go hunting. Ready?"

Each of the men acknowledged while Cotten gave a tentative wave. Then Ivanov turned and started up the steps.

The climb was slow since the steps were steep and irregular. And because the stone was permanently moist and slippery, the going was extra treacherous.

After five minutes of cautious climbing, they came to a confined, rectangular-shaped space just big enough for them to crouch in. The ceiling was an iron grate similar to the one protecting the cliff-side opening to the back door. Ivanov turned off his light and signaled the others to do so as well.

The now familiar sound of dripping water surrounded them. Cotten felt sure she heard a squeak, and the scurrying scratch of claws on the stone floor was unmistakable. Rats.

Ivanov motioned to Alexei. The two positioned themselves and pushed the grate up with their backs, then slid it out of the way. A few seconds later, everyone stood in the basement. Quickly, the men pushed the grate back into position.

An acidic stench assaulted Cotten's nostrils as she shivered in the cold. In the beams of their flashlights, she saw narrow cubicles lining a wall to her right. Each had a metal-barred prison door covering the entrance. To the left was a large open area with a handful of long wooden tables. She made out wrist and ankle clamps on each, and realized this was more than a basement. It was a dungeon—a torture chamber.

The group crept along, taking care to cause as little sound as possible. Ivanov suddenly held his fist up and everyone froze. Then he motioned to a nearby prisoner's cell, its door agape. They moved inside, cramming their bodies together in the confining space. Cotten stood beside the colonel in the front, with Victor, Alexei, and Krystof behind them.

"What is it?" she whispered. From behind, Victor's hand slipped around and covered her mouth. Then she heard voices, at least two individuals, both male. Their words were faint and hard to understand as they echoed off the basement walls.

"This is one of the most frightening places I've ever seen," the first voice said.

A pale light appeared from around a corner to Cotten's right. Two men walked into her line of sight and entered the area containing the torture tables. One carried a lantern and wore a military uniform. The other was dressed in dark trousers and a heavy coat.

Cotten's hiding place was just on the outer fringe of the men's lantern light. If the two turned and came in her direction, she and her friends would be exposed. Cotten felt Victor pull her deeper into the darkness of the cell.

"This room has been the final place on earth for thousands," the military officer said. "Starting with Dracul, right through the height of the Cold War. If you listen carefully," he said with a chuckle, "you might still hear the echo of their screams."

She watched them walk around the torture chamber as if they were touring a museum after hours. At one point, they paused thirty or so feet away with their backs to her.

"The priest is unsure what happened," the officer said. "I suggested to him that it was the ghost of Dracula who stole his precious cross."

"It would have proven a hindrance if we were forced into a confrontation and he still had it," the other man said. "The crucifix is a powerful weapon. And the priest has had the fortitude to use it against us in the past—in an altercation with the Son of the Dawn."

The officer said, "He doesn't come off as being that strong."

"Don't let his appearance deceive you. Most of the time, it's a disappointment that so many lack true courage. But, if more had the strength of the good cardinal, it would make our job harder."

"I've been informed that the distracter has worked," said the officer. "The Stone woman has dropped her investigation."

"So far. But that doesn't mean we can let down our guard. Remember that the priest is the least of our problems. He only serves as the diversion to keep our target preoccupied."

"Are you confident the Koreans can accomplish their goals in the time frame?"

"The scientist leading the project is driven by hate, the truest form of motivation. We have rarely seen anyone so consumed by it. She will complete her task. But her health is failing. We must make sure she has no further interference until she is finished."

"What are you going to do with the cross?" the officer asked.

"I'll keep it hidden away."

"Just destroy it. There's an ancient well located near the old castle stables. Dispose of it there."

"Excellent." The man with the heavy coat wrapped himself in his arms. "Thank you, my brother, for the tour. I've been most curious about Dracula's dungeon. But I've seen enough. Besides, it's freezing down here."

They turned to leave, and as they did, Cotten saw their faces illuminated before they disappeared around the corner. She didn't know who the officer was, but she recognized the other man from the ransom photo. He was one of the kidnapped priests.

A terrifying dagger of fear pierced her soul. Both the officer and the priest were either Nephilim or Fallen. It meant pure evil had found her. Now she understood why John was kidnapped, and who was responsible.

The Son of the Dawn.

THE WELL

"NEPHILIM OR FALLEN," COTTEN whispered when the echo of the footfalls faded away.

"Quiet," Ivanov said softly.

The basement was as black as the darkness Cotten felt in her heart. She had been tricked. They knew she would not stand by and let harm come to John. She would drop everything and race to his rescue. And the thing they wanted her to abandon, to leave behind, was her investigation of T-Kup, Calderon, and the Korean connection. Now it became the second most important issue in her life, next to getting John out of this horrible place. But first, she must grab hold of her emotions. She had to somehow make Colonel Ivanov and his KGB friends realize that they faced far more than gangsters in Wolf Castle. In fact, gangsters would be welcomed adversaries.

But how would they react to her? Certainly, she would sound like she had lost her mind. The simplest explanation for now would have to do. Any lengthy explanation involving God and Satan and Fallen Angels would distract them from their mission. But at some point, she would have to face the priest and the man dressed in the military uniform. And in doing so, she would be confronting her father's kind and her own—the Fallen and Nephilim.

Ivanov pushed the cell door forward an inch at a time. After it stood open, he waited in the darkness another few moments before flipping on his flashlight. With caution, he took a step forward. Making his way to the end of the row of prisoner cells, he looked around the corner in the direction the two men had left. Finally, he signaled for the others to follow.

"Okay," Ivanov said. "Now we go up to top of tower." He started to take a step.

"Colonel, I recognized one of those men," Cotten said.

"So did I," he said. "Major General Nikolai Borodin. Big shot gangster general in former Soviet army. Most corrupt prick of all. I am not surprised he is behind this."

"Well, the other man is one of the hostages. He is a Catholic priest. I saw him in the picture of the captives sent to the Vatican by the kidnappers. Now I know he is a traitor, probably responsible for setting up the abduction."

"Birds of feather," Victor said with a huff.

"Borodin is corrupt," Ivanov said. "Now, so is priest. Both need to go meet God tonight." He was about to turn and lead them on, but he paused and looked at Cotten. "What was strange word you said back in cell?"

She considered lying to him so they wouldn't lose their momentum. Instead she said, "Nephilim."

"It means?"

"Offspring of Fallen Angels."

"Interesting," he said. Ivanov lifted his brows and nodded. "Will Nephilim die if bullet go through brain?"

"Yes."

He shrugged. "Fuck Nephilim."

Motioning the group to follow, Ivanov headed across the torture chamber to a set of wooden stairs, arcing the floor ahead with his flashlight beam. Cotten saw tiny red spots as the light reflected off the retinas of rats caught in the beam. They took one look and scurried to the safety of the darkness.

The stairs were circular and extended upward for twenty feet or so. The group came to a wooden platform and a large, bulky door. Ivanov pushed, and with a creaking of rusty hinges, it opened. A blast of frigid air rushed in, smacking Cotten and throwing her off balance. She started to teeter on the edge of the steps when Victor's strong grip grabbed and steadied her.

"Thank you," she said and squeezed his arm.

"Would be bad fall," he said.

One by one, they slipped through the door into the darkness of the freezing night. The wind howled across the top of the mountain and raced around the castle's walls. Crouching below the upper lip of the parapet wall, the group waited for Alexei to unfasten his sniper rifle from his back and open his supply bag.

Cotten rose just enough to take a quick look over the wall. She saw the main entrance down to her left. It appeared that the drawbridge was in the up position. In addition to the tower they were gathered beneath, she saw three other tall, round towers connected by thick walls forming a large polygon-shaped fortress. The battlements protected what she estimated to be at least two acres of stone and wood structures. Inside the confines of the fortress the main buildings were capped with steep roofs that would shed the snow. Most of the structures were spotted with dozens of arched windows. A few lights were on behind the windows. Snow-laced wind whipped across the top of the medieval structure bringing a cold, damp edge that cut deep.

Cotten watched Alexei as he pulled a long, slim cylinder from the bag and screwed it onto the end of the rifle barrel. Then he removed a tubular-shaped device that attached to the top of the weapon. She assumed it was a night vision device of some kind. Alexei grabbed a magazine clip from the bag and pushed it into the bottom of the weapon. Pulling back the bolt, he slowly stood and peered over the top of the stone battlement wall. Sighting through the scope, he scanned the courtyard below. Back and forth he moved in a slow sweeping motion, stopping now and then to examine particular areas. Then he slipped back to his crouching position.

"Two men on front gate," he said to Ivanov. "One on back wall."

"Start with one on wall," the colonel said.

Alexei stood and re-aimed his weapon.

A moment later, Cotten heard a muffled thud.

He shifted his aim, and two rapid thuds followed. The three shots, along with the clinking sound of the metal shell casings dropping onto the stone walkway, were swept away in the howl of the wind.

"Done," Alexei said, as if he had just swatted an insect.

"Stay here and cover us," Ivanov said. "Victor, go down to drawbridge and get ready. Krystof, hostages brought here in limousine. Find it and warm up." He turned to Cotten. "Ready?"

As ready as she would ever be, Cotten thought. "Yes."

"This way." Ivanov led her, along with Victor and Krystof, down steps that hugged the inside battlement wall. At the bottom, he motioned for Cotten to follow while the other two headed off in different directions. As she and the colonel rounded a corner of a large structure, they both froze at the sight of a figure walking out of the building and heading across the courtyard.

"It's the traitor priest," Cotten whispered. "I want to follow him."

"That would waste time," Ivanov said.

"I have to."

He shrugged, then waited until the man was past them.

"I think I know where he is going," Cotten said.

"And where is that?"

"To the well to dispose of John's cross."

"We don't have much time. Too much delay and you risk friend's life."

Without hesitation, she started after the priest. Ivanov gave out a grunt and followed.

They hugged the side of the buildings, staying in the darkest of the shadows. Cotten stopped when she saw the priest standing beside the round stone well alongside the old horse stables. She watched as he raised one of the wooden planks covering the opening and held his hand out.

"Give me your pistol," she whispered to Ivanov.

He pulled his gun and handed it to her.

Boldly, Cotten stepped forward until she was a few yards from the priest. "Stop," she said with as much authority as she could muster.

The priest turned around, the gold cross glittering as it dangled from his fingers. Staring at Cotten, he said, "You're early."

RESCUE

"Give it to me!" Cotten snatched the crucifix and chain while still keeping the gun aimed at the priest. "You're too young to be Archbishop Roberti. So I assume you're Michael Burns."

"You're not really going to use that?" he said.

Cotten glowered at him as she slipped the crucifix and chain in her pocket. Then she handed the gun back to Ivanov. "No, but my friend will if you don't take me to Cardinal Tyler."

"Drop the weapon."

The voice came from behind Cotten and Ivanov. As they turned, Ivanov said, "Borodin, you piece of shit. Why am I not surprised you are big shot here?"

"Hello, Vladimir." The General aimed an automatic pistol at the former KGB agent. "You're up past your bedtime. Now hand over your weapons."

"I give you one chance to surrender," Ivanov said. "You accept generous offer?"

"Do I look like a fool?" Borodin almost laughed.

"No," Ivanov said. "You look like dead man." He raised his arm as a signal, and in the next instant a pink cloud appeared from the side of Borodin's head.

Cotten gasped as she realized what Alexei had done. The sniper's bullet passed through the general's head, blowing most of the back portion of his skull away as it exited. Borodin fell to the ground like a puppet whose strings were snipped.

Colonel Ivanov bent and pried the pistol from the general's grip. He turned and gave it to Cotten. "Souvenir." Then he said to Burns, "You want to be dead man, too?"

Burns held his hands up in a gesture of surrender as he glanced over his shoulder in the direction of the sniper.

"Take me to Cardinal Tyler." Cotten raised the gun and pressed the barrel to Burns' chest. "I've never killed anyone in my life," she said. "But I'm willing to start tonight."

Burns backed away, then started walking toward the main building.

As Cotten passed Ivanov, he grinned at her as if to say he was impressed. "What did he mean by being early?"

"They didn't expect me to show up this quickly," Cotten said.

"Maybe Nephilim not so smart," Ivanov said. He cocked his head as the wind carried the sound of an engine cranking and then starting. "Krystof find limousine."

Burns headed toward the main building but the colonel stopped him. "No, not that way." He pointed to the side of the building not far from the steps where they had descended into the courtyard. "We go through side door."

With Burns in the lead, the three moved around the side of the building, their feet crunching in the newly fallen snow covering the flagstones.

"Here," Ivanov said and motioned to the portico. Opening the door, Burns led them down a hallway. The colonel shined his flashlight at the far end. He pushed Burns and they continued on until the three stood in the middle of the castle's kitchen. "Where are guards?" he said.

"You seem to know a lot about this place," Burns said. "Why don't you figure that out—"

Ivanov moved within inches of Burns' face. "I don't care if you are devil himself, and according to her, you might be. But I have cut off balls of men who would scare devil out of you. Tell me location of guards or there will be another head on stake."

Burns backed away. "Calm down. There are two on the front gate, one inside the entrance to the main hall, one on the back battlement wall, and one upstairs guarding the prisoners. Borodin's driver and another guard are sleeping in the servants' quarters."

"Odds getting better," Ivanov said, winking at Cotten.

Burns turned to her. "You have no idea who you're dealing with."

"I know what you are."

"Stubborn little prick." Ivanov grabbed Burns by the shoulder. "We take back stairs to prisoners' rooms. Go." He shoved Burns forward, and they headed across the kitchen to a set of narrow, wooden stairs. "Very quiet," he whispered as they started up.

When they came to the top of the stairs, Ivanov said to Burns, "Open door slow. If you see guard, call him to come help you."

Burns obeyed. As he opened the door, Cotten saw over his shoulder a hallway lit by a handful of lights along the walls. From her angle she spotted four doors, all closed. A man sat in a chair at the opposite end of the hall. His head leaned back against the wall, and he appeared to be asleep.

"Call him," Ivanov whispered to Burns. "Quietly."

Burns stepped out into the hallway. "Hello," he said just above a whisper. "Hey."

The guard shuddered awake and sat up with a start. "What is it?"

"Borodin needs you," Burns said. "Now."

The guard rose, still obviously trying to shake the sleep from his head. He started walking toward Burns. When he was a few yards away, he suddenly stopped and glared down at his chest. A dark bloom formed on his shirt as his arms went limp. Dropping to his knees, he fell over face first onto the hallway floor.

Ivanov stepped into the light of the hall, a wisp of gray smoke drifting up from the barrel of his silenced automatic. He turned to Burns. "Which room?"

———

Still dressed, John lay on the bed staring at the faint patterns on the ceiling cast there from the fireplace. Suddenly, he heard a scratching at his bedroom door. The lock was being manipulated and the knob was turning. Was it the night visitor again?

He reached for the small lamp on the bedside table. At the same moment, he saw the door open. A figure stood in the doorway.

He switched on the light.

Michael Burns walked in, his hands held in the air.

"Michael, what's going on?"

Then John saw a second figure behind Burns—a small-frame person dressed in bulky clothing. The face was hidden beneath a ski mask.

He sat up and swung his legs off the bed.

The figure stepped forward, a pistol in one hand. The other hand reached to pull away the ski mask.

John's mouth opened in shock. "Cotten!"

ESCAPE

JOHN GOT TO HIS feet and Cotten rushed to throw her arms around him. "Thank God," she whispered.

John held her tightly. "How did you find me?"

"The photo, your hand on your neck."

"It was a long shot. I never thought anyone would figure it out. Such a dumb clue."

"It worked. That's all that matters."

John looked at Burns, then at another man standing in the doorway, a man with a pistol in his hand. "Whoever you are, I can't thank you enough." Then he turned to Burns.

"He betrayed you," Cotten told John. "He set you up."

Ivanov pulled the ski mask from his face. "Time to go."

"Archbishop Roberti? Is he safe?" John asked Burns.

"Where is he?" Ivanov poked Burns in the back with his gun barrel.

"Next room." Burns motioned toward the wall.

"Why did you do it?" John asked.

"He's Nephilim." Cotten stepped away from John to face Burns. "This whole thing was to distract me from a much larger issue. But it didn't work the way they planned. They never figured I'd show up here so soon."

Ivanov moved into the hall. "Hate to spoil reunion, but time to go."

John grabbed his coat. "I'll go awaken Luigi." He headed into the hall with Cotten behind him. Stopping short, he saw the dead man. Making the sign of the cross over the body, he went to the next bedroom door.

"Want me to shoot Nephilim piece of shit?" Ivanov called to them as he aimed his pistol at Burns.

"Lock him in the room," Cotten said. "If they thought it was a good enough prison for John, then it'll do for him."

Ivanov locked Burns in, using the key he had recovered from the dead guard. He followed John and opened Roberti's room.

"Luigi, wake up," John said. He shook the priest until the man turned and stared at him.

"What's going on?" The older man looked terrified.

"You're safe, Luigi." John threw back the blanket and helped Roberti swing himself out of bed. "It's good you slept in all your clothes."

"It was freezing," Roberti said.

"Put on your shoes and coat," John said. "We're getting out of here."

"What about Michael?" Roberti asked. "We must awaken him."

"He's already awake," John said. "Luigi, Michael betrayed us. He was in on our kidnapping."

Roberti's eyes grew big, and he seemed even more confused than when John had burst into the room. "Impossible."

"Discuss later," Ivanov said.

Roberti stared at the man with the gun.

"He's a friend," Cotten said.

For the first time, the archbishop noticed Cotten. "Sweet Jesus, what are you doing here?"

"She and this man have rescued us," John said. "But we must leave now. Please, Luigi, hurry. We'll explain everything later."

"This must be a nightmare," Roberti said, tying his shoes. He stood and John helped him into his coat. "All right, I am ready ... I think."

"This way," Ivanov said. He directed them to the stairs leading to the great hall.

"What about the guard at the entrance?" Cotten asked the colonel. "The one Burns told us about."

"Victor has relieved him of duty."

"Are you sure?" Cotten asked.

Ivanov stopped short and turned to her. "Trust Vladimir, future mayor big shot of Chisinau."

She smiled. "Forgive me, Vladimir. I trust you with my life."

He looked at John. "Smart lady." Then he turned and started down the stairs.

At the bottom, they entered the great hall. Ahead, near the main doors, Cotten saw a dark heap on the floor. Standing nearby was Victor, his machine pistol at the ready. As they got closer, Cotten noticed the spreading pool of blood and gaping slit in the guard's neck.

"Nice work," Ivanov said.

"Caught him sleeping on job," Victor said with a smile.

They burst through the doors into the snow-blown night. Cotten spotted the limousine near the front gate, clouds of steamy condensation billowing from its exhaust. The drawbridge was down and Krystof was in the driver's seat. From across the courtyard, Alexei ran toward them, his sniper rifle in his hands.

Everyone converged on the ZIL at almost the same moment. "Quickly," Ivanov ordered. "We must go."

Once they had piled into the car, Krystof shoved the accelerator to the floor, and the old engine roared as the car barreled through the gate and across the bridge.

With sickening thuds, bullets slammed into the metal trunk lid. Ivanov turned to look out the back window. "Last two guards woke up," he said.

Cotten peeked above the back seat for a second and saw the muzzle flashes as the two men fired from the steps of the main hall. But just as quickly as the bullets hit the old car, it swerved around a curve and raced down the steep mountain road. Cotten leaned into John next to her and rested her head on his shoulder.

Behind them, the imposing silhouette of Dracula's Castle disappeared into the driving snow.

SETBACK

"Careful, you idiot," Ivanov shouted as the ZIL swerved around a sharp bend in the narrow mountain road. "Long way to fall."

"You want drive, big shot future mayor?" Krystof wrestled with the steering wheel of the cumbersome limousine.

"Who are your interesting friends?" John asked Cotten as he tried to maintain his balance in the back seat of the swerving car.

"This is Colonel Vladimir Ivanov, formerly of the Soviet KGB, currently considering a career in politics. And these are his colleagues, Krystof, Alexei, and Victor. I would predict they might also have a future in local government."

"Never work for lazy prick like him," Alexei said, motioning to the colonel. "Unless I become director of whore house inspection."

"That is all you are good for," Victor said.

"Well, whatever you gentlemen do in the future," Roberti said, "we cannot thank you enough for assisting Ms. Stone and coming to our rescue tonight."

"Rescue easy," Victor said. "Getting back into Moldova a bitch."

"We are almost to turn-off," Ivanov said to Cotten. "Must get off road before border crossing."

"Won't the two soldiers back at the castle have already notified the border guards of our escape?" Cotten asked.

"Maybe, but Vladimir is smart guy." Ivanov smiled broadly. "Once they find old limousine, we will be back across river."

Krystof slowed the car as they rounded a turn and took a sharp left onto a narrow forest road. At the lower elevation the snow had slowed. The road wound through a mile or so of thick evergreens on a gradual descending grade. Finally, it ended in a tangle of underbrush. He switched off the lights and ignition. The heavy darkness of the forest rushed in and surrounded the old car, while the howling wind replaced the rumble of the engine.

Ivanov turned and peered out the back window watching for any sign they were followed. "Okay, everyone out," he said. "Don't want to spend rest of life in big Russian coffin."

The group exited the limousine and gathered around the front of the car trying to absorb the last of the warmth radiating off the engine block.

"Victor and Alexei bring up rear," Ivanov said. "Krystof, take point. Everyone watch step. Many hidden rocks under snow."

With only their flashlights and the moon to light the way, they zigzagged down a hillside on an unseen path beneath a shallow crust of snow. Although the grade was manageable, the fear of twisting an ankle or tripping over a hidden root or rock kept their progress slow.

Within fifteen minutes, Cotten realized that she recognized a few rocky landmarks. They had rejoined the original mountain trail leading to Wolf Castle and the back door. Next, they moved onto the hunting trail and left the incline behind. A hundred paces later, she saw the reflections of the moon on the river. Moving down the embankment, they stood at the water's edge. Before them sat their rowboat, the netting shredded, the hull filled with enough water that the stern disappeared under the gentle lapping waves.

Sucking in her breath, Cotten knew they were in trouble.

Like mourners at a funeral, the group gathered in silence on the riverbank and stared at the half-sunken boat. Despair, like the numbing cold, seeped deeper into Cotten as she shoved her hands into her coat pockets. She couldn't believe that their luck had run out after coming this far.

"What happened?" John asked.

"River patrol," Ivanov said. "Tugboat captain must have called them. Sometimes get reward for turning in smugglers. Patrol shoot holes in boat to prevent crossing back to Moldova."

"Is there another boat available?" Roberti asked.

"No chance," Victor said. "At least not on this side of river."

"Could we get to the bridge and walk across?" Cotten asked.

"Not without proper papers," Ivanov said. "This is bad news."

"What if the kidnappers were not really part of the Transnistrian army?" Cotten said. "Do you think they would have notified the border guards of our escape?"

"Cardinal Tyler said they passed through crossing with no hassle. Tells me someone at crossing part of conspiracy."

"But maybe not everyone?" Cotten asked.

Ivanov shrugged.

"Borodin would probably not want to split the ransom with any more people than he had to, right?" Cotten asked.

"True." Ivanov rubbed his chin. "General was stingy bastard. Doubt he would spread money around."

"Then what we need is to catch everyone at the crossing by surprise and hope that whoever is in charge is not part of the conspiracy." Cotten pulled her cell phone from her coat. "How long will it take us to walk to the Dniester River bridge?"

"One hour, give or take," Ivanov said.

"We couldn't take the car?" Roberti asked.

"Impossible to back out," Krystof said.

"And for someone to drive from Chisinau to the bridge. How long would that take?" Cotten asked.

"Same," Ivanov said.

Cotten opened her cell phone and checked the signal strength. Two out of five bars. She gave her friends a smile. "I know how to get us across."

CROSSING

Just before dawn, the buttermilk clouds thinned and broke to the east. Sunrise painted gold and orange streaks across the sky causing the surface of the Dniester River to appear ablaze. Even the wind settled, allowing the river to catch its breath on its eight-hundred-mile journey from the Polish border to the Black Sea.

One of the four soldiers stationed at the Transnistrian border crossing on the eastern end of the bridge turned and stared into the celestial lightshow, sipping his black coffee. A few yards away, a fellow soldier checked the papers of a transport truck bringing fresh produce from Moldova. Soon, the truck rattled on and disappeared around a curve along the forest highway.

Being Sunday morning, the traffic was light, though it would pick up as the day went on, with families traveling to visit with relatives for the day.

As the border guards started to settle back into their morning routine, a low, distant rumbling sound drifted across the river. A large box-shaped truck pulled onto the western end of the bridge. It had bright golden lettering on its side and front that read: *Satellite News Network*. On the roof was an uplink dish folded to lay flat against the top of the box. As soon as the truck was on the bridge, a second appeared and followed. This one was from *First Channel Ukraine*. A third from the German international broadcaster *Deutsche Welle* fell in line, followed by others bearing the logos of networks from Russia, Romania, Italy, and Poland. By the time the SNN truck ground to a halt in front of the border-crossing gate, twenty-three international television remote broadcast trucks formed a line on the bridge.

Almost immediately, doors were flung open and men with portable television cameras on their shoulders jumped to the pavement and headed toward the gates and the border guards. Reporters with microphones rushed forward. Like the opening of metal flowers, the dishes on the roof of each truck started to unfold as their motors lifted the uplinks into position. Even from yards away, reporters were already shouting out questions.

"Have they arrived yet?"

"Where are the hostages?"

"Who's in charge?"

"How did they manage to escape the castle?"

"Was anyone killed?"

"Is it true that Cotten Stone rescued them?"

"Were KGB agents involved?"

The first soldier dropped his coffee cup as the mob of reporters and camera operators surrounded him and the other guards. Trying to establish some sense of order, he held his hands up and called out, "Wait! Stop!" He was immediately the focus of attention as microphones were thrust in his face. Questions came at him like automatic weapons fire.

"Quiet," he shouted. "One at a time. What's going on here? What do you think you're doing?"

A reporter at the head of the pack said, "The Vatican hostages. We're here to cover their rescue and release."

"There are no hostages here," he said. "There has been no—"

"Look!" called one of the reporters, pointing over the soldier's shoulder.

Like the start of a marathon race, the pack rushed past him. He turned to see what had caught their attention. A small group of people emerged from the forest a few hundred feet away. They looked tattered and fatigued. A woman led the group, and a few of the men carried weapons.

As they approached and were surrounded by the press, the soldier called, "You can't do this. You cannot cross without the proper papers."

A passing cameraman stopped and said, "The whole world is watching, my friend. Be careful what you say."

———

Smiling from ear to ear, Ted Casselman stood in SNN master control and watched the video feed from Moldova. Every once in a while, he glanced at one of the technicians in the room, pointed to the monitor, and chuckled.

Ted watched Archbishop Roberti say, "Once again I wish to thank the government of Moldova for its gracious hospitality in welcoming us here today." Roberti stood on the steps of the Moldovian parliament building. Beside him was the president of Moldova, the U.S. ambassador, members of the government, and the commander of the Moldovian armed forces. A light snow fell as over fifty reporters amassed in front of the building.

"As you can imagine," Roberti continued, "we are anxious to get on with the work we came here to do. This afternoon, I will meet with the president and also representatives of the Ukraine and Transnistria to start a dialogue on a solution to the ongoing border dispute. We are optimistic that the Vatican can assist in mediating this into a peaceful conclusion."

"Way to go, kiddo," Ted said when Cotten appeared on camera to finish the report.

———

Cotten, John, Colonel Ivanov, along with Victor, Alexei, and Krystof stood in the back of the large crowd of press and onlookers. The former KGB agents beamed with pride, a result of being informed earlier by the Moldovian president that they would be awarded gold medals for their bravery.

"Thank you for kind endorsement on news report," Ivanov said to Cotten. "I start collecting campaign funds to run for office now that everyone heard of Vladimir."

"Just don't forget your colleagues," Cotten said, motioning to his friends.

"He will get big head power crazy and turn up nose at men who do real work," Victor said.

"Not if I call and check on him every so often," Cotten said with a smile.

"Nice lady keep you in line," Alexei said, and slapped Ivanov on the back.

Escorted by Chisinau police, a government limousine arrived. "Here's our ride," John said. He turned to Ivanov. "Thank you." He shook the colonel's hand, then the hands of other three men. "I don't know how I can ever repay you, all of you, for saving my life." He blessed them before holding the door open for Cotten.

She wrapped her arms around the colonel and kissed his cheek. "Goodbye, Mr. Big Shot."

"Goodbye, Cotten Stone. Next time you want big adventure, call us. By then, we will be bored and ready for new killing spree." He gave her a wide grin. "Joke."

Cotten shook her head in mock disgust, then hugged each of the other KGB agents before getting into the back of the car.

With blue and red lights flashing, the police escort led the limousine away from the parliament building. Cotten waved to her friends through the rear window. As she turned back around, her cell phone rang.

Looking at the caller ID, she said, "Ted."

"Hey, you looked great. Every news organization on the planet has picked up the rescue story."

"So my theory about Dracula wasn't so farfetched after all?"

"You won this round."

"Have you pulled all the info on T-Kup?" she asked.

"And then some. I came across a story out of the remote Amazon region of Brazil. An anthropologist just returned from spending a stretch with the locals down there while he worked on his doctorate. He witnessed a death of a native that matches the symptoms of Jeff Calderon."

"So we might have a lead to another victim?"

"It looks that way," Ted said.

"Any idea what it all means?"

"Nothing concrete yet. I need you back here to work on it."

"We're headed for the airport right now. John has to return to Rome to brief the pope on what happened, then on to London to do the same with MI5 and the CIA. But I'm coming directly home. I'll see you tomorrow."

"Stay safe."

"Yeah, I've heard that one before." She was about to close the phone.

"Cotten?" Ted said.

"I'm here."

"I'm glad you're okay."

"Thanks."

She ended the call and turned to John. "Things are really starting to heat up."

"Just the fact that Burns was part of the Darkness means we're in for a fight. We'll need all the help we can get to confront whatever they've got in store for us."

"Then you're going to need this." She reached into her coat pocket and pulled out his gold crucifix and chain.

EASTERN PASSION

COTTEN AND TED WALKED through the busy News Department on the eighth floor of SNN headquarters.

"It's getting cold out there this morning," she said, shedding her coat as they entered his office.

Ted hung her topcoat on the rack next to his before shutting the door and taking his seat behind the desk. "Still got to be warmer than the mountains of Moldova."

"That's an understatement." She sat in a chair facing him. "I've never been so cold in my life, especially on the cliff ledge looking up at Dracula's Castle in the middle of the night. There were gale-force winds and driving snow trying to blow me into a thousand-foot-deep chasm. Made my walk to work this morning feel like a summer stroll." She noticed his coffeepot was half empty and a drained mug sat on his desk. "You must have come in early."

"I get a lot done when nobody is around." He lifted a brown envelope with her name written on it. "Fame follows you like a puppy." ·

"Everybody gets their fifteen minutes."

"I think you exceeded your fifteen minutes a long time ago, kiddo. Every talk show wants an interview—Leno, Letterman, even Oprah's people called." He handed her the envelope.

Cotten glanced inside at a collection of message slips. "I'm much more comfortable as the interviewer."

"I know. Just roll with it." Then he slid a document across his desk. "I put together an initial report on the Amazon death."

Cotten scanned it. "You figure this anthropologist, Pierre Charles, has something of value?"

"Could be. He mentioned the same symptoms as Calderon. Plus, just like here, nobody else got sick. Might be a long shot, but I think it's worth looking into."

Cotten skimmed the report again. "Doesn't say much."

"I know, but you're good at digging."

She glanced to confirm that his office door was closed. "Ted, there are some things that I didn't tell you on the phone. When I was in the castle's dungeon, I overheard Burns and General Borodin talking. They said that the whole kidnapping and ransom thing was a diversion meant to pull me off this investigation. They also referred to a Korean connection and a woman scientist who is involved in some secret experiment. They said that she had health problems and didn't have a lot of time left to finish whatever she is doing. So it sounds like we may be on a short fuse here."

"And you think she's tied to the deaths?"

"Not sure, yet. But I haven't told you everything."

"There's more?"

"Ted, you're one of the only people on earth that knows about my ... legacy."

"Are you going to tell me that this is connected to The Fallen?"

"Burns is Nephilim. I couldn't confirm it, but I suspect that General Borodin was, too."

Ted leaned back. His brow furrowed as he rubbed his face. "If that's the case, then you need to talk to the anthropologist as soon as possible."

"Exactly. No phone interview. I want to fly down there and meet him face to face. Let me see if I can book a flight."

"I'll do you one better. The brass upstairs owes you a big one for all the PR you did for us in Moldova. I'll get authorization for you to fly to Gainesville in the corporate Gulfstream. How soon can you leave?"

"Just need to grab a few things from my office."

Ted picked up the phone and buzzed his assistant. "I need one of the Town Cars brought around to the front for Cotten Stone." He glanced up at her. "You still here?"

———

Cotten pulled up in front of the Gator Lofts apartments and parked her rental. It was located two blocks behind "The Swamp," the nickname for the Ben Hill Griffin Stadium, home to the University of Florida Gators. The apartment wasn't much on the outside, but then again, college students lived on a shoestring budget.

She climbed the stairs to the second floor and knocked on the door to Pierre Charles' apartment. A moment later, the door swung open.

"Ms. Stone?"

"Yes," she said.

"Come in. Sorry the place is a bit of a mess. I've been trying to get back in grad school mode this past week." The anthropologist wore flip-flops, a pair of Gator orange sweats, and a T-shirt with a picture of the starship *Enterprise* on the front. He had dark eyes and an unruly mop of hair, but a warm smile.

Looking around, Cotten felt the apartment seemed tidy. Nothing for *Better Homes and Gardens,* but certainly a classic example of functional beauty. In a college student tradition that spanned decades, bookshelves were made from CBS concrete blocks with slabs of unfinished one-by-eight pine shelving. The floors were real wood but needed refinishing. To his credit they were clean. Furniture was sparse and simple.

"Mr. Charles, I appreciate you agreeing to meet with me." Even with his delightful French accent, Cotten found that his English was perfect.

"Please," the young man said. "Call me Pierre. And it's an honor, Ms. Stone. I have seen you on television many times and followed your amazing adventures. Didn't some writer recently call you a female Indiana Jones with a press pass?"

"I do have a press pass," she said with a chuckle, "but I'm afraid the rest is fiction."

"Nevertheless, you certainly have a way of capturing the headlines. So, please have a seat." With a hand gesture he indicated a boxy sofa with a blue slipcover.

Cotten sat and took out her miniature digital recorder. "Do you mind if I record our interview? I have a terrible memory."

"It's fine with me."

"All right then, Pierre, would you tell me about the mysterious death you witnessed in the Amazon. Start at the beginning. I know you've already spoken to someone at SNN. But I'd like to have the entire story myself. Okay?"

"Yes."

"Just start when you're ready." Cotten turned on the recorder.

Pierre cleared his throat. "I was in the Yanomamo village for more than two years. During that time, I had never seen much sickness. Not even common colds. These people are so pure, so unaffected by the rest of the world." Pierre rubbed his knees. "I hate to think what this report might bring on them. They should be protected."

"Unfortunately, the word is already getting out. I'm just trying to find the source of the sickness, I suppose like everybody else. The case you cited isn't the only one of its kind, and that's why so many people are already concerned."

"I understand." He closed his eyes and shook his head as if the memory was vibrant. "It was a terrible thing. *Catastrophique*."

"Tell me what happened. How old was the victim and how long had she been ill?"

"She was maybe in her mid-thirties, maybe a little younger. It is hard to say. She had been feeling poorly for several days and the village shaman tended to her. First she had a fever, headache, chills, and general myalgia. Then she developed a rash on the trunk of her body. But still she did not appear morbidly ill. I didn't pay much attention after that, but was told later that she had experienced vomiting and delirium. And at the end, that is when I saw her, saw the horror of it." Pierre wiped his face with his hands. "It was the worst death. She bled from her nose, her ears and eyes, bloody diarrhea, every orifice seeped blood. Horrible. Horrible."

Pierre visibly shuddered at the recollection and stared in the distance. "You know their mortuary practice is to cremate their dead, then crush and pulverize the bones and make a drink of it. They believe it keeps their loved ones with them forever." He looked at Cotten. "I couldn't bring myself to take part, even though I was extended an invitation."

"No, I suppose not. And you say no one else in the village had been sick or became sick that you know of?"

He shook his head. "Not even the shaman who was in such close contact with her. He had breathed her breath and put his mouth to her nostrils and mouth. He didn't become ill, nor did anyone else. It took me a few days to get out of there. Scared the shit out of me. But nobody else showed any symptoms. The shaman blamed me, not me personally, but said it came from my world, meaning the outside culture that had infiltrated his remote village."

"Had anything unusual happened in the village prior to this woman getting sick?"

"No, nothing."

There was a pause in the conversation. *This is looking like a dead end.* Cotten realized that Pierre had no more answers than she did. He was only a witness to the dreadfulness of whatever this disease was, just like she had been.

"Anything else you can remember?" she asked.

"Nothing. I am sorry."

"Thank you for taking the time to talk to me. And I have to say, I appreciate your passion for caring so much for these people and trying to keep them protected. Man does so much damage in the name of research and progress."

"You're right. I had that exact conversation with an anthropologist who passed through the village just a week or so before all this happened. Dong-yul agreed with me. We had quite a discussion on the topic."

"Dong-yul?" A spike of adrenalin shot through her. "That's an interesting name."

"It's Korean. Said his name meant Eastern Passion."

LUTHER

"And finally, in a follow-up story," the SNN Headline News anchor said, "you may recall an incident that recently occurred right here at our New York studios."

A graphically bloody photograph appeared electronically over her shoulder.

"This man, identified as former pharmaceutical salesman, Jeff Calderon, collapsed in the SNN lobby and later died of what appeared to be the last stages of a mysterious, extremely lethal infection. The subsequent disappearance of his body before authorities could perform an autopsy is still under investigation by the New York City police and health departments and the Centers for Disease Control in Atlanta. Because of the severity of Mr. Calderon's symptoms, authorities are understandably concerned for the safety of the public. Until recently, no other cases had surfaced. For a special report on this we go to senior investigative correspondent, Cotten Stone."

Luther Sutton sat in the threadbare La-Z-Boy recliner and drained the last drops of Miller beer from the can. He was dog tired and his back had flared up again. Shoveling snow, chopping wood, many of his routine chores aggravated his lower back. And the West Virginia wind made his arthritis agonizing. Some of the teenage grandkids would have to start coming over and help him out. But since they buried Big Thelma, no one came around much anymore. Big Thelma's sickness had caused a rift in the family that Luther didn't see any hope for being repaired.

He started to get up and shuffle into the kitchen for another Miller but paused when something caught his eye on the Sylvania. A reporter woman was yapping away about some native person down in South America that had died from an awful disease. He recognized the reporter. Stone was her name. He'd seen her on TV before.

"So the only connection we have so far," Cotten was saying, "is the unusually severe symptoms exhibited by Mr. Calderon and the Yanomamo native. Anthropologist Pierre Charles described it as the worst death he had ever witnessed. He said that she bled from her nose, her ears and eyes, bloody diarrhea, every orifice seeped blood. Experts from the CDC are asking for the public's help in trying to determine if anyone knows of other cases. If so, please contact the Centers for Disease Control at the number on your screen or visit w-w-w-dot-satellite-news-dot-org for additional information."

Luther let out a grunt as he pushed his heels and lower calves against the footrest of the recliner, bringing it upright. Slowly, he braced his tired hands on the arms of the chair and stood. His dusty boots scraped across the well-worn wooden floor as he moved toward the kitchen. He opened the old Frigidaire and wrapped his skeleton fingers around another can of beer, snapped the top open, and downed half.

"They might want to dig her up," he said to himself. "Rest of the family won't allow it." He stood in the dark by the Formica-top dinette and drank the rest of the beer. Nobody but he and his baby brother, Ellis, had seen her at the end. The rest didn't understand how bad it was. They didn't know about the devil's death.

Placing the can on the table, he went to the rotary dial wall phone and lifted the receiver.

DEAD IN THE WATER

THE NEXT MORNING, COTTEN was in her office going over her facts and suspicions of the investigation. After the Gainesville interview with Pierre Charles, there was no doubt that the Calderon and Yanomamo deaths, T-Kup, Black Needles, and North Korea were all connected. The big question was: how?

She turned to her desktop computer and Googled hemorrhagic virus. The first link on the list was Ebola.

Ebola is one of the deadliest groups of viral hemorrhagic fevers that begins with fever and muscle aches and progresses to where the patient becomes very ill, suffers from breathing difficulties, severe bleeding, and organ failure. The source of the virus remains unknown. It is transmissible by direct contact with infected blood, body fluids, and semen.

Cotten bounced her pencil eraser on the desk before clicking the browser's back button. She followed links to other hemorrhagic viruses like Marburg and Omsk. Marburg was transmitted like Ebola. Omsk, however, couldn't be passed from human to human. Transmission of Omsk was by the bite of an infective tick, but there was also the possibility of direct transmission by muskrats and contaminated water. It wasn't as deadly as Ebola or Marburg, and was pretty much limited to Russia.

She read about others, but none quite fit. The thing most perplexing about Calderon and the Amazon woman was that nobody around them got sick. The cases were isolated to those two individuals. Calderon was probably sexually active, and a nearly penniless addict, therefore sharing needles was likely. So where were the sick sexual partners or fellow junkies? He could have been infected by a tick, but others would have been also. And the woman in the Amazon—Pierre had said he thought she was in her thirties, so she most likely had a sexual partner, and the shaman's treatment would have certainly put him at risk of contracting the disease. Cotten assumed there were ticks in the Amazon, but why would the woman be the only one contracting the disease? And what was Black Needles? Was it the name of the disease? Or were those words just the ramblings of a dying man? As far as she knew, there were no documented cases of multiple infections that matched the symptoms—

"Oh, shit." Cotten dropped the pencil and it rolled off the edge of her desk. She picked up the phone and dialed Ted.

———

"Okay, run it," Ted said after pushing the intercom button on his phone. He and Cotten sat in his private conference room. On the wall in front of them was a large flat-screen video monitor.

An engineer in the SNN video distribution center two floors below pressed play on the digital video recorder. As the image sprang to life on the plasma monitor, Ted swiveled his chair around to watch.

An electronic slate appeared: *W. J. Phillips interview. C. Stone. Mayport, Florida. Camera 1. Cassette A. 12 minutes. NTSC. Satellite News Network.*

Cotten saw herself sitting in a chair opposite one that was occupied by USN Commander Walter J. Phillips. It was an interview she had conducted a year ago. She and Phillips were surrounded by a half-dozen lights set up by her crew. A few large pieces of white foam board were clamped to tripod stands and used to reflect soft light back at Cotten and the naval officer.

"Are we ready?" Cotten asked in the video.

"Anytime," the cameraman said. "We're rolling and we've got speed."

Cotten turned to the officer. "Thank you for taking the time to talk with us, Commander Phillips."

"Glad to be here," Phillips said, sitting straight in his starched whites. He was a slim academy officer with nineteen year's experience at sea. His current command was captain of the Perry class missile frigate, USS *Robert G. Bradley*.

"I'd like to start by asking you how you felt about launching an international incident. There are still lawsuits pending and international outcries addressing North Korea about why they have not returned the bodies that were on the *Pitcairn*."

"At the time, it didn't seem all that unusual," Phillips said. "The entire encounter took less than an hour. By the time it was over, we had documented everything, handed it off to Pacific Command,

and resumed our patrol. I don't think anyone anticipated the North Koreans refusing to release the bodies."

"Do you think they just wanted to provoke the United States?"

"That's for the politicians to decide, Ms. Stone. As far as I was concerned, the incident was over and it was no longer my problem. Only later did we learn about the controversy when it showed up all over the news."

"Can you give me a description of the events?"

"We were heading up the western coast of North Korea after putting into the South Korean naval base at C-F-A Chinae. The weather was dicey at best. A heavy front had moved through that morning, and there were still scattered squalls and thunderstorms. Just after noon, communications alerted the bridge that we had received a distress call. It came from a location twelve miles to our starboard."

"In the direction of the Communist coast?"

"Correct. My ensign said it was a fairly large stationary target. I asked him to punch in the coordinates on my video monitor, and then I used my binoculars to scan the water in the direction of the contact. A squall line blurred the horizon with a wall of rain and I saw nothing. I asked radar if there were any other vessels in the area."

"Were there?" Cotten asked.

"Two North Korean patrol boats about twenty-two miles from our location. I ordered the ship to change course toward the point where the distress call originated. I also ordered the crew of our Sikorsky Seahawk to prepare to launch in the event we needed to conduct a search and rescue mission. We finally spotted the faint outline of a vessel emerging from the edge of the storm. It drifted on rolling swells, dead in the water. At that point, I had the helm slow to one third and take us to within a thousand yards of the target."

"Did you see any signs of life?"

"None. I half-expected a panic-stricken crew or smoke from an explosion or fire. What I saw was a lifeless ship drifting out of the squall."

"Were you able to identify the vessel?" Cotten asked.

"It didn't take long. She was the Oceanautics research vessel *Pitcairn*. Port of registry, San Diego. Our database showed that she had a normal crew of six and a contingent of twelve students and scientists. Oceanautics was contacted and confirmed that they were performing deep water drift current studies and island botanical research, and the ship was reported late in arriving into Dandong, China."

"So you ordered the launch of the rescue helicopter?"

"Yes. The Seahawk sits on our aft helo pad. She's got a pilot, co-pilot, and two special-ops Navy SEALs. Tango X-Ray—the call sign for the Seahawk—took off and made three circuits around the *Pitcairn*. Their video cameras transmitted close-up images back to us. When we spotted the bodies on deck, we recalled the Seahawk and outfitted the SEALs with Level A hazmat gear or bunny suits as they're sometimes called. You see we didn't know if the people on the ship were dead, injured, sick, or what. Could have been anything at this point, including contagious illness or they may have come in contact with a deadly toxin. Level A gear is completely airtight. We had to take all precautions, and it's a good thing we did. After outfitting the SEALs—"

"Their names were Bennet and Richards?"

"Correct. They re-boarded the Seahawk. The *Pitcairn* was a fairly large research vessel, and it also had a stern-mounted helo pad. Tango X-Ray put down on the *Pitcairn* and the SEALs disembarked. Once they were safely on the ship's deck the pilot lifted the Seahawk up to hover at a safe distance. Using the video feed from Tango X-Ray, I could see my men move to the ladder leading up to the vessel's bridge."

"Who was the first to relay back what they'd found?"

"Bennet. He said that it looked like everyone onboard was dead." Phillips shook his head, obviously reacting to the memory. "I asked him to repeat, and he said that he was checking for signs of life but it didn't look good."

"How many bodies did he find?"

"At that point, four—two on deck and two on the bridge. He believed those four were the captain and members of the crew."

"Did your men find any vitals on any of the victims?"

"None. Then Richards radioed that he had discovered six more bodies below deck. He said they appeared to be college age or a little older. They had to be the students and scientists."

"What condition were the bodies in?"

"He reported their flesh had turned yellow and that there was blood clotted around their nostrils, mouths, and ears."

"But if everyone was dead, who activated the distress beacon?" Cotten asked.

"Bennet found it on a table in the radio room—one of those handheld, personal transmitters. He reported a dead body on the floor. Probably the person who set off the beacon. And he said that it looked like there had been an extensive fire in the electronics

186

rack. Could have been why they didn't call for help on the normal frequencies."

"At that point, could your men determine cause of death?" Cotten asked.

"Negative. Bennet said that all the bodies showed the same signs of excessive bleeding from every orifice."

"So when did the Korean missile boats show up?"

"Right after Bennet's assessment of the condition of the bodies, we received a radio communication. The voice identified itself and informed us that we were in North Korean waters. They declared that we had violated international law and demanded that we reverse course and leave immediately."

"That must have taken you by surprise."

"Ms. Stone, I was so preoccupied with the discovery of the dead bodies, I had temporarily dismissed the Koreans. Radar called up to the bridge that there were two targets—Houdong missile boats. They were coming at us at a pretty good clip. I ordered radar to confirm our location."

"So you were definitely inside Korean waters?"

"We were holding steady at five hundred yards inside their territory but the ocean current was pushing the *Pitcairn* farther toward the coast. She had already drifted over two thousand yards across the boundary."

"And that's when you got the second warning?"

"They said it was a final warning, that we were violating the sovereign territory of the Democratic People's Republic of Korea, and to reverse course and leave immediately or we would be fired upon."

"Didn't you think they were pressing their luck threatening an American warship?" Cotten asked.

"Yes and no. Right about then, radar confirmed that there were two more missile boats closing in on us. At that point we were in close quarters with the targets and the fact is, we *had* violated their territory. It seemed fairly certain that the people on the *Pitcairn* were dead, so there was nothing I could do for them. My main concern was for the safety of my two men onboard the Oceanautics vessel along with my ship and crew. Conducting any type of armed conflict at that point was without merit."

"So you ordered Bennet and Richards to abandon the *Pitcairn*?"

"No choice. Tango X-Ray landed on the vessel and recovered the SEALs. As soon as I saw them safely inside the helicopter, I told communications to acknowledge to the North Koreans that we were complying with their demands. And I instructed the helm to back us off to five thousand yards beyond the line."

"That must have really riled you to have to leave?"

"I would have preferred to finish searching the ship and see if there were any survivors."

"Of course, we now know there were none," Cotten said.

Phillips shrugged as if not sure.

"Were you able to maintain sight of the *Pitcairn* and the Korean boats?"

"For as long as we could. We steamed west until we were well into international waters before we came about. Unfortunately, another squall line moved in between us and the target, and we lost visual contact. By then radar had confirmed that a number of North Korean vessels were converging on the *Pitcairn*."

Phillips paused, seeming to be in deep thought. Finally, he said, "You know what they reminded me of, Ms. Stone?"

"You mean the Koreans?"

"They looked like sharks circling a kill."

BODY COUNT

COTTEN CROOKED HER NECK to hold the phone in place while she skimmed through papers on her desk and waited for John to pick up. She'd been put on hold by his secretary.

"Hey, Cotten," he finally said, answering.

The connection was clear, as if he were just next door instead of an ocean away. As always, John's voice was warm and comforting. "Hey, yourself," she said, grabbing the phone with her hand, leaving the papers in a heap.

"It's great to hear from you."

"Same here. Are you coming this way anytime soon?" She closed her eyes and hoped for a *yes*.

"No, I'm just back from the MI5 briefing in London and am pretty tied up here for a while. Maybe I'll see my way clear in a month or two."

"I'd like that," she said. "I think I'm going to need your help."

"The T-Kup thing?"

"Yeah. It's growing. I was sitting here thinking about Calderon and the Amazon woman and did a little research. The strange thing about them was that they were isolated cases and worlds apart. Nobody else around them became infected. Then it hit me. I had done a piece on that research vessel, the *Pitcairn*. Do you recall that event? It caused quite a stir for a while."

"Yes. Everyone on board was dead. North Koreans grabbed the ship."

"Right. They still haven't returned the bodies. The families have filed lawsuits against the North Korean government to get the bodies back, but no results. I thought I remembered the description of the bodies, but wanted to make sure. So, Ted and I watched my interview with the U.S. warship's commander again. The description of the dead given by the SEALs who went on board appeared to match those of Calderon and the Yanomamo woman."

"No kidding. Looks like the North Korean connection is getting stronger."

"Sure does. We're trying to tie down a link, something that might pull this whole thing together. It's more than obvious that Calderon was attempting to give me some clue when he said Black Needles. But I can't figure it out. When I do, I believe it will all come together."

"What's the CDC been able to scrape up?"

"Nothing. There are no bodies to examine or autopsy. Calderon's disappeared, the Yanomamo woman was cremated in keeping with the Indian tradition, and the North Koreans still have the bodies from the *Pitcairn*."

"There's no dealing with their General Secretary, I can tell you that. He has total control. He's like a god. And nobody really knows what's going on over there. He says anything he wants but that doesn't mean what he says is true. After such an in-your-face, aggressive attitude about their nuclear ambitions, he suddenly succumbs to pressure to curb the program? He agrees to allow the Nuclear Regulatory Commission inspectors to go in and disable their main nuclear facility? Seems way too easy. And now you've made me think I know why. Cotten, what if the nuclear threat is simply a decoy?"

"That's our thinking, too. We just don't know what they're up to. But if Calderon is an example of the results, we'd better find out fast. Maybe they were just simply testing the waters, or maybe Calderon and the native woman were accidents. But I think it comes down to the fact that they are up to their necks in some type of germ warfare experimentation. Personally, it scares the hell out of me."

"Have you talked to anyone in the government about this possibility?"

"Ted said he spoke to someone and was told the FBI and CIA get hundreds of calls with all types of suspicions. Mostly from crackpots. Right now we have nothing to give them. No hard evidence. They'd just brush it off at this point. Probably think we were trying to *create* a story for network publicity. We have to get something firm, first."

"I can talk to someone. I'll get Archbishop Montiagro to—"

"Not yet. Let me see what else I can come up with."

"Cotten, don't wait too long. You and I both know there is more to this. Something much larger is behind it, and much more terrifying."

Cotten's call waiting beeped. "John, hold on a minute, let me get the other line."

She hit the flash button. "Cotten Stone."

She held the phone intently to her ear and listened for a few moments.

"I'm sorry," she said. "Okay. Yes. Give me a number where I can reach you. I'll take care of everything and get back to you."

She scribbled a phone number on a pad of paper, thanked the caller, and hit the flash button again.

"John, are you still there?" Her voice was laced with excitement.

"Everything all right?"

"Yes. I think we have another victim. And this time, it looks like we have a body."

BLACK NEEDLES

MOON STOOD AT HER kitchen counter and lifted the pot of coffee.
The brew was rich and dark, and she anticipated its strength and
bitter taste. She had altered the recipe of one scoop per cup and
one for the pot, to one scoop per cup and three for Moon. She
needed the staggering dose of caffeine. Caffeine, as well as more
specific antagonists of the adenosine A receptor, had been found
to attenuate neurotoxicity in mice. She suspected her disease was
linked to toxins rather than being hereditary. For some time now,
the evidence suggested that caffeine lowered the chance of developing Parkinson's. Even if there was no current evidence that caffeine would slow the progression of the disease, she felt there was
nothing to lose in trying.

The coffee steamed, sending up pungent aromatic swirls to her
nostrils. Moon set it aside and reached for the clear bottle of grain
alcohol, the second component of her morning medicinal cocktail.
Whether or not alcohol could protect a person from developing
Parkinson's was a hotly debated topic. And of course she already

had the disease, but if there was some slight chance that alcohol and caffeine might give her a little more time, she would pursue it. Again, what did she have to lose?

Moon measured the grain alcohol into a shot glass and then poured it into the mug of coffee. If nothing else she would relax a little before the meeting.

She put away the alcohol, emptied and washed the coffee pot, then sat at her kitchen table with the mug cupped in her palms. Taking a small plastic pill bottle from the center of the table, she spilled one salmon-colored Stalevo tablet into her palm, one of eight that she would choke down throughout the day. Moon popped it into her mouth and chased it with a gulp of her coffee. She sat back and meditated for the next ten minutes, sipping from her mug until the coffee was all gone and the alcohol had kicked in.

Finally, she rinsed the mug and thought to herself how this was the best time of her day—the morning. She was not going to feel any better than she did right now. The remainder of the day would be filled with anxiety and unpredictable tremors.

Beside the sink was a plastic tote containing a dozen pill bottles of vitamins, herbs, and other sources of immune boosters and protectors. She shook one pill from each into her palm and wolfed them down in groups of three with a large glass of tap water.

Thirty minutes later when she had dressed, she called for the car to be brought around to the front entrance.

———

Upon being introduced by the General Secretary, Moon entered the converted WWII hangar that now served as an auditorium for large meetings of her staff and the Black Needles recruits. It was one of a dozen buildings making up the high-security government laboratory complex north of the city. Narrow rectangular windows let the morning light spill in while a large contingency of heavily armed military police were posted inside and out.

The General Secretary had taken his seat up front on a raised platform. Behind him, stretching across the back wall was a fifty-foot-wide flag of the Democratic People's Republic of Korea. Sharing the platform were a dozen military officers and Workers Party dignitaries.

One thousand Black Needles volunteers sat in rows across the middle of the room. All had been handpicked for their zeal and loyalty, and had undergone extensive background checks. When tapped for service, they were only told the minimum information needed at the time and were sworn to secrecy. Today they would learn all they needed to know to complete their missions.

The General Secretary nodded as Moon approached. She acknowledged him before walking to the podium. Then she turned to face the men and women who waited to hear the details of their fates.

"Good morning, comrades," Moon said. "Friends of the new revolution, we are on the brink of bringing the world of the imperialist aggressors to their knees. At last they will pay for the atrocities committed on our people. Soon they will grovel before us. Our glorious day is almost at hand, and you, dear comrades, will have the satisfaction of knowing you are an integral part. As Dear Leader has just said, the people must have independence in thought and politics, economic self-sufficiency, and self-reliance in defense. Soon, we will have all of this and more. Our *Juche* ideology and outlook requires absolute loyalty to the party and Dear Leader. You have proven to us that this exists in the very fiber of your souls. Amongst tens of thousands of your countrymen, you are the chosen ones. Your sacrifice will be the supreme example of absolute loyalty. And it is my humble task to lead you." Moon's voice spiked. "Who among you embraces this passion in your heart?" She thrust her right arm in the air. "Who is with me?"

With a thunderous roar, the recruits shot to their feet in applause and a resounding cry of "I am with you!"

Moon bowed her head in gratitude and pride, then motioned for the volunteers to settle back in their seats.

"You will be the first of a new breed of warriors. You and the names of your honorable families will be etched in our history books, a proud legacy to pass on for generations. The legacy of Unit 731."

Her left hand trembled at her side, and she hid it in the folds of her long skirt.

"But before you take on this mission, we must be clear. You need to understand the mechanics and details of what will be required of you. Today this knowledge will unfold."

She paused until there was utter silence in the high-ceilinged aircraft hangar. She wanted them to realize the seriousness of her words.

"First, I must take you back in time to when I was a young girl. As many of you know, by heredity, I am not Korean, but rather the daughter of Japanese parents who spent many years working with what was called Unit 731."

There was a subtle muttering of acknowledgment amongst the recruits.

"When my homeland surrendered at the end of the great Pacific war, the government turned its back on many of the Japanese people who had served them so well. Enraged at the amity developing between Japan, the United States, and their allies, my parents fled to Korea, and later, more specifically, North Korea, to carry on their work. After their deaths I took up their task, and at last have found a most perfect way to bring about the revenge for my mother's death and so many fellow countrymen."

The General Secretary rose to his feet. "Dr. Chung means that she has found a way to make our great country one to be reckoned with. We will at last become a world superpower."

Moon bowed her head. "Yes, Dear Leader. That is what I meant to say."

He gave a quick motion of his hand for her to carry on before taking his seat.

"A year ago when our courageous navy captured the American research vessel *Pitcairn* and discovered all on board were dead, it presented quite a quandary. How had this happened? When we reviewed the ship's log and watched video taken by one of the student passengers, it became clear that the ship had anchored near a small island off our west coast, one where my parents had spent years at the secret Unit 731 facility researching biological warfare for Japan. I thought perhaps there was a connection between their work and the deaths of the ship's crew, and so I returned to the island with my research team. Protected by our hazardous materials gear we discovered that the laboratory had been abandoned at the end of the war. But I found there were some things left behind, originally hidden but exposed by a recent earthquake. These things included canisters of what was believed to be a rather benign virus, not much more than what causes the common cold. When I returned here to our laboratory, I studied the Unit 731 samples and discovered that this seemingly innocuous virus had mutated over time. In itself, it was still rather harmless, but the mutation was significant for a totally different reason."

She watched their young faces as they seemed to hang on each word.

"You see, comrades, all of us—all humans—have scattered across our DNA the remnants of an ancient retrovirus, one much more virulent than the one found on the Unit 731 island. In essence we are all carrying in the human genome what can be considered as time bombs."

The eyes of her audience grew wide in wonder.

"When a person is infected with the Unit 731 virus found on the island, the body's immune system immediately attacks it and renders it impotent. In itself, it is no threat. But here is the secret it harbors. When it infects someone, almost instantaneously, before the immune system destroys it, this otherwise benign virus reacts with that ancient retrovirus we all carry in our genes. That prehistoric retrovirus reassembles, mutates, and becomes a hemorrhagic virus killer."

Moon paused for dramatic effect as she sipped water from the glass on the podium.

"Are you following me so far?" She surveyed the pool of nodding heads. "Then I will proceed. Under the code name Black Needles, I spent the last twelve months manipulating and engineering the Unit 731 virus, which I call the T-virus, or trigger virus, so that it will do our bidding. And you are the heroes chosen to deliver it."

EXHUME

"THIS IS NOT RIGHT, and you know it," Ellis Sutton said, stabbing the air with his finger in front of Luther's face. "You're letting them strangers desecrate our mother's grave."

"Will you just pipe down," Luther said. "We ain't got no choice. They come with a court order signed by the judge."

"Well, they wouldn't have no court order if you hadn't gone and called that New York woman." Ellis pointed at Cotten standing on the other side of the parlor in Thelma Sutton's farmhouse.

Cotten said nothing as she turned to the window looking out over the West Virginia farm. Through the white veil of snow gently falling across the hills, she watched hazmat-suited state police agents moving like ghosts around the newly opened grave. Not long after she arrived, a backhoe had broken through the frozen ground and made a pile of mahogany-colored earth off to the side. The men were in the process of tying heavy straps around the casket to lift it from the hole.

Cotten had listened to the ongoing exchange between Luther and Ellis for the past half hour. Ellis was a much smaller man than his older brother, and she felt like she was witnessing a modern day version of David and Goliath—Luther planted like a tree trunk growing out of the wooden floor while Ellis circled him.

Beside her stood the Calhoun County sheriff. Scattered around the room, along with a few other members of the Sutton family, were the county medical examiner, the family pastor, and a local funeral director.

"And I told you we should of called the mortician when Big Thelma died," Ellis said to Luther. "They don't like folks burying bodies in homemade coffins and just anywhere they please."

"She said she didn't want no one seeing her in that condition," Luther said, his voice bellowing across the room.

"Yeah, well, tell that to the sheriff," Ellis said. "Jesus, Luther, what were you thinking?"

"Ellis Sutton," the pastor said, "I won't stand for you taking the name of the Lord in vain."

"Sorry, Reverend." Ellis bowed his head. "I'm just so upset." He dropped down onto a wooden, ladder-back chair. Talking to the room, he said, "They're out there digging up our mother. It just makes me sick."

"Are they in a lot of trouble?" Cotten quietly asked the sheriff.

"Probably not." The sheriff was a tall man in his late forties with premature gray hair. He stood with his hands stuffed inside his parka. "West Virginia state law is largely silent on burials. So not withstanding any local ordinance, you can have yourself laid to rest pretty much anywhere you'd like. They frown upon doing it near a water supply, though. But that's not the case out here in such a rural setting. I think the younger Sutton just likes to raise a ruckus." He glanced over his shoulder at the family members. "Burying their mother up there on the hill is the least of the problems here. What we need to know is what killed her."

"You're absolutely correct, Sheriff," the medical examiner said, standing behind Cotten. "Fortunately, because of the freezing weather, her body should be well preserved. Even without proper embalming, the temperature in the frozen ground would have slowed down decomp. We should have a good chance of determining cause of death."

"What about the question of who signed the death certificate?" Cotten asked the sheriff.

"Under state law," he said, "only a licensed medical, surgical or osteopathic physician can sign. According to Luther, they had a doctor come out here and complete the death certificate."

"That would be the mysterious Asian doctor who has since left the area?" Cotten asked.

"I'm afraid so," the sheriff said. "He treated Thelma Sutton while old Doc Benson was away on a two-week trip. The Doc used what's known as a temporary physician service. They send a licensed doctor to fill in while a local doctor is away so he don't have to close down and lose business."

"Is that a common practice," Cotten asked.

"I've heard of it," said the sheriff. "This is a small community with lots of elderly folks. We can't afford to go without a doctor for two weeks. I can understand Doc Benson using the service."

"Does he have records of who the Asian physician was?" she asked.

"Already checked," the sheriff said. "The company that sent the temporary physician here said it was the first time they used him and he never reported back after this assignment. He has since disappeared." He turned to Cotten. "I know, the whole thing stinks to high heaven."

She glanced out the window in time to see the backhoe lift the plain pine coffin from the hole and set it down beside the mountain laurel that had also been dug up.

"Have you ever heard of a death like this before?" Cotten asked the sheriff.

He shook his head. "Not in these parts. Nothing that comes close to the description of Thelma Sutton."

The medical examiner motioned to the activity on the distant hillside. "They've got it open."

Cotten watched the hazmat-clad agents gather around the open casket. They stood motionless for a while, then one knelt and appeared to study the inside. He turned and looked toward the farmhouse. Then he removed his protective headgear and brought his radio to his mouth.

"What the hell?" the sheriff said. "Why did he take his mask off?"

His two-way radio crackled and a metallic voice said, "Come on up."

The parlor emptied as everyone headed out the front door and across the snowy field toward the hillside cemetery.

Cotten walked beside the sheriff. She could see that all the agents had removed their masks. A few had turned and started walking toward the state crime scene forensics truck a few hundred feet away.

With every step, Cotten felt the familiar pang of dread growing in her gut. The same one that cut into her each time she came in contact with the handiwork of the Fallen.

The group gathered around the pine coffin and stared inside. Cotten saw delicate snowflakes already collecting on the bare wood bottom of the empty box.

THE SWARM

As a whole, Moon thought, the recruits had digested everything she had told them so far. This was going as well as she had anticipated. She stared out across the hangar at the thousand eager faces as she paused for a sip of water. A hand went up.

"Yes, comrade."

"Will the ancient retrovirus not be difficult to control? Could disease spread even to our own people?"

"Ahh, a very smart question. This is why you were all handpicked, because of your intellects."

A scattering of smiles and applause rippled through the crowd.

"The beauty of this is that the ancient retrovirus, once reassembled, still has not made the leap which allows it to be passed from human to human. You will be delivering to these specific targets the T-virus that will cause the ancient virus to reassemble and mutate into a killer. Once the targets receive the T-virus, their bodies will attack and destroy it, but not before it causes the ancient virus to reassemble— but they cannot pass on that deadly disease to another human. This keeps our countrymen and friends from falling prey."

Moon looked across the room again. "We have satellite medical preparation labs already assembled and in place around the world. You and your teammates will each be provided a passport and proper identification that will allow you to enter and move freely in the country of your assignment. Once at your designated lab, you will begin the process of chemotherapy and radiation. This is necessary so that when you are infected with the T-virus, your natural immune system will not quickly destroy it. Remember that it is a relatively weak virus on its own. And so your bone marrow must be impaired, in fact, eliminated. Once infected, you will only have a few days to reach your targets before the reassembled ancient virus inside you rapidly disables you."

She waited to see if there were any negative voices or rumblings of dissent. None came.

"Also included in the packets you will receive today will be two small containers of pills. The first is blue and holds an exceptionally potent drug that produces an extreme amount of energy. It will help you compensate for the weakness you will experience resulting from the immune system medical procedure. The second is red. Once you have delivered the T-virus to your targets, you are to take the red tablets. This will prevent you from suffering after the reassembled retrovirus attacks your body. It is a painful death, and we do not want any of you in this special group to endure discomfort. Taking the pills will mean that death comes swiftly, peacefully, and painlessly. You, faithful comrades, are giving your lives to preserve our beautiful way of life in Korea. Your families' hearts will swell with pride. You are the finest of patriots and will be remembered eternally for your sacrifices."

She took another drink of water, then said, "One last detail. Once you are on station and ready to go forth to strike your designated targets, you will receive a command to launch. That command is the number 731."

Another hand went up.

"Dr. Chung, how will we deliver the T-virus?"

"Another smart national hero," she said. "And the answer to that question is the amazing beauty of our Black Needles project. Unlike the crude, barbaric suicide bombers who blow themselves up in the market places and mosques of the world, you are the next generation of avengers. For you will carry within your body the breath of death. Your weapon cannot be detected or identified, for it is invisible. Those around you will see only a man or woman sitting in a church or riding in a bus or traveling on an airplane, shopping in a mall, or attending a sporting event. Just another face in a faceless crowd. And with something as innocent as your breathing or simply by a cough or sneeze, you will strike out and wreak havoc upon our enemies. Then you will casually walk away from your targets, leaving them totally unaware that you have just dealt them a fatal blow. Once our enemies learn of the terrible plague cast upon them, they will be afraid to leave their homes, go to their jobs, or send their children to school. We will hold the world to our terms. You are about to become the most powerful and deadly force on the face of the earth. And for that, I salute you."

This time, not only did the hangar erupt with a thunderous roar, but the General Secretary and his delegation stood and applauded as well.

Once the reaction died down, Moon turned to face the General Secretary. "Dear Leader would also like to express his gratefulness by rewarding each of your families with a monetary remuneration of one thousand won."

A collective "Ahh," sounded in the room. Moon knew they would be pleased. The average income was sixty won per month, so one thousand won was more than any would earn in a year.

She scanned the audience. "Are there any questions?" When no one spoke, she said, "Then we will begin the final processing. Please stay seated until your name is called. You will then join your team and be given a brief orientation along with your packets and information about your final destination and approximate launch windows."

The room broke into yet another mighty wave of applause. Moon went to stand beside the General Secretary. As they watched the reaction from the Black Needles recruits, he leaned in and whispered to her, "They are like swarming bees destined to die once they sting."

DEAD END

"I'M REALLY SORRY, LUTHER," the sheriff said. "There's just not much else we can do right now. If and when we locate your mother's body, we'll perform an autopsy and hopefully figure out what killed her."

"I know you done your best," Luther said.

"Good God Almighty," Ellis said. "Who'd-a-gone and taken Momma?"

Cotten glanced at the sheriff. He shrugged and shook his head.

"Why would somebody go and do that?" Luther said.

The sheriff ran his hand over the top of his head, then replaced his cap. "Was she buried with any heirlooms, valuables, jewelry?"

"We put her in her blue dress," Ellis said, glancing at the pastor. "Her Sunday best. She liked that one."

"Big Thelma didn't have no fancy jewelry," Luther said. "Only them cultured pearls she got to wear when she married our daddy, Hubert. But I don't believe they was worth much."

"I just want Momma back in her final place beside daddy," Ellis said. "It don't make no sense. If there's some scumbag who wanted our momma's pearls, why didn't he just take them and leave Big Thelma to rest in peace?"

No body, no evidence, Cotten thought.

Luther stared in the distance, his expression showing that he was deep in thought. He turned back to the pile of dirt beside the grave and blinked. "I planted that mountain laurel the same day we buried her." He tipped his head toward the dug-up shrub. A melancholy smile emerged on his face. "It was her favorite. Blooms so pretty—I thought she'd like that. In the spring I was gonna plant a sugar maple. Give her some shade, you know. Me and the rest of the family come out here about once a week or so, and I haven't noticed any dirt piles or anything that would make me think somebody had been fooling with her grave. And nobody else has said nothing. Whoever did it would have had to dig up that laurel. I'd have noticed. So I figure it had to be right after we put her in the ground, before the soil settled." His eyebrows arched, and the corners of his mouth turned down. "Could have been somebody from church. Nobody else would know about them pearls."

"But Luther, they ain't worth shit—sorry, pastor," Ellis said.

"Somebody must have thought different," Luther said.

Ellis kicked the ice-crusted ground. "Son-of-a-b. Anybody that needs a couple of bucks that bad—"

Luther looked at Cotten. "So I guess we won't be finding out if Big Thelma died of the same disease as that New York City fella you told us about?"

"Doesn't look that way," Cotten said. "Sorry your family has gone through all this."

Luther gave her an appreciative nod.

"I'd have to agree with Ms. Stone," the sheriff said. "All we have is the description of your mother's symptoms. But the state police plan to get the forensic boys to do a complete analysis of the coffin for any evidence. And we'll start an investigation into the disappearance of the body."

"Let's hope it was just for the pearls," Cotten said to the sheriff as they shook hands.

———

Cotten checked the speedometer as she drove down Interstate 79. The light traffic let her keep the cruise control on eighty. She could easily make her 2:30 flight out of Yeager. As soon as they discovered that Big Thelma Sutton wasn't in her grave, Cotten had switched her flight back to New York, changing it instead to Atlanta.

She probed the center console for her cell, found it, snapped it open and said, "Ted, work." In an instant she heard the tones of the phone dialing Ted Casselman at SNN headquarters. She only had a few of her contacts programmed for voice recognition, numbers that she called often, especially when on the road. *Great feature.*

"Hey," Ted said, picking up.

"I'm on my way to Yeager. You're not going to believe this, but Thelma Sutton's grave was empty. No body in the coffin. And how about this, it was an Asian doctor who treated her and signed the death certificate. And of course he has since vanished. This is getting more intriguing by the minute."

"Are you kidding? Someone stole the body?"

"No joke. I've got a contact in the CDC. Pete Hamrick. I interviewed him back during that anthrax incident at the America Media building in Boca Raton. I'm flying to Atlanta this afternoon. He said he'd do what he could to get me in to see the director. I believe it's a task that would fall under their shop's responsibility anyway. Somebody with authority has to get involved now. With this new turn in events, it's more than just suspicion or coincidence. They'll have to listen. You agree?"

"Definitely. Let's keep our fingers crossed. It sounds like we're on the brink of blowing something heinous wide open."

"These cases, even the *Pitcairn,* are either amazing coincidences, sheer accidents, or someone is testing the water. We know who is behind this, and they have to know we're sniffing around. That might push their buttons and cause them to make a mistake. We just have to find them and whoever else they've gotten involved."
Cotten was quiet for a moment. "This really scares me."

"Me, too. Be safe, kiddo."

She pushed the *end call* button. This was going to wind up being much more than she could handle. She held down the call button and spoke into the phone.

"John, cell."

THE TARGET

"We have an emergency," the Old Man said.

"Excuse me?" Moon looked up with a start, not hearing him enter her office. She had been making notes in her log after the morning meeting when she heard his voice. Out of respect, she started to rise.

With a wave of his hand, he stopped her, then walked to the window near her desk and stared out across the farmlands surrounding the secret government complex.

"What kind of emergency?" she asked.

"I need one of your young recruits to move up his launch date as soon as possible. He must leave today. And I need to change his target."

"With all due respect, we have their schedules precisely timed and their targets have been chosen well in advance under the impeccable supervision of Dear Leader. Some are individuals but others are groups involved in scheduled events like Times Square on New Year's Eve and Midnight Mass at St. Paul's Cathedral in

London—they are dependent on the calendar. Your request is out of the question."

He turned to her. "I can understand your hesitation. After all, you have no desire to interrupt your meticulously designed schedule. But trust me, Dr. Chung, not reacting to this emergency could jeopardize your entire program. You recall that I told you early on that you and your project were stepping stones to my ultimate goal of returning a family member to the fold? What you have created can deliver my loved one to me. But if you do not cooperate, then I will seek another solution. I assume that you don't want to do anything that might endanger the success of Black Needles?"

"Of course not. I would never risk the project. But what is about to take place as our recruits go forth is the result of a year of hard work and careful planning. Besides, having a target hit before our designated launch date will expose our hand and attract unwanted attention. A documented case of the Black Needles virus would alert the authorities and cause them to go on the defensive before we have everyone in place. I cannot alter our timetable in any manner without just cause."

There were two chairs in front of Moon's desk. The Old Man went to one and sat. "Let me enlighten you on a few things that might give you a clearer view of what is at stake here."

"At stake?" With a huff, she straightened in her chair. "You have no idea what is at stake. You did not watch your mother being tortured and gang-raped by barbarians as I did. You did not witness the murderous acts of cruelty against my countrymen as I did. What is at stake here is the retribution for years of pain and suffering at the hands of the imperialist aggressors. And I will not budge from my objective. It's a part of every breath I take, every minute of every day."

She folded her hands on her desk in confidence, proud of her display of courage to stand up to this … person. She had one goal, and one goal only—to inflict the most death and destruction on her sworn enemies as possible. And that was what she was about to do. Black Needles would be her legacy, her masterpiece. It would secure her a place in history.

The Old Man's gaze suddenly made her uncomfortable. She felt an uneasiness that grew in intensity, heating her body on the inside. Her hands shook, and she wondered if it was because her medication was wearing off or because she feared she had overstepped her bounds.

A change in reasoning occurred to her. Perhaps she was being foolish and overreacting. If ignoring his request would jeopardize the project, then maybe she should choke back her pride a bit and listen to what he had to say.

"I apologize for the outburst," she found herself saying, the words awkwardly tumbling out her mouth. "We are on the verge of the culmination of a project that has been in the making for two generations. I must protect it at all costs. There is little else in life that is of value to me."

When he said nothing, she continued, "It's just that I don't have a lot of time left. My body is not cooperating. It is deteriorating each day, making it harder for me to do my work. A setback now might cause me to lose focus and the ability to see this through."

Suddenly, Moon had another surge of confidence. "I didn't ask questions in the beginning, taking your word that you would divert attention from the Calderon-T-Kup incident so that I could complete this project unhindered. I didn't ask you how you would do this or even what you would gain." Moon took a deep breath and swallowed. "But now I feel I must..."

Moon's gaze settled intently on his, ready to identify clues that would divulge his internal reaction to her forthcoming question. She locked in her own flat and controlled expression. He would be able to read nothing in her eyes or face. Finally, she said, "Who are you?"

"Misunderstood."

"What?"

"I am misunderstood."

Moon held her hands up in a gesture of confusion. "That tells me nothing. Explain, please."

The Old Man sighed. He seemed to sink into the chair as if he were weary of repeating the story. Steepling his fingers and tapping his chin, he said, "There was a time when I basked in the glory of ... Paradise."

Moon intercepted her gut-level response to anticipating where he was going with this, and she only blinked.

"In my youth I was considered beautiful—perhaps the most beautiful. Those around me compared my beauty to the brilliance of the dawn. In fact, my former name meant light—the luminescence of the heavens—the Light-Bearer. I was called the Son of the Dawn. Along with my brothers and sisters, we filled the void before the great creation with a radiance that can only be described as complete, absolute, total."

Moon's earlier wave of confidence crashed on the shore of what she was dealing with and a trickle of deep fear leached away the strands of her self-assurance. She was playing with something way out of her league. She never should have asked the question.

"But there came a time," the Old Man continued, "when one among us declared that he was supreme, the god of gods. Without any concern for our feelings or our stature in the ranks of our legions, he professed to be our superior. For lack of a better word, he declared himself God. Some of my brothers and sisters agreed with Him, bowing down, succumbing to His will. I did not, for I saw no need. We were all equal. There was no one god over us. There was only … us."

Moon felt a growing nausea mounting in her belly. Her right hand shook so fiercely that it bumped the bottom of her desk. A runnel of sweat ran down the track of her spine. She had been so wrong to begin this questioning. Now there was no turning back.

"Those who didn't agree with Him chose to side with me. We tried to reason with Him but it was to no avail. We banded together to prove our determination, and a bloody confrontation resulted in many of us being banished from our home, the only home we had ever known. For simply standing up to an unreasonable tyrant, we were made to pay a price that far exceeds any price you have paid, Dr. Chung. For not only were we exiled from our home, but forbidden to ever return. The place where my brothers and sisters now live is a wasteland of disappointment. For every moment there, we are reminded of what we lost and how unfair it was. So, when you speak of cruelty and revenge, Dr. Chung, let me assure you that I am the king of cruelty and revenge. I am the almighty god of vengeance. I am the fist of retribution and the blade of reckoning. And Dr. Chung, when I tell you that we have an emergency and you must alter your schedule, it is not a suggestion."

As he leaned forward, Moon envisioned a cobra about to strike. He slipped a piece of paper across her desk. She stared at it as if it would burst into flames.

"What is that?" she asked.

"The name of the target."

COMMUNION

Dear Father,

I write with deep regret that I have never accomplished anything worthwhile for you in my short life.

I was selected quite unexpectedly for a special duty to Dear Leader and am now within moments of fulfilling his request. Once his order was given for my one-way mission it became my sincere wish to achieve success in fulfilling this duty. Even so, I cannot help feeling a strong attachment to our beautiful country. Is that a weakness on my part? On learning that my time had come I closed my eyes and saw visions of your face, mother's, grandmother's, and the faces of my close friends. It was heartening to realize that each of you wants me to be brave. I will do that!

My training in the service of Dear Leader has not been filled with sweet memories. It is a time of resignation and self-denial, certainly not full of comfort. As a singular reward for my service, I can see only that it gives me a chance to die for my country. If this seems bitter it is because I had experienced the sweetness of life before volunteering for this mission.

The other day I received Dr. Chung's lecture on life and death. It seems to me that while she appears to have hit on some truth, she was concerned mostly with superficial thoughts on avenging the past. It is of no avail to express it now, but in my twenty-three years of life, I have worked out my own philosophy. But I am willing to take orders from Dear Leader and Dr. Chung because I believe in our noble country.

The Korean way of life is indeed beautiful, and I am proud of it, as I am of history and mythology reflecting the purity of our ancestors and their belief in the past, whether or not those beliefs are true. That way of life is the product of all the best things which our ancestors have handed down to us. And the living embodiment of all wonderful things out of our past which is the crystallization of the splendor and beauty of Korea and its people. It is an honor to be able to give my life in defense of these beautiful and lofty things.

My greatest regret in this life is my failure to tell you that I love you. I regret not having given any demonstration of the love and respect which I have always had for you. During my final moments, though you will not hear it, you may be sure that I will be saying I love you and thinking of all you have done for me.

I did not ask you to come to see me in Pyongyang because I know that you are comfortable at home and do not like to travel. I also know your health is failing and that is why I did not ask.

I leave everything to you. Please take care of my sisters.

I pray that you will live long. I am confident that a new Korea will emerge from my actions and those of my brothers and sisters preparing themselves to go forth into the world on our special mission. We must not be rash in our desire for death, but proceed in a belief that our actions are for the best.

Fondest regards, just before my final act of heroism,

Your loving son, Kang

———

He folded the letter, placed it in the envelope he had prepared back in his hotel room, and slipped it into the yellow *cassetta postale* mail drop box. It was getting cold as the evening shadows gathered. Despite the blue pills he took to overcome the debilitating effects of the medical procedure, he felt weak and lethargic. Working hard so that his appearance did not look out of the ordinary, Kang shoved his hands inside his overcoat before turning to walk the last few blocks along Via dei Quercetti to his target.

———

Resembling a medieval fortress, the fourth-century Basilica of Santi Quattro Coronati emerged from the tree-covered heights of Coelian Hill. Despite being near one of Rome's busiest markets, the Basilica of the Four Crowned Saints was isolated and reclusive. Passing the high, thick walls and buttress-supported towers, Kang entered the main building of the ancient complex.

The Mass honoring the feast of St. John of the Cross was already underway. He sat in a pew near the rear and waited, focusing most of his attention on the half-dome apse forming the high ceiling over the sanctuary. Candle smoke and incense gave the appearance of a gray veil between him and the grandeur of the frescoes behind the altar commemorating the four Roman soldiers who gave their lives as martyrs under the Emperor Diocletian.

Soon, the congregation stood and formed a line down the center aisle to receive communion. Kang pulled the small tube of concentrated pepper essence from his pocket, opened the top, and squeezed a few drops onto the palm of his right hand. Returning the tube to his coat pocket, he rose and joined the end of the communion line.

Slowly, the procession of the faithful moved forward until only one woman remained in front of Kang.

"Body of Christ," the priest said and placed the small wafer of unleavened bread into the recipient's outstretched palm. Beside the priest stood a young altar boy who held a silver paten beneath the woman's hands to catch the communion host in case it dropped.

As the woman turned to walk back to her seat, Kang stepped forward.

The priest removed a communion host from the chalice-like ciborium and held it for Kang to see. Then he said, "Body of Christ."

Kang stared hard into the priest's face, then said, "Cardinal John Tyler?"

The priest gave him a perplexed expression. After a moment's hesitation, he responded, "Yes."

Kang brought his palm to his face and breathed deeply. The potent pepper essence entered his nostrils and his body reacted.

He sneezed.

PEACHTREE

COTTEN PEERED OUT THE window of the Atlanta Sheraton Midtown Hotel at a view looking through brick archways into the garden courtyard and pool. In forty-five minutes she was to meet Pete Hamrick of the CDC downstairs in the bar for a drink. There was plenty of time to freshen up.

She closed the blinds and lifted her purse from the floor beside the nightstand. Digging through it, she pulled an envelope out—a letter she'd gotten several days ago. She stared at it for a moment before running her fingertip over the handwriting.

John's writing.

Cotten stacked both pillows together at the headboard, stretched out and propped up on the pillows. Gingerly, she took the letter from the open envelope. The stationery already showed signs of wear, a bent corner and a couple of creases. She had read the letter many times, etching every word into memory, but it was never enough. Just to see it again and picture John holding the pen and picture John holding the pen and writing…

Dear Cotten,

I hope that all is well with you. I have missed you since returning to Rome. I always find it difficult to leave you, but know that this is the way it must be. You are such an incredible woman, and I care about you very much. As we have said so many times, if things were different … perhaps another time, another place.

I do not mean to sound unhappy, as I am not. For so long I searched for the best way to serve God, at one time even taking a leave of absence from my duties. But at last I feel I have found my way and I believe that is mostly due to knowing you. Yet, still, there is a void inside me that is unfulfilled, and will remain so for the rest of my life. I must settle for spending short times with you, hearing your voice during brief phone calls, and clumsily attempting to express myself in letters. The time we live in is difficult as the forces of good and evil come closer to the final end. These times define us, who we are, what we do, and we have both found our places. I know that at times you feel you have put me in harm's way, but that is not true. We both battle the same enemy. And so we are living our lives as God has destined us to live and as we have chosen. We have made personally tough but virtuous choices.

I am thinking of you every day.

Devotedly,

John

She touched his signature, tracing the sweeping J, then pressed her fingertip to her lips. "If things were different, another place, another time," she whispered.

The jangle of the phone startled her as sharply as if she were awakened from a deep sleep by a sudden blare of a horn. She flinched, clutching the letter to her chest.

"Damn," she said, then answered the phone.

It was Pete Hamrick. He apologized for being a few minutes early.

"No, that's fine," Cotten said. "Give me five and I'll be right down."

———

Pete Hamrick waved at Cotten as she entered the Peachtree Bar. He sat at a small, low table and already had a drink in his hand.

As she walked over, he stood.

"It's great to see you again," Pete said, pecking her on the cheek. "You look terrific as always."

"Thanks." Cotten sat. "I appreciate you taking the time out to see me, especially on such short notice."

"No problem." He took his seat across from her. "What's your poison choice?"

"Absolut on the rocks."

He got the waiter's attention and placed her order. They made small talk, discussing the cold weather, some of Cotten's travels, and the birth of Pete's third child before the waiter returned with her cocktail.

Cotten sipped the drink and felt the warmth of the Swedish vodka reach her belly. "Perfect," she said. "So tell me, what ever happened to the American Media Building? Bring me up to speed since our interview."

"Actually, it sold not long after the anthrax attack. A developer named David Rustine bought it for forty grand, but spent millions on maintenance and decontamination. Renamed it the Crown Commerce Center. Turned it into a really beautiful office building. Applied Card Systems purchased it from him and they occupy it now. It's probably the cleanest office building on the planet."

Cotten laughed. "I'll bet you're right."

Pete stared at her for a moment and Cotten felt the awkwardness of the silence.

"I know you aren't here to catch up on American Media," he finally said. "You were a little mysterious on the phone, telling me just enough to intrigue me."

Cotten took another sip before setting the glass on the table. She leaned forward and spoke softly. "I really need to talk to the director. I have reason to believe that a biological warfare attack is being tested right now and will soon be launched."

"Tested? You mean like clinical trials?"

"No. More like guerilla trials. Innocent victims."

"Where's it coming from? Who's doing the testing?"

"I have a good idea—actually more than just a suspicion. Listen, I don't know how many tests they've done already or how it is being controlled, but I can assure you the first cases are out there. People have died."

"Look, Cotten, we haven't seen any major outbreaks of anything since SARS."

"You haven't seen any major outbreaks of anything else *yet*. This will make bubonic plague look like the common cold. You've got to get me in to see the director."

"You're going to have to tell me a little more than that. I can't go to her based only on general speculation and vagueness. She'll think you're some kind of kook and that I'm an idiot."

Cotten let out a sigh. "If I tell you, and you don't believe me, you won't get me the appointment and I'll lose all around. I can't let that happen. There's too much at stake. You're welcome to remain in the room when I speak to the director. Then you'll both hear it all at the same time."

Pete leaned over his knees, resting his arms on his thighs, and cradling his glass in his hands.

Cotten reached across the table and touched his forearm. "I swear to you, this is real, and we can't afford to ignore it. We have to snuff it out before it's too late."

"I don't know," he said, drawing a finger across his mustache.

She knew Pete probably remembered the embarrassing scandal she went through a few years back with what the press called the creation fossil hoax. It was her exclusive story and was supposed to prove the creationist's theories to be true that man and dinosaurs had co-existed. In reality, it was an elaborate setup meant to disgrace her. The goal was to destroy her credibility regarding any future investigations into the Darkness. The incident made international news, cost her her job, and almost her career. Only she, Ted, and John knew the truth—that it had all been orchestrated by the Old Man and the Fallen.

For Cotten, it was a hard climb back to respectability. Pete had to be wondering if this was also a hoax she had gotten caught up in to further her career.

"You've got to trust me. Pete, I learned my lesson long ago. I don't jump to conclusions, and I don't grab on to things just for notoriety. Please trust me."

He swallowed the last of his drink. "Well … I can't promise anything, but I'll see what I can do." He put his glass down on the table.

"I'll be waiting for your call."

"Yeah." He started to throw a couple of dollars on the table.

"I've got it," she said.

Pete stood and turned to leave, but then paused and looked back. "Don't make me look like a fool."

SWAN SONG

"Dr. Swan, this is Cotten Stone from the Satellite News Network," said Pete Hamrick. "Cotten, I'd like you to meet Director Charlotte Swan."

"Thank you so much for seeing me on short notice." Cotten shook the woman's hand. She had arrived at the CDC campus off Clifton Road twenty minutes earlier and was greeted by Pete at the main security center before being ushered to Swan's tenth-floor office.

"Please, have a seat," Swan said, indicating the leather chairs facing her desk.

As she and Pete took their seats, Cotten guessed that Charlotte Swan was in her late forties. And she was definitely all business—as evidenced by her attitude and appearance—navy-blue tailored suit and blonde hair pulled back tightly into a small bun at the base of her neck. Her desk was just as meticulously groomed.

How did anybody work like that, without stacks of papers, file folders, staplers, scattered paperclips, pencils and pens? Cotten pictured her own desk at SNN. Whenever she was deep into a project, especially when conducting research, her entire office gave the appearance of being as organized as an explosion.

"Dr. Hamrick suggested you be a priority on my schedule today, that you have something to discuss that would be of concern to the CDC." The director leaned back in her chair with an inquisitive expression. "I pressed him for details, but he said I should hear it from you. He also assured me that you were here in the capacity of a private citizen, not as a network news correspondent. So I assume that what we discuss is off the record?"

"That's correct," Cotten said.

"I am most curious to hear what you have to say, Ms. Stone, but I have a video conference with the director of the World Health Organization in twenty minutes. That's all the time I can give you."

The woman's tone was cordial but to the point. Swan didn't seem irritated by the interruption in her schedule, but Cotten knew she had one shot at this, and it had to be good.

Even before the first word came out of her mouth she detected the signs of her nervousness. Her feet were cold, her mouth felt dry, and her hands clammy. She brushed a stray strand of tea-colored hair behind her ear. "Do you recall the incident last year with the discovery and subsequent loss of the Oceanautics research vessel *Pitcairn*?"

"Vaguely," the director said.

"The ship was found drifting off the west coast of North Korea," Cotten said. "The crew and student scientists were found dead by specialists from an American warship. The *Pitcairn* ended up falling into the hands of the North Koreans who still have it according to satellite images."

"Oh, yes. I remember. The description of the bodies got our attention. It sounded like a hemorrhagic fever."

"Right," Cotten said. "Well, it seems that other people have recently died with physical symptoms similar to those on the ship." She explained in detail the deaths of Jeff Calderon, the Yanomamo woman, and Thelma Sutton, her empty coffin, the abandoned T-Kup labs in New York and now in California, the other T-Kup holdings around the world, and the possible Asian connection to them all. "I believe these deaths are connected. And I fear that it signals a possible biological threat, perhaps to this country or one of our allies."

Cotten anticipated Dr. Swan's questions and concerns, and attempted to head them off. "I know there are no bodies to examine, but that reinforces my premise. Just think, Calderon's body mysteriously disappeared from a major New York City hospital, and Thelma Sutton's body was stolen from her grave. Somebody doesn't want those bodies examined. No autopsies mean no trail of evidence. Add to that the fact that the North Koreans refused to release any medical details on the cause of death from the *Pitcairn* bodies."

"Are you saying this is the doing of the North Koreans?" the director asked.

"I don't know."

"They thumb their nose at the world all the time. That's no surprise," Pete said.

Dr. Swan folded her hands on the top of her desk. "The work of the CDC is heavily weighted on the empirical side, not theoretical."

Cotten felt her shoulders slump. "Dr. Swan, so much is at—"

"However," Swan continued, "it has been my experience that gut intuition often leads to the right hypothesis, and from that point on you can prove or disprove. It's that first inkling that starts everything in motion."

Cotten found herself smiling in relief. "Then you agree that there is a strong possibility these deaths might indicate a connection? That there might be a threat?"

"You have to understand, dealing with political issues is not within the CDC's authority or domain."

"Does that mean you're not going to investigate?" Cotten asked.

"I didn't say that. What we will do is look into what kind of outbreak this might be and then what we can do about it."

Cotten took out her wallet and pulled a card from it. "This is the number for the county sheriff in West Virginia. Thelma Sutton's coffin is being examined for any residue or evidence. You might want to take a look at the results of the forensics report."

Dr. Swan took the card. "We'll get in touch with the sheriff and the Sutton family, and request access to their home, especially Ms. Sutton's room."

"Thanks," Cotten said. "If you can nail down the disease, maybe we can find out how to stop this."

Dr. Swan stood. "I'll be in touch."

They shook hands and Cotten said, "Please keep me in the loop." She removed her own business card from her purse and handed it to the director. "And Pete, you have my number, too."

"Thank you for coming in," Dr. Swan said.

Pete escorted Cotten out of the office to the elevator. Just as the doors slid open, Cotten's cell rang. She looked at the caller ID, then closed the phone.

"Thanks again, Pete," she said as she entered the elevator. "Call me with any news."

A few moments later, she handed in her visitor badge at the security desk and stepped out into the bright Georgia sunshine. Opening her cell, she pushed *call back* on the missed call.

"Hi, Ted. What's up?" she said.

"When are you back in New York?"

"I'm headed to the airport right now."

"Then come straight to the office. What I've discovered is going to blow you away."

UNIT 731

COTTEN WALKED INTO TED'S office, having come directly from Kennedy. She took a seat and gazed out the large window behind his desk. "I've wondered about something for a long time but never asked you—what good is an office with a view if your desk is faced away from the window?"

"If I look out the window all the time," he said, "I don't get my work done. Makes me daydream." He spun his chair 180 degrees. "And I can always do this when my brain needs a short hiatus from the job." He swiveled back around to look at Cotten.

"So tell me what you found."

Ted opened a file folder on his desk revealing a stack of papers. He spread them out. Some were handwritten notes on yellow note-pad paper and others were hardcopies printed from the Internet. "I was researching biological warfare to see what I could come up with. This is the thread I ended up following. We've got to go back to the year 1925 and the Geneva Protocol that banned gas and germ warfare—which, by the way, was approved by all the great powers except the United States and Japan. The U.S. signed, but didn't ratify it until fifty years later, in 1975. The Japanese never signed it. Anyway, the Japanese were so impressed that such warfare was so heinous that it had to be banned under international law that they decided germ and chemical warfare must be the ultimate weapon. In 1930, Japan's biological weapons program began under the direction of an officer named Lieutenant General Shiro Ishii."

Ted looked up from his notes. "I'm going to try to give you a timeline to follow. Bear with me."

"Should I make some notes?"

"No, just listen for now." Ted shuffled through the papers. "1932. Japan invaded Manchuria and Ishii began preliminary experiments. Soon after that, he established Unit 731, a biological warfare unit disguised as a harmless government agency. He razed eight villages to build a huge compound in Pingfan near Harbin, a remote part of the Manchurian Peninsula. The compound consisted of 150 buildings covering about four square miles. There were barracks, labs, operating rooms, crematoria, and more. And get this, a theater, bar, and Shinto temple. There were at least seven other similar units scattered across Japanese-occupied Asia, all under Ishii's command. By the time he was promoted to full general, he had over three thousand people working under him. The atrocities Ishii and his colleagues committed are right up there with the likes of Joseph Mengele. As a matter of fact, some of the research I came across referred to it as the Auschwitz of the East."

"Really?" Cotten said. "I've never even heard of Ishii or Unit 731."

"Most people haven't, and there's a reason. I'll get to that in a minute." Ted waved a paper with his notes scrawled on it. "Unit 731 experimented on humans. They nicknamed their victims *marutas,* which means logs. That's how they saw their prisoners, nothing more than inert logs."

"Sounds like a good brainwashing technique so their consciences didn't get in the way," Cotten said.

"Nobody with a conscience could have committed what I found. Let me give you some examples."

Ted searched the papers, finally ending up with one in particular. "Some prisoners were given electrical charges which slowly roasted them. Others were decapitated in order for the Japanese soldiers to test the sharpness of their swords. Limbs were amputated on live victims to study blood loss."

Ted sat back and rubbed his shoulder as if it ached. "Want to know how sick these guys were?" He didn't wait for Cotten's response. "Sometimes they would stitch the limbs back on the opposite side of the body. They would remove all the organs, and for whatever reason I can't imagine except for some perverted kick, they'd reattach the esophagus directly to the intestines." Ted peered over his glasses at Cotten. "Too much for you yet?"

She shook her head in silence.

"They hung prisoners upside down to determine how long it would take them to choke to death. Prisoners were locked in high pressure chambers until their eyes popped out. The *marutas* were even put in giant centrifuges and spun to death."

"Jesus," Cotten said. "What the fuck kind of medical research is that?"

Ted didn't give a direct answer. "I found out that the Japanese had what they called *comfort women*. The military operated brothels for its soldiers. But when venereal disease became an issue, Ishii took it on. He had his scientists bring a prisoner infected with syphilis together with another who was not infected and demand they perform sex or be killed. Then they would track the progress of the disease from the moment of infection." Ted looked away and breathed out a loud breath. "Instead of just looking at the external signs, like examination of genitalia, they performed live dissections—vivisections, most often without any type of anesthesia. They would cut the *marutas* open and note the effect of the disease on the internal organs. The babies of those women who they did not kill by vivisection were also used in unspeakable experiments. Or they were given to the soldiers to practice tossing them with their bayonets while the infants were still alive.

"And there was more; many of the prisoners were infected with plague, cholera, typhoid, and a myriad of other diseases so they could study the progress of the diseases as well as vaccines. Again, live dissections were the norm. In the end, all the data was to be used to find a way to attack the United States. Near the end of the war, Unit 731 came up with the plan, codenamed, Cherry Blossoms at Night, to use kamikaze pilots to infest California with plague-infected fleas. The plan was for a submarine to take them near the coast of Southern California. A plane carried by the sub would be flown into San Diego and the insects released. But before that could happen the war ended. They had formulated many other attack plans as well—to release infected animal feed and all kinds of disastrous disease on the United States, but luckily, didn't get to carry them out. In the final days of the war, Ishii ordered the last 150 *marutas* killed to cover up their experimentations. The Japanese blew up the secret labs and headquarters of Unit 731."

Cotten stared at Ted. She could think of nothing to say as the horrible images swam in her mind.

Ted engaged her eyes. "When I started this research I couldn't believe what I was reading."

"Why hasn't there been the same horrendous outcry as there was against Hitler and the Holocaust?"

"I can only assume it was a massive cover-up. From what I've read the United States believed the information collected by the Japanese on biological warfare far outweighed prosecution for war crimes. In the fall of 1945, General MacArthur granted immunity to members of Unit 731 in exchange for the research data on biological warfare."

Cotten felt sick to her stomach. "How could they? How could we?"

"Listen to what happened to some of the major players of Unit 731 in the postwar years. This will blow you away." Ted flipped through the papers, then lifted one and adjusted his glasses. "Asahin Masajjiro, a member of the typhus team, went to work for the National Institute of Health as did Murata Yoshisuke who was part of Unit 1644. Futagi Hido, the vivisection team leader, became the cofounder of Green Cross Corporation."

"What's that?" Cotten asked.

"It was Japan's first commercial blood bank, which later became a big pharmaceutical company, merged with other corporations, and now even has subsidiaries in the United States." Ted pushed the papers back into the folder. "The list of those who got away with murder goes on and on."

"So where does this leave us? How does this fit in with T-Kup, Calderon, and Sutton?"

"Oh, kiddo, I've saved the best for last."

MEGA-MART

THE FOREST PARK MEGA-MART west of Chicago was packed with holiday shoppers now that the blizzard had finally let up. The Cadillac Escalade circled the huge parking lot. Behind the wheel, the woman regretted she had waited this late in the season to start her shopping.

"Mom, I'm bored," her eight-year-old said from the back seat.

"We're here already," the mother said, glancing from side to side, searching for an empty spot. "I just have to find a parking space. Keep watching your *Shrek* DVD."

"You brought the wrong one," her son said with a whine. "I wanted the new one."

"And whose fault is that? How many times did I tell you to get ready to go and pick out a movie?"

"But I've seen this one already."

"It's your favorite."

A small import started pulling out of a space just ahead. She switched her blinker on. The guy was taking his own sweet time backing out, she thought. Another car turned into the row from the opposite direction. She eased forward. The import finally cleared the spot and turned to pass her. Before the driver coming toward her could make his move, she shot forward turning wide to block him and pulled her big SUV into the space.

Finally, this first challenge to Christmas shopping was complete—finding a parking place.

Mother and son bundled up and got out. The headlights flashed as she pressed the lock button on her remote, and the two headed across the parking lot. The crust of ice and snow crunched under their feet as they passed rows of automobiles and abandoned shopping carts.

With a whoosh, the sliding doors opened, and the welcome warmth of the store surged over her. The greeter, a gray-haired lady in a wheelchair, nodded at her as she did to everyone entering Mega-Mart.

"I wanna go to the toy section first," the boy said.

"We've got a lot of gifts to buy for both your grandmas and grandpas, and Auntie Sue, and Uncle Jack. And we've got to get something for Daddy. Sugar, I don't think we have time to look at toys this trip."

"But you said we could."

"I said if we got everything else done first."

"I can go look at the toys while you shop. I promise I'll stay right in that department. You can come get me whenever you're ready to go."

"I don't think so. You need to stay with me," she said, pulling out her shopping list from her purse. "No discussion." She looked up and searched the section signs for one that said *hardware*.

"Wait." Her son pointed to a boy and his mother walking down a side aisle. It was one of his neighborhood friends and mother. "Can I go say hello?"

She waved at the other mother.

"Sure, but make it quick." She watched him navigate through the flow of customers to his friend. A moment later, he ran back to her.

"They're going to look at the toys. Can I please go hang out with them. His mom said it was okay."

His mother glanced down the aisle. The neighbor waved and mouthed that is was okay.

"I promise I won't leave that section," her son said.

She could probably get more done faster without him complaining the whole time, she thought. "You promise to stay with them?"

"Yes!" He raised his arms in a victory gesture as he ran off dodging the knot of shoppers that clogged the store.

She headed for the hardware section, knowing her father-in-law had hinted he wanted a new cordless, reversible drill for Christmas. Her husband said to only get one made by Black & Decker. That should be easy enough.

The aisles were so congested she had to almost shoulder her way through to the hardware section. There were six different drills to choose from, making the decision process harder. She was reaching for a mid-priced model when she heard a shout. It sounded like it came from a few aisles over. She started reading the features list on the box when she heard a woman shriek.

A few people at the ends of the row started walking toward the commotion. She realized that the disturbance was coming from the direction of the toy section. Placing the drill back on the display, she hurried to the end of the row. A number of people, including employees, were rushing in the direction of the toys displays.

Someone yelled to dial 911.

She picked up her pace, feeling her heart rate increase. It was probably nothing, but people were so crazy during the holidays. She should have made him stay with her. She scanned the crowd, searching for her son's face, the back of his head, his plaid jacket.

Customers gathered in a mass at the end of one of the aisles in the toy section. She pushed her way through until she could see what was happening. About halfway down the row, three employees knelt around a man who was sprawled on his back on the floor. Thank the Lord, it wasn't her son. The man appeared to be Asian, maybe Chinese or Japanese. They all looked alike to her.

"Mom?"

She turned to see her son standing next to her. "Thank God, you're all right," she said, hugging him.

"Yeah, I'm fine."

She squeezed him again, then let him go.

"I was looking at a Spiderman action figure and this guy was standing a few feet away when he started coughing and stuff. Like he was having some sort of allergy attack. You know, like when Auntie sneezes around our cat? He kept coughing, and all of a sudden he just fell on the ground—looked like he was trying to take a red pill. This one lady called 911 on her cell."

Across the way she caught sight of the neighbor who shrugged, lifting both hands like she had no explanation of what happened.

The mother ushered her son away, excusing themselves as they moved through the onlookers. "Let's leave the sick man to the paramedics. Come on, I need you to help me pick out a drill for Grandpa."

CONNECTION

"THIS IS THE PART that made my head swim," Ted said. "I was totally appalled at everything I read about Unit 731, but couldn't specifically attach any of it to our investigation. Then, strictly by accident, I ran across a tiny article. Seems that two of the most zealous members of Unit 731 defected to Korea just after the war. The code name for the germ warfare project they worked on was Black Needles."

"You're kidding," Cotten said.

"Nope, here's the article." He pitched it across the desk to her. "This man and wife team was adamantly opposed to the Japanese cooperating with the United States in any way, so after the war they got majorly pissed off. And guess where they ended up? They fled to North Korea and changed their last name from Nakamura to Chung. In North Korea they continued the work they had begun with General Ishii."

Cotten scanned the article then glanced up. "But they'd probably be too old now to be of any consequence, if they aren't dead already."

Ted smiled. "Right. But guess what, they had a daughter, Chung Moon Jung. It took a couple of days to get any kind of info on her, but our research team came up with a few references. There isn't much you can find out about the goings-on inside North Korea, especially individuals, so we were lucky we came up with anything at all. It appears that Dr. Chung is a high-ranking official working for the Democratic People's Republic of Korea. She's got a couple of doctorates, including one in biochemistry from the University of Beijing. She's fluent in a number of languages, including English." Ted nodded as he arched both brows. "We also found out that her health is failing. Parkinson's disease among other ailments. Is it coming together for you now?"

Cotten's jaw dropped. "This Chung Moon Jung might be our Korean woman connection."

"Exactly. Unfortunately we don't have anything terribly substantial to go on, but it makes sense. It makes even better sense when your hear this. The facility in Pingfang is the one mostly associated with human experimentation, but the actual designation of the term Unit 731 didn't come into use until 1941 or '42—I can't remember." Ted tapped the folder of papers with the tip of his index finger. "It's in here somewhere. Anyway, Unit 731 became kind of a generic term that embraced not only the Pingfang-based unit, but also all the satellite facilities. Some of those who were involved with Unit 731 have come forward in recent years and provided testimony. I ran across one account of a nurse who said she worked in a facility on an island in Korea Bay under the supervision of Doctors Nakamura, a husband and wife team."

Ted's mood darkened, and he folded his hands on top of the folder.

"There's something else, isn't there?" Cotten said.

"Unfortunately. We went back through the Navy transcripts and found that before the confrontation with the North Koreans, the *Pitcairn* had been anchored off a remote volcanic island in Korea Bay. They were there for several days while they tried to repair damage to the electronic navigation and communication system caused by an onboard fire. Remember, the *Pitcairn* was a research vessel. Among the passengers were some young botanists."

Suddenly, Cotten put the puzzle pieces together. "Oh, Christ," she said. "Those kids went on the island and found the ruins of the Unit 731 lab."

"And stumbled across Black Needles."

THREE-WAY

COTTEN SAT AT HER desk, making notes on a yellow legal pad about everything Ted had just gone over with her. Pieces were coming together and forming a huge complicated picture. Maybe she should fill Dr. Swan in on the latest.

She retrieved Charlotte Swan's card from her purse and stared at it a minute, wondering if the CDC director was the right contact. Maybe she should try the FBI.

Let's see where the CDC is taking this first. Cotten dialed, and after getting Dr. Swan's secretary, she was finally connected.

"Hi, Doctor Swan. This is Cotten Stone. If you recall I—"

"Of course I recall. Funny you should phone. I was just looking over the forensics report on the Sutton coffin."

"That was fast."

"I had them fax me a copy. Got it maybe thirty minutes ago."

"Find anything?" Cotten asked.

"Nothing definitive, but there are a few suspicious results."

"Like what?"

"Possible traces of pathogens. I think it warrants further investigation. As a matter of fact, I was just about to assemble a team to go to West Virginia."

"I'm so relieved. I was afraid you would come up with nothing or wouldn't see the need to follow up."

"Oh, absolutely not."

"Dr. Swan, I have more to tell you. I know it isn't within your jurisdiction, but I think you need to know what you might be looking at here and what it involves."

"I appreciate that."

Cotten revealed everything Ted told her about Unit 731, the *Pitcairn*, Dr. Chung, and her family. Swan seemed to listen intently with only a few questions.

"What do you think?" Cotten asked when she finished.

"I think it's scary as hell and I'd better do my end of the job quickly. Actually, I think this goes way beyond the CDC. I'm going to get in touch with some friends at Health and Human Services along with the FBI. Homeland Security will probably need to get involved as well. They're all going to have to help carry the ball."

Cotten leaned back in the chair, her hair tumbling over the back. She closed her eyes. "That would be great. I really want to thank you, Dr. Swan."

"No, I want to thank *you*. I'll get back in touch as soon as I know where we are with all this. I'll talk to you soon."

"You bet," Cotten said, letting the receiver slide down the side of her cheek and come to rest on her jaw. *Thank God, someone is listening to me.*

———

"Heard anything?" Ted asked as the elevator door closed and began its journey up the shaft in the SNN building.

Cotten watched their reflections in the polished bronze doors. "No. Three days ago Dr. Swan sounded like she was gung-ho. She seemed to really believe we were onto something more than just a new flu strain."

"Have you called her?" Ted asked.

"Twice yesterday afternoon, but her secretary said she wasn't in. I don't want to be a pest. She said she'd get back to me. I guess I should be patient. I did call Pete Hamrick, and he said he would check up on the status, but I haven't heard back from him either."

The elevator stopped on the fifth floor, and a new hire from post-production got in with them. Cotten couldn't remember his name but offered a greeting as did Ted.

Cotten discontinued her conversation about Charlotte Swan until she and Ted got off on the eighth floor and went into his office.

Ted eased the door closed behind them. Cotten took off her coat and laid it over a chair.

"I simply don't get it," she said. "Swan was so ready for action. She even said she was going to take this to various Washington agencies. I felt relieved, like we had handed it off to people who could take care of it. I mean Washington, for Christ's sake."

Ted chuckled and sat behind his desk. Then his face turned serious. "I think I know all your secrets. Right?"

"Mmm," Cotten said, sitting opposite him.

"I believe you've pushed something important to the back of your mind, like you're trying to ignore it."

Cotten tilted her head and bit away a hang nail.

"Don't forget who and what we believe you're up against. Shit, it freaks the beejesus out of me. I go home every night and check out the sunset, wondering if it's the last one I'll ever see or when I see the next one will I be thrashing on the floor under my window bleeding from every hole in my body like Jeff Calderon. I have frigging nightmares and there's not a damn thing I can really do about it. All this shit is going on in the background of everybody's life like white noise. Who'd believe us if we told them? Who would listen if we got in their faces on our evening newscast and said demons and devils are plotting our demise? Even if we gave specifics, we'd either cause mass hysteria or the FCC would find a way to revoke our license."

"So what are you trying to tell me, Ted?"

"Okay, I'll say it and lay it out there, but I know it's already stapled to the very front of your brain. Those agencies in Washington may not be the answer at all. Give Director Swan another call and then make a decision. But you're the one who has to make that call. You are the only one. And you know it."

Cotten knew Ted was right. "I'll call Pete Hamrick and see what he knows."

Ted picked up his phone and handed it to her. "Know his number?"

"I've got it in my cell," she said.

"Look it up and use this phone. I want a three-way on speaker."

"What?"

"See if you can get John on the line first."

Cotten glanced at her watch and did the math. "He should be available." She opened her list of contacts on her cell and found John's. Then she punched the number into Ted's phone.

After waiting for his secretary to put her through, Cotten heard John's voice. "Hey, any news?"

"I have you on speaker. I'm here with Ted. This whole T-Kup thing has blown up. Like I told you earlier, I've been in contact with the CDC, but haven't heard back. Director Swan was going to get a number of government agencies involved, but now Ted and I are wondering if that's the right course. You know what I'm getting at? I'm going to call Pete Hamrick again and see what he knows. Ted thought you should be on the line." She paused a moment, then said. "I'm glad I called. It's so good to hear your voice."

"Yours too."

"Hold on." She pressed the flash button, dialed Hamrick's number, and when it started to ring she brought John back on line.

"Pete Hamrick," the voice answered.

"Hi, Pete. It's Cotten Stone. I have you on speaker with Ted Casselman, SNN news director." She didn't see any reason to mention John and have to go into a long explanation. "I was wondering if you have heard anything from Director Swan?"

There was a long pause.

"Cotten, I'm not sure how to tell you this. I didn't call you earlier because I've been wrestling with it."

"Spit it out, Pete. What is it?"

"I talked at length with Dr. Swan this morning, and she says they are dropping the investigation, that there is not enough evidence to go on, that it's only conjecture at this point."

Cotten smoothed the hair from her face, feeling the dampness of perspiration breaking out at her hairline. "What do you mean? She said there was possible evidence of pathogens from the coffin forensics. She was sending a team to West Virginia and calling authorities in Washington. She definitely thought it more than conjecture."

"I don't know what to say, Cotten. To put it bluntly, she said the whole thing sounded like a crock, concocted by you and your network to boost your ratings." There was a long silence. Then he said, "I'm really sorry. I gotta go." The line clicked off.

"John, you still there?" Cotten asked.

"Yes."

"What are your thoughts?"

"Sounds dubious to me. Very suspicious."

"I agree," Ted said.

"Dr. Swan was anxious to move ahead with the investigation when I last spoke to her," Cotten said. "Something happened. Somebody shut her down. Why?"

"Had to have something to do with her Washington connections," Ted said. "As soon as she started singing to somebody over there, the roadblocks went up."

"But why?" Cotten said.

"It doesn't matter," John said. "The CDC isn't going to do anything."

"So where does that leave us?" Cotten said.

"I have an idea," John said. "It's a long shot, but I'm going to call in some favors. Plan on me flying out of Rome late tonight or first thing in the morning. I'll call you with my flight info as soon as I know."

"To New York?" Cotten asked.

"No, Washington."

CAMP DAVID

When Cotten first caught sight of John coming through customs at Dulles, the compelling desire to run to him whirred within her, starting deep inside, then prickling its way across every nerve and out to her fingertips.

Instead, she smiled and waved.

Cotten realized she had stopped walking and was glued in place, watching him approach. Finally, within touching distance, John stood his rolling Travelpro on end and hugged her. "Hello, Cotten Stone."

She felt his breath on her cheek. "Hello, John Tyler," she whispered into his shoulder.

Then his arms released her, and the bite of cold air replaced the warmth of his embrace. "How was your flight?" she asked, tossing back her hair and tying to regroup her emotions.

John grasped the handle and towed his bag behind as they walked. "Not bad. It actually gave me some undisturbed time to think and prepare for what I'm going to say."

"Do you think you can persuade President Brennan to get involved?"

"I think so. We know his background. He ran his campaign on moral and religious platforms. An evangelical Catholic is in the White House."

"But you can't just blurt out that the legions of evil are behind a couple of mysterious deaths—" She corrected herself. "No, considering the number of bodies on the *Pitcairn*, it would be a whole host of deaths and their unobtainable or disappearing bodies. No matter, he would still think you're nuts."

"Yes, he would," John said. "But I believe I've come up with a convincing argument. Scary, but convincing."

"You're not going to tell him about me, are you?"

John turned to look at her. "No. He'd definitely have us both sent to the funny farm if I did that."

"Sometimes it doesn't seem real. Even to me it sounds ridiculous. There are moments I wonder if this is all a weird dream and any minute I'll wake up and my life will be normal. No more Nephilim or Fallen Angels. The next moment I realize it's no dream, and my stomach churns. Thank God for you and Ted. You two keep me sane."

"Somebody has to," John said.

Cotten elbowed him. They exited the terminal and boarded the car rental shuttle. A half hour later, they were on I-270, heading northwest toward Maryland.

The hour-long ride took them through Frederick, north to the Catoctin Mountain Park which surrounds the Presidential retreat at Camp David. The drive gave them plenty of time to plan their strategy. The rustic 125-acre mountain retreat was colder than it had been at Dulles, and the rental's heater didn't seem to be able to keep the car warm.

Cotten kept one hand on the steering wheel and banged the dash with her free hand, hoping to jar the heater into cranking out more warm air. "My feet are freezing," she said. "And my nose feels like if I flicked it, it would shatter."

John leaned forward and fiddled with the temperature controls. He held a hand in front of the center vent testing for any change. "At least we're almost there. Enjoy the scenery and try to take your mind off the cold. If you want to stop for a minute, I'll get you a heavier jacket out of my bag in the trunk."

"It's okay. I want to hurry up and be there. Besides I don't want you to open the door and let in more cold air." Cotten watched the snow-powdered hardwood forest flow by. "You're right. The scenery is lovely. Even in the winter, the mountains are beautiful. So you've been here before?"

"Twice, once with Brennan, the time before that with his predecessor. The last time was to brief the President on secret talks between the Holy Father, the Israelis, and the Palestinians."

"I wasn't aware that the Vatican was involved with Middle East peace negotiations."

"That's why they're called secret talks."

She glared at him then smiled. "Touché."

Up ahead, she spotted the sign marking the turnoff to the main entrance of Camp David. It read, *Camp #3*. Cotten made the turn, and a short way down the road passed the first of three black SUVs. Next, they drove by two fully armed Humvees parked on each side of the forest road, their .50 cal machine guns aimed at the approaching car. Finally, a high metal gate and fence resembling the entrance to a maximum security prison emerged out of the forest. A U.S. Marine dressed in full combat gear held his hand up as Cotten slowed the car to a halt. Additional Marines, all carrying assault rifles approached from both sides.

Cotten lowered the driver's side window and the officers leaned down. "Identification, please."

She removed her license and SNN press ID from her purse and handed it to the Marine. At the same time, John handed his Vatican City passport to Cotten who gave it to the officer.

The Marine scrutinized the documents while he spoke into a tiny microphone that protruded from an earpiece. A moment later, he gave the IDs back to Cotten. "Please proceed through the gate and follow that vehicle." He pointed to a Humvee that had just positioned itself onto the entrance road up ahead. "Welcome to Camp David."

———

President Brennan sat in front of the fireplace in Aspen Lodge. His old friend, John Tyler, had been intentionally vague when he called and said it was urgent that they meet. Brennan and his advisors had discussed the upcoming visit from the cardinal, and the President prayed it had nothing to do with the dropping of the CDC's investigation of the death in West Virginia. But, he was well aware of John's association with Cotten Stone, so he anticipated the worst. Shutting down Charlotte Swan had been difficult enough. This would be even harder.

An aide opened the door. "Mr. President, Cardinal Tyler and Ms. Stone are here."

Brennan closed the file folder marked *Top Secret*, stood and went to a decorative secretary desk. He slipped the folder into a drawer, then laced his fingers, cracked his knuckles, and rocked his head from side to side to loosen his neck. Finally, he glanced at the aide. "Show them in."

The man left, reappearing in a moment with Cotten and John.

"John," Brennan said, striding toward him and extending his hand. "So good to see you again." They shook hands. "Sorry, I have a hard time calling you anything but John, though I know it should be Your Eminence."

"I'm honored that you still call me John, Mr. President. And that you've agreed to see us."

Smiling, Brennan turned his attention to Cotten. "Ms. Stone, your reputation precedes you. I'm glad to finally have the pleasure."

"Thank you, Mr. President," Cotten said, shaking his hand.

"Please have a seat and enjoy the fire. I find when I'm out here at the retreat, it's one of the most soothing things I can do. Staring into the fire is mesmerizing, almost primeval."

Cotten and John chose two armchairs that formed a semi-circle grouping in front of the fire.

Brennan took a seat in a third. He felt a spear of anxiety poke at his throat and rolled his head again, hearing it crack and a sound like sand being grated between his cervical vertebrae. "Tension affects the whole body."

"And you certainly have a stressful job," John said. "Exercise helps. But you're in good shape."

"Actually my health is good. The First Lady keeps me in line. I eat right. Jog or fast walk every day. But I haven't done any real running since track in Boston." He paused a moment, then locked his eyes on John's. "Might as well get on with the rat killing, John, don't you agree? I'm sure you didn't come all this way for small talk. So shoot."

"Mr. President, I think the United States and its allies are in grave danger."

Immediately Brennan knew that his fears were justified. They had come about the investigation.

John went on to explain what they knew and how they had gone to Director Swan at the CDC. Cotten chimed in now and again, adding details.

When they finished briefing him, Brennan sank deeper into the chair and bit his bottom lip in a grimace. The integrity of the United States was at risk if this investigation went forward. He was the President, and it was his duty to protect the nation. He had to come up with some legitimate-sounding response. He had to stop this from going any further or the country would be forced to reveal a dark secret long buried. It could irreparably damage the United State's position with respect to human rights in the eyes of the world.

Brennan gathered his thoughts. "This is alarming. Especially your suspicion of a Korean connection. Know what's really scary about that? The DPRK is a closed society. Try as we might, we have little success penetrating their world. Might as well be on another planet. Frankly, I wouldn't put this or anything past that nut-job tyrant."

"Mr. President," Cotten said, "we don't know why, but we suspect that somebody shut down Director Swan's investigation on purpose. But at this point it probably doesn't matter. We're asking that you consider bypassing the forensic investigation and move to take action to stop North Korea and the Black Needles threat before it's too late."

"Dr. Swan is excellent at what she does," Brennan said. "If she dropped the investigation, I'm sure it was for good reason." He ran a finger under his collar, loosening it from his neck.

"But you can do something, Mr. President," Cotten said. "Forget about Dr. Swan, it's bigger than that. If North Korea is planning a biological attack on this country, it's your sworn duty to try to stop it. Don't you see they've been field testing their weapon? Black Needles has already claimed innocent lives."

Brennan gave a patronizing smile. "If you're correct, the thought is frightening. But where is the evidence? I can't act on supposition. I can't go to the Joint Chiefs and Congress and say, hey, I've got this funny feeling that North Korea is up to no good." He laughed. "It would be dead on arrival."

John swiped his hand over his face and stood. "Mr. President, we go back a long way, and I know how strong your faith was then. I'm depending on it being even stronger now. I'm going to reveal something to you that I think will change your mind. I need you to not only listen to what I'm about to say, but also *hear*. The future of the world may be dangling from a thread hanging from your soul."

GRAND TOUR

It had been a fairly quiet morning at Golden Ridge Elementary School in Chino Hills. Even the traffic in the front office was slow.

The secretary was listening to a parent on the phone who wanted to cancel a teacher conference when a cough at the front counter got her attention. She looked up to see a man standing there. The secretary nodded to let him know she would be right with him. "I'll get the message to your son's teacher," she said into the receiver, then hung up.

"Can I help you?" She got up from her desk and walked over to him.

"Yes. I purchase home next to Hidden Hills Park. My children attend this school? Correct school, yes? And I have questions." He coughed again, covering his mouth with his hand. "Sorry. Bad cold."

The man spoke with an accent. Vietnamese, Chinese, Japanese, one of them, she thought. She hated to be prejudicial, but Oriental accents all sounded alike to her, just like Spanish accents—Mexican, Columbian, Cuban, Venezuelan—she couldn't tell the difference.

"That's definitely in our boundaries." Poor guy seemed to be miserable. "Everybody's had a bug lately," she said. "Stuffy head and cough. We had three teachers and a ton of kids out last week."

"I thought I am only victim," he said grinning.

It was an odd smile, the secretary thought, as if he had put something over on her—slipped something by like a private joke. "When you come to register the children you'll need proof of age, such as their birth certificates, passports, baptismal certificates along with proof of residence address, and immunization records. Are they up-do-date on their immunizations?"

The man didn't answer and seemed distracted, surveying the office.

She asked again. "Are the children's immunizations up-to-date?"

The man glanced over his shoulder out the glass doors. "Yes," he said, turning back.

Oddball, the secretary thought. She hoped the kids weren't as bizarre as their daddy. She took a couple of brochures from the stand on the counter. "Here's information on bus routes, and this one is about after-school care. Some other basics you'll want to look over." She held them out.

He took the pamphlets. "Thank y—" He couldn't finish, instead sneezing several times in succession.

The secretary reared back to avoid the spray of droplets she saw in the air. Even so, she felt a fine mist on her face.

"So sorry," he said when the coughing subsided. "I came here yesterday but school already closed. I like to take tour. Now, please. Tight schedule. I like see classrooms, maybe cafeteria? Must do today."

"Sure." The secretary glanced up at the wall clock. "Lunches started about twenty minutes ago. Let's get you signed in, Mr. . . . ."

"Choi."

"Okay, Mr. Choi, I'll need your driver's license, and here, sign in on this log." She pushed a clipboard with an attached ballpoint toward him as he took his wallet out of his pocket. *Mr. Choi is really Mr. Weird*, she thought.

A few minutes later Choi had a visitor's pass sticker to put on the front of his shirt.

"Have a seat and I'll get someone to take you around. It shouldn't be but a few minutes. We'll give you the grand tour."

———

"I can't believe I'm really standing here looking at it," the elderly, gray-haired tourist said to his wife. He had recently retired, and they were visiting London on the first leg of an around-the-world vacation. They stood a few feet away from the Rosetta Stone on display in the British Museum. "You know how when you buy an appliance or tech device, you get an instruction manual in multiple languages?"

"Sure," she said, holding on to his arm.

"Well, let's say a thousand years from now, archaeologists lost the ability to read and write English but they know how to speak and read Japanese. So, let's say they come across the owner's manual for your blender. If they compare the Japanese version of the instructions to the English version, they would probably have enough information to learn English."

"That's how the Rosetta Stone works?"

"Right. After Egyptian hieroglyphs went out of use, the knowledge of how to read and write them soon disappeared. Now, jump forward to Napoleon's time. His army discovered the Rosetta Stone while digging the foundation of a fort in Egypt. What's inscribed on the surface is actually nothing earth shattering. It's something about some royal event commemorating the coronation of a pharaoh. The big deal is that the decree is inscribed three times just like your blender's owner's manual. It's in hieroglyphic, some other Egyptian script, and Greek."

"So, the Greek version was the key."

"You got it. Scholars realized they had a means of decoding Egyptian hieroglyphics by comparing the Greek version to the glyphs on the stone. That started the whole—"

They both turned toward a commotion coming from the tour group exiting Room Four that housed the large collection of Egyptian sculpture. The tour group opened up around an Asian man who was bent at the waist as he threw up on the marble museum floor.

Even from a dozen yards away, the retiree could see that the vomit was bloody.

ASPEN

JOHN PACED IN FRONT of the huge Aspen Lodge fireplace while President Brennan's eyes tracked him.

What on earth was John getting at? Brennan wondered. Why such high drama?

John gazed into the flames, his back to Brennan. "Steel yourself for what you're about to hear, Mr. President. Listen with an open mind." He turned around. "Can you do that?"

"Of course."

"We did some Bible study together, so I know you're familiar with the scriptures. Go back to the original battle for Heaven. God cast the rebellious angels out of Paradise, never to return. And what does Genesis tell us about those Fallen ones?" He removed a small Bible from his jacket pocket and opened to an earmarked page. "In Genesis, chapter six, verse four: *The Nephilim were on the earth in those days, and also afterward, when the sons of God went to the daughters of men and had children by them. They were the heroes of old, men of renown.*"

"I'm familiar with that verse," the President said.

"The Nephilim were the offspring of the Fallen and mortal women. They were half human, half angel, described as giants. Goliath of Gath was believed to be one. The Nephilim aren't just an Old Testament legend, Mr. President, they're referred to in myths of almost all cultures including the Egyptians, Hindus, South Sea Islanders, American Indians—across the globe, giving credence to their existence."

"Yes, John, I know that. Where are you going with your Bible lesson?"

"Think about this, Mr. President. What motive did the Fallen have to populate the Earth with their hybrid children? Was a plan orchestrated by Satan to interrupt Abraham's bloodline because the Seed of the Woman, Jesus Christ, was to come through Abraham? God responded with the Great Flood to cleanse the earth of this corrupt genetic race. Only Noah and his family were spared because they had not been defiled. No Nephilim in their family, and so they were saved."

John continued reading: "Genesis, chapter six, verses five through seven: *The Lord saw how great man's wickedness on the earth had become, and that every inclination of the thoughts of his heart was only evil all the time. The Lord was grieved that he had made man on the earth, and his heart was filled with pain. So the Lord said, I will wipe mankind, whom I have created, from the face of the earth, men and animals, and creatures that move along the ground, and birds of the air, for I am grieved that I have made them.*"

John stopped and looked up. "Can we agree that the Fallen and Nephilim existed in Noah's time?"

Brennan shifted in his chair. "If you take the scripture literally, then we can agree. But I ask you again, what has that got to do with the suspected virus threat and the North Koreans?"

"Be patient," John said, holding his hand up. "Matthew, chapter twenty-four, verses thirty-seven through thirty-nine: *But as the days of Noah were, so also will the coming of the Son of Man be.*"

"Some would say that the Nephilim were wiped out by the Great Flood," the President said.

"They were, but the Fallen will be with us until the End of Days. They continue to have offspring who have grown as many or more in number today as they were prior to the Flood. We're told to pay attention to how things were in Noah's day." John stared hard into Brennan's eyes. "The Nephilim do walk among us, as do the Fallen. You have to believe me. I know. I've seen it first hand."

"John, I'll concede that there's more than enough evil in the world..." Brennan wasn't certain he wanted to hear more. And he didn't want to keep sounding negative to John's theories, even though he had no choice. He glanced over at the desk and thought of the *Top Secret* folder.

"So you do accept that Satan's legions exist today?" John asked.

"You know I do. You and I share the same faith." He did believe it, but he still wasn't getting the connection to the biological threat.

"What are some of the signs of the Tribulation, the terrible times we will suffer before the Second Coming?"

The President thought for a moment. "Wars, famines, earthquakes."

"Right," John said. "And false messiahs. How many of those have we seen over the last generation? But these are only the birth pangs. The end is still to come. Also from Matthew twenty-four:

There will be famines and earthquakes in various places. An increase in false messiahs, an increase in warfare, and increases in famines, plagues, and natural disasters." John paced again before stopping directly in front of Brennan. "Plagues. I don't think it's just the North Koreans behind Black Needles. I'm certain it's much bigger than that."

Brennan blinked, and a wave of uneasiness swept over him. He had to end this discussion soon before he was pushed into a corner. John was right, there were bigger things here. Things that could irreparably harm the reputation of the United States.

"You see where I'm going, don't you, Mr. President?"

Brennan didn't answer, but simply stared at John.

"Let me bring it all together for you. The Fallen and Nephilim are still at war with God today, and what is happening now was prophesied in the book of Revelation." He turned to another page in the Bible. "Revelation, chapter sixteen, verse two: *And the first went and poured out his vial upon the earth; and there fell a noisome and grievous sore upon men which had the mark of the beast...* I believe that refers to Unit 731's work. Revelation, chapter sixteen, verse three: *And the second angel poured out his vial upon the sea; and it became as the blood of a dead man.* Could the *sea* be a reference to the *Pitcairn?*"

Brennan's throat and mouth went dry, and he found it hard to speak. "Stop." His voice sounded to him like sandpaper on raw wood.

"Revelation, chapter sixteen, verses eight and nine: *And the fourth angel poured out his vial upon the sun; and power was given unto him to scorch men with fire.* Could the *sun* be the rising sun of the Japanese flag? Japan, where this disease originated? And does *scorch men with fire* refer to the raging fever brought on by Black Needles?" John closed the Bible and slipped it back in his pocket. "If all that isn't enough to convince you, Mr. President, then listen to one more quote from scripture."

President Brennan's throat constricted, as if a noose were tightening around it. *I'm the President of the United States. How could I possibly betray my oath of office? But this... this theory of John's, if it were true, protecting the integrity of the United States would be no more than an insignificant trifling.* The room suddenly seemed to lack oxygen.

This time John spoke from memory. "Revelation, chapter sixteen, verses ten and eleven: *And the fifth angel poured out his vial upon the seat of the beast; and his kingdom was full of darkness; and they gnawed their tongues for pain, and blasphemed the God of heaven because of their pains and their sores, and repented not of their deeds.*"

Brennan sat forward. "What do you think it means?"

"It took me most of the flight to Washington to understand it. I believe it means that the North Koreans are using their own people as weapons. Helped by the Fallen, they are somehow infecting their people, then sending them out to deliver the virus to their targets. That's what I think it means by *And the fifth angel poured out his vial upon the seat of the beast; and his Kingdom was full of darkness.* They don't repent. They are like Japanese Kamikaze pilots or radical Islamic suicide bombers. But unlike those terrorists, these suicide bombers are carrying weapons that are undetectable, invisible. Their weapons are the germs inside them."

Leaning back, the President groaned, then muttered, "I need time to think."

Cotten stood. "But there isn't any time, Mr. President. The suicide bombers could be out there right now sitting next to innocent people in buses and airplanes, theaters or supermarkets, or schools—"

Brennan's head shot up as he saw a possible flaw in the theory. "No, that can't be. They'd have no way of controlling it. It would eventually infect their own countrymen as well."

"Maybe they have developed some kind of vaccine," Cotten said.

"Do you know how huge an undertaking it would be to inoculate the entire population of North Korea, not to mention their allies and all those in countries whom they don't regard as enemies," Brennan said. "And on top of that, how would they keep something that huge a secret? Impossible."

"Then Dr. Chung has found a way—" Cotten suddenly stared at John. "No one else got infected! That's it! That's why the people around Calderon and Thelma Sutton and the others didn't get sick. Dr. Chung has somehow engineered Black Needles so it can't be passed from man to man. Like the Avian flu, or at least the way we think the bird flu is transmitted. Man can get it from a bird, but can't pass it along—yet. The suicide bombers are like the birds. Someway, they cause the infection. This is how they can pick and choose their targets." Cotten slapped her palm to her forehead. "How stupid of us. She's a biochemist after all. That's what she does." She looked at the President. "Please, Sir, you have to intervene."

The President glanced back at the desk, his hands sweaty and his skin crawling. *If they had any idea what was in that folder.* "I'm sorry, but despite your colorful and imaginative argument, there's really nothing I can do. You have no proof, no compelling evidence. It would be worse than the Iraq WMD debacle. We can't make such serious accusations on a whim. John, you and I both know you can interpret scripture a million ways from here to Sunday and back."

"Damn it, don't you see?" Cotten said. "The attacks could already be underway. And when mothers start seeing their children die horrible deaths, how do you think they will feel when they find out you knew and did nothing?"

Brennan rose. *It was a terrifying scenario that John painted. But the likelihood that it was true was still remote. Regardless, it was the investigation that he feared most. That's what could open up a festering sore and cause irreparable harm to the United States in the eyes of the world. He had no choice.*

"I'm sorry, Ms. Stone. Thank you both for coming to me with this. Your concerns are commendable. And I promise I will weigh each fact uncovered against your points, John." He motioned to the door. "The military escort will take you back to your vehicle."

"Steve," John said, calling the President by his first name as they walked to the door. "If you don't believe me, believe your heart and the word of God. Don't wait too long to act. There's too much at stake."

———

President Steven Brennan collapsed in the armchair, blankly staring at the fire. After a few moments, he went to the desk, removed the folder, and returned to his chair. If he allowed this whole issue of Unit 731 to resurface, the hideous secret that had been hidden away for nearly an entire generation would raise its filthy head. All he could do was pray that John's premise was wrong, that he and

Cotten Stone would realize it, and that they would drop the matter. It might prove to be the biggest gamble of his life.

He opened the folder and scanned the intelligence assessments again. 1951. America was drowning in the Korean War. A miserable war in a miserable place. MacArthur's campaign had resulted in the loss of over 60,000 United Nations troops in North Korea, and the American people were in a frenzy anticipating the threat of "Yellow Mongol Hordes" marching into the homeland. Something had to be done. Brennan's eyes read and reread the October 1951 order.

OPERATION CODE NAME——TAKE OFF.

The U.S. Joint Chiefs of Staff hand-delivered an order to General Ridgeway to begin experimental, limited germ warfare in Korea. It was followed by a second JCS directive in February 1952. *JCS# 1837/29* authorized larger field tests. The order was given verbally so there would be no paper trail, no archival evidence.

Brennan's stomach churned at the thought as he once again reviewed some of the horrific details.

Using much of Unit 731's research, the United States had dropped their standard ordinance bombs, but then followed in the last wave of planes with germ-laden bombs. After the air raid, the North Koreans converged on the site to rescue their injured.

The germs were intended for the rescuers.

But it wasn't limited to germ bombs. It was even more hideous. Infected food was dropped on major populations to kill the hungry civilians.

It wasn't until the U.S. troops accidentally became infected that it finally ended.

Brennan closed the folder, wishing he could close the book on one of the country's blackest stains as easily. He knew that the government had been vigilant in keeping it covered up. Only one other time had it come this close to being exposed to the public. It was in 1953 when a germ warfare specialist from Camp Detrick was ready to blow the whistle. He was found dead in a hotel room. *Suicide.* His children never accepted that their father had taken his own life. Forty years after his death, the body was exhumed and reclassified a homicide.

Brennan stared at the presidential seal above the fireplace, then dragged himself to the bar and poured three fingers of eighteen-year-old scotch. He downed it in one gulp, knowing he was faced with the biggest question of all—what to do about Cotten Stone and John Tyler?

JET LAG

"WE GAVE IT OUR best shot," Cotten said to John, taking her eyes from the road a minute as they drove to Washington from Camp David.

"But it wasn't enough." He leaned his head back against the seat.

"Maybe President Brennan just needs time to think about all that scripture you quoted before he reconsiders. It was a lot for him to take in at one time. I watched his face, his eyes, as you talked, and he definitely seemed to be grasping what you were saying. Near the end, he appeared downright nervous."

"Maybe," John said.

"You look tired. Why don't you use this time to rest a little? Jet lag has to be hitting you."

Without lifting his head from the headrest, John turned to look at her. "I'm okay."

"Yeah, right. It wouldn't kill you to doze off while I drive. Then I won't feel bad about asking you to go with me to dinner when we get to the city." She grinned at him. "Go on. Humor me."

Cotten turned on the radio and found a station playing smooth jazz. The light piano and strings hummed along with the song of the tires on the road. A few minutes later she looked over at John. His beautiful blue eyes were closed.

———

They checked in at the Washington Dulles Airport Marriott, both of their rooms on the second floor.

"Say in about forty-five minutes," Cotten said as they got off the elevator. "I need to freshen up first. We can just grab a bite in the hotel restaurant if you like."

"Better idea," John said. "There's a great Japanese restaurant about two miles from here. Feel like sushi?"

"Perfect. I'll knock on your door when I'm fit to go out in public. How's that?"

"Sounds like a plan."

Cotten slipped her card key in her door lock then swiftly removed it. The small green light flashed on, and she opened the door. "See you in a bit," she said.

Over the years of reporting from every corner of the globe, she had gotten used to living out of a suitcase. Like always, she packed light and only clothes that didn't wrinkle.

Cotten pulled the long-sleeved, black jersey sheath from the suitcase and hung it up in the bathroom to steam while she showered.

Poor John, she thought, turning on the water and adjusting the temperature to a comfortable hot. She stripped and stepped in the shower, letting the water cascade over her from the crown of her head to her toes. *He was ragged from the trip from Rome to DC. He hadn't stopped since early this morning, and he had added an additional six hours to a normal twenty-four because of the time zone difference.*

After shampooing, lathering up, and shaving her legs, Cotten wrapped a towel around her head, turban style, and another around her body and got out of the shower. She stared at the steamed-up mirror. Someone who had stayed in the room previously had apparently steamed up the mirror during their stay and drawn a heart in the condensation. Like magic, the heart and the initials reappeared in the fog on the mirror. Maybe it was a honeymoon couple or a teenager missing her beau while she and family vacationed. There were hundreds of stories she could imagine.

Cotten dried her hair and got dressed. She didn't wear much makeup, just some blush, mascara, and lipstick. She smoothed the clinging jersey dress over her hips.

Satisfied she was ready, Cotten picked up her handbag and left the room, heading down the hall to John's.

She stopped in front of his door and knocked. When he didn't answer she knocked again and called his name. *Probably had the television on and didn't hear her.*

The door finally cracked open.

"John?"

He stepped out from behind the door, wearing his bathrobe.

"You take a nap, sleepyhead?"

"Yeah, I did. I hate to do this, but I think I'm going to have to beg off."

"Boy, jet lag really took its toll." Cotten stepped into the room, closed the door, and tossed her purse on the dresser. "Want me to order something from downstairs?"

"No, thanks. You go ahead. I think I'm going to call it a day. Sorry. I'm just whipped."

"No problem. How about if I bring you something back when I come up?"

"No, no. I'm fine. Breakfast in the morning?"

"You got it," Cotten said, retrieving her purse. "You call me when you get up." She gave him a hug. "See you mañana."

———

Cotten sat curled up in the chair watching the SNN late news and sipping on an Absolut over ice she picked up at the bar. She had on her comfort pajamas—a lightweight sweatshirt, sweatpants, and socks. The black dress lay in a heap on the floor at the foot of the bed. One black heel on its side, the other upright, her stockings and bra next to the shoes. She was disappointed they hadn't gone to dinner, and she kicked herself for feeling that way. The poor man was exhausted.

She wondered if she had guessed right about Black Needles and the method it would be delivered. Had the attacks already started? Would Brennan see the light and launch measures to protect the country? She fully understood his hesitation. After all, it was only conjecture and speculation. But she knew that once the element of the Fallen was added into the equation, conjecture could easily become tragedy. Where would she and John turn next? Who else would listen?

The vodka warmed her, and she felt her body loosen the kinks it had acquired during the day. She was tired, too. Downing the last of her drink, Cotten set the glass on the nightstand and crawled under the covers. When she clicked off the TV with the remote, the room fell into darkness and almost as quickly, she drifted off.

———

The sharp jangle of the phone ripped Cotten out of a heavy dream that she couldn't remember. She fumbled for the lamp on the nightstand and switched it on. The digital clock radio display read 3:47.

Cotten lifted the receiver. "Hello." Her voice was husky with sleep.

"Cotten?"

"John, what is it?" She sat up. "What's wrong?"

"I'm not sure," he said. "I think ... maybe ... I'm coming down with something."

"What do you mean?"

"I'm sick."

Cotten swung her legs over the bed. "John, open your room door. I'm coming down."

She dropped the handset onto the base, grabbed her card key from her purse, and headed out the door.

John's door was ajar, and Cotten pushed it open. The bathroom light was on, but the door closed. "John, are you all right?"

A moment later the door opened and he stood illuminated by the bathroom lighting.

His eyes were red-rimmed and glassy, his lips void of color. She touched his forehead. "Jesus Christ, you're burning up." Her eyes caught a quick glimpse of pink in the sink and toilet.

Suddenly, he bent forward, covered his mouth with one hand, held his chest with the other, and coughed—a deep rumbling cough. Then he collapsed.

OFFSPRING

Cotten and the Georgetown University Medical Center's infectious disease specialist stood outside John's hospital room.

"Has Cardinal Tyler been around any exotic animals?" the doctor said, peering over the top of his glasses. "More specifically primates? Chimps? Monkeys? Gorillas?"

"No. Nothing like that," she said.

"Maybe visiting a mission in a remote area of Africa?"

Cotten shook her head. "He was recently in Eastern Europe, but there aren't any of those kinds of exotic animals where he was. What are you getting at?"

The doctor tapped his pen on the metal clipboard that held John's chart. "What we believe is that this is some type of hemorrhagic virus—"

"Like Ebola," she said.

"Right. Typically, these types of viruses are transmitted by contact, though we don't know the natural reservoir, or origin of how they first appear in a human outbreak. They are believed to be zoonotic, animal borne, and from then on transmitted by contact with blood or secretions or objects that have become contaminated. But Cardinal Tyler's case is somewhat of an enigma. It doesn't appear he has transmitted the disease to anyone. To tell you the truth, I'm not quite sure what we're dealing with here."

"What's the prognosis?" she asked.

"Not good, I'm afraid. We don't have any experience with this particular disease. We haven't been able to identify it. We can only surmise that because of the likeness in symptoms to Ebola, this disease will run the same or similar course. But we can't say for certain."

"People survive Ebola," Cotten said.

"True." He glanced at the clipboard.

She read his grave expression. "But it has a high fatality rate, correct?"

"Yes."

"What are you doing for him? You've got to do something." Her voice was sharp and rising.

"About all we can do is keep his fluids balanced, watch his electrolytes, oxygen levels, and blood pressure. Mostly just support therapy."

"What about an antibiotic? Can't you give him—"

"Antibiotics are not effective against viruses, only bacterial infections." The specialist pushed his glasses up the bridge of his nose. "I'm really sorry, Ms. Stone. But I promise you we are doing all we can."

———

Cotten sat on the couch in the visitor's lounge. She stared blankly at an empty Styrofoam cup someone had left behind.

Hospitals all had that distinct mixed antiseptic and medicine smell, an odor Cotten associated with death. She hadn't really taken notice of those smells or what they conjured in her mind until after her mother's stint and eventual death in the hospital. And hadn't she heard somewhere that smell is the sense most profoundly tied to memory? And those memories provoked by smell are the most emotional laden? She felt positive that was true.

Emotionally and physically exhausted, Cotten hoped she could catch a few moment's sleep. She lay down on the couch, her mind spinning. It didn't take long for her to realize it was useless to try to sleep, knowing that John was just down the hall dying. Because of her. The Fallen's signature was all over this. John had been singled out as a target. She was sure of it.

She'd fought them before and won. Or at least thought she had prevailed—that goodness had prevailed. John was the goodness. Not her. Her heart pumped the blood of her father. It didn't matter that her father had repented. He was not human. And neither was she. At least not completely.

Cotten squeezed her eyes at the sting of tears and sat up. She needed fresh air. The odor of the hospital and the thoughts of John's condition, her father's legacy, and her mother's death—it was all too much.

She pulled her coat on and headed to the lobby and out the doors into the night.

The cold, fresh air hit her like a slap, and it felt good, not cluttered with sour smells and troubling memories and dark thoughts. Cotten breathed in a deep lungful and let it out slowly as she walked away from the hospital entrance. A few moments later, she stopped and stared up at the stars. "Haven't I done what you've wanted? Haven't I suffered enough for my father? I didn't ask to be conceived or come into this world. If life is a miracle, then everything that's happened is all your doing. Why are you punishing me? How can a compassionate, loving God ... What else do you want from me?"

Her anger and frustration raged inside like torrid winds. "Maybe I have turned to the wrong—"

Cotten sobbed into her hands. "Why? Why?" Finally, she smeared the tears from her cheeks and wiped her nose with a tissue from her coat pocket. She stretched out her arms and turned in a circle. "I give up. You win!" she shouted, not knowing exactly to whom she called. Had God won or had the Fallen? She just wanted an answer, for someone to hear her pleas, and she didn't care who.

Finally spent, her energy purged, her will broken, she felt barren, like some empty husk.

The sudden chime of her cell startled her. Cotten shoved her hand in her pocket and pulled out her phone. Without even looking at the caller ID, she flipped it open. "This is Cotten."

The voice on the other end made her recoil.

THE OFFERING

"DAUGHTER OF FURMIEL?" SAID the voice on the phone.

Cotten held the cell to her ear, unable to speak. She felt weak and lightheaded. Finally, she formed the words, "Yes."

"You do remember me, don't you? It has not been that long."

She tried to swallow but her mouth was suddenly Sahara dry. His voice was easily identifiable. She'd heard it before. It was the voice of her immortal enemy, the Son of the Dawn.

"What do you want?" Her words sounded feeble and unsteady to her.

"What do I always want? I want what is good for you."

"No, you don't. You are what my father rejected."

"I am your family now. No matter how much you try to dismiss it, ignore it, pretend it is not true, you and I share the same blood-line. And I take care of my family. You are not meant to be just of this world. You have special gifts and privileges because of your fa-ther." He sighed. "It is regrettable that Furmiel was so weak. He could not take losing Paradise. No adaptation skills. And when his God did him such a *great favor,* he could not handle mortality. You, on the other hand, have proved yourself strong under the most pressing conditions. I am proud that you are part of my family."

"I'm not your family," she said with conviction. "My father repented and was forgiven."

"Oh, he repented all right. But do you think he was really forgiven? God played a cruel trick on your father. Do you not see that? Furmiel gave up his immortality. He surrendered your twin sister at birth, and promised you to Him. Your father did not even give you a choice. Did God take care of you? Did God make the drought end and save your family's farm?"

There was a pause, then the Old Man lowered his voice. "I do not understand humans. They believe that God is all-powerful, and so many worship Him without question. Doesn't logic follow that if God is all-powerful, then who do you think brought about the drought to begin with that threw Furmiel into a downward spiral? If He loves Man so, why does He allow pain and suffering? That just does not make sense to me."

Cotten felt as if she were loosing her balance, that her knees were giving way. "Leave me alone. Don't do this to me."

"I would have left you alone, but I know you are hurting right now, that you are tormented and distressed. It pains me to know that. I care about you. And I still believe that deep in your father's heart he would want me to come to you now. He would want me to help you in any way that I could. He would want me to relieve you of this anguish. Family members do that for one another. No questions asked. No hesitations. No matter past feuds. Daughter of Furmiel, I can help you. Will you not at least listen to what I have to say?"

Cotten didn't want to listen. She wasn't in the right frame of mind to argue or agree with anything, no matter what he offered. Her mind was too frayed. "I've got to go. Don't contact me again."

"Slow down. Take a deep breath. Do that for me."

"Please, leave me alone. Just leave me alone."

"You need to hear what I have to tell you."

The voice seemed to echo, as if coming from the cell and from behind her. She turned around to see a figure emerge from the darkness to stand only a few feet away, his frame now backlit by the distant hospital lights. Cotten lowered her phone and closed it.

"Why have you come? What do you want?" she asked.

The Old Man smiled. "You are confused. You have it all wrong."

"What are you talking about?"

"I came because you asked."

Cotten glared at him, shaking her head.

"I do not *want* anything," he said. "It was you who called out for help."

He paused while Cotten struggled to make the connection.

"Just a minute ago you cried out for answers. And who listened?" He stepped closer. "God?" His expression was that of a caring and consoling grandfather. "Look at me. I am the one who has come to your aid. Not God. You have had enough, have you not? Your cup runneth over."

Cotten tried to look away but was held transfixed.

"I never turn my back on one of my own."

"My father was what you call family," she said. "But not me. And he gave that up."

"It destroyed him. God did not come to his rescue, did He? The drought—the loss of the farm—was the last straw for your father.

Furmiel finally felt the only way to end his suffering was to take his own life. First, he deserted me and the rest of his brothers and sisters, and then he did the same thing to you and your mother. Left you to fend for yourselves. You cannot compare yourself to him. The only part of him that resides in you is his blood. And that bonds you forever with me. You are Nephilim, and your God cannot change that."

"I don't know what I am. Half of this, half of that."

"If you would only acknowledge the truth, a great peace would settle over you. You would not have this turmoil. You are trying to live a lie."

The Old Man peered into her eyes. "You are a renowned journalist by choice and Nephilim by birth. I can make good use of those characteristics. But first, for your own protection, you must travel to a place that is safe. I want you to go to North Korea. Once there, I will start you on a journey that will bring you great fame and raise your stature to that of the global voice of a new world that is about to become reality."

"I don't need fame," Cotten said, wondering why he didn't think she was aware of the Korean connection to Black Needles? And what did he mean by referring to her own protection. "So why would I want to do that?"

"In the coming days, few places on earth will be safe. Despite your ties to me, you are not immune to the danger of the sickness that is about to strike so many. I always protect my family, and I want you to be in a place that is safe and secure. The second reason is that North Korea is about to become a world power whose dominance will be undeniable. You are destined to play a part in my future plans. I want you safely at my side to tell the world the story of

North Korea's great leader. It will be your first assignment in a long list of opportunities I will provide you."

"Assignment? I haven't agreed to anything. I don't even know what it is I'm agreeing to. And even if I did, I don't think I'm interested."

The Old Man smiled. "I have a peace offering."

Cotten looked confused. "What do you mean?"

"If you *come home*, be who you really are, you will be pleased with your reward."

"You aren't hearing me. Money and fame don't matter to me. You should know that by now."

"Money and fame are not what I offer, although you will find those are waiting for you, as well. No, I offer something much, more precious."

Cotten gave a smug smile. "I can't imagine how you can offer me anything that would make me happy."

The Old Man raised a brow. "I offer you the priest's life."

DEATHWATCH

COTTEN STOPPED BESIDE THE Venatori agent posted outside John's room on the fourth-floor isolation ward of the hospital. "Any change?" she asked as she put on the protective gown over her street-clothes.

He shook his head.

Cotten stared at all the precaution signs posted on the door, then put the mask over her nose and mouth, and pulled on the gloves. When she entered the room she gently pushed the door almost closed, leaving a crack wide enough to allow a slice of light to come in from the hall. She stood overcome by the reality.

Deathwatch.

She sat in a chair next to the bed and glanced at the monitor recording John's respiration and heartbeat, then at the IV pole on which hung several bags, slowly dripping their contents into his arm. She knew it was a futile attempt to save his life.

Cotten removed her mask, gambling on the fact that Black Needles could not be transmitted from one victim to another. John must have been specifically targeted by one of the bombers—a ploy to bring her to her knees. And if she was wrong and could contract the disease from him, it would already be inside her.

Hemorrhagic viruses set off such red alerts that sometimes she thought the medical profession couldn't see the forest for the trees. This was no typical virus, not Ebola or Marburg. This one had not naturally evolved. It was orchestrated. Why weren't they concentrating on the obvious? None of the documented cases indicated that this mysterious virus was contagious. The only exception was onboard the *Pitcairn*. None of those exposed to Calderon at SNN, and not even Jimmy Franks who lived with Jeff Calderon had become sick. No, this virus was like a handcrafted bullet with someone's name etched on it. And one of the bullets bore John's name.

The anger surged inside her as she massaged her temples. There was so much hate and rage building within her. No *good* person could have such feelings, she thought. And that confirmed the rightness of her decision. She was who she was.

"John," she whispered.

His ashen face matched the white pillow beneath his head. She wished he would open his incredible ocean-blue eyes so she could see them once again. At this point she would even settle for any sign that he recognized her presence and could hear her. But there was no movement, nothing.

"This is all because of me," she said. "All the bad things that have come into your life are because of me." Her voice strained and cracked as she unsuccessfully fought back the tears. Wiping them away Cotten looked at the ceiling and bit her bottom lip trying to compose herself. Finally her eyes traveled to John's face again, a face she had burned in her memory. Every line, every angle, every contour. If somehow she was stricken blind, she could still place her palm on his cheek and know it was him.

Cotten smoothed his hair away from his face and briefly touched her fingertip to his lips. "I am so sorry."

Her tears came again. "You mean more to me than anything in my life. I can't let you die. I won't, no matter what I have to do. I suppose I am glad you can't hear me because I know you would try to stop me. I only hope that you will be able to forgive me."

She paused, tilting her head and looking at John, drinking him in. Though she knew she could never have him, she loved this man with every fiber in her body and would do anything to save him.

Anything.

"John, you know who I am. You know my heritage, and that my father promised me to God in exchange for his redemption. I am the only blood enemy of the epitome of evil on Earth, and though they can't kill me because I am Furmiel's daughter—one of their own—they will destroy me by destroying you. I have caused them too many problems over the years. They want to be rid of my interference permanently. I am tired, and I can't bear what is happening to you."

Cotten rested her face in her hands for a moment before looking back at him. "I can end this. Just as my father was given forgiveness and mortality for his repentance, I will be rewarded for my repentance with your life. All I have to do is give myself up to my legacy, to the Darkness. No matter how much I strive to do what is good and right, in the end, I am Nephilim and nothing can change that. I have been given a choice. If I will return to my Nephilim heritage, then your life will be spared. It is a small price to pay. And when you get well, maybe then you will have peace, and maybe I will, too. I can't watch you die when I know I can stop it. I have tried to live up to my end of my father's bargain, but I've failed. I have brought nothing but pain and misery to those I care about the most. I can't do it anymore. Your life is too precious. You are the goodness in this world that I could never be."

Cotten bent over the rail and kissed his cheek. "I guess you might say I'm going home where I belong."

The door opened and pale light from the hall flowed in. A nurse entered wearing a white nun's habit, a mask, and gloves. She touched Cotten's shoulder and then checked John's vitals.

Cotten looked up at her with an expression that begged any news.

The nurse shook her head. "Pray," she said.

"Sister, I don't think God will listen to *me*."

"He listens to everyone."

Cotten looked back at John and touched her fingertips to his cheek.

"Perhaps you should also ask his patron saint to intercede for him with God."

"I don't know who his patron saint is. I didn't even know he had one."

"Cardinal Tyler's patron is Saint John of the Cross," the nurse whispered as she pulled the door closed behind her.

Turning back to John, Cotten wondered if she was beyond praying at this point. Why would God listen to her prayers? She was about to turn her back on Him forever.

She sat at his bedside for over an hour, coming to terms with what she was about to do. She had only one hope, and needed to talk to Ted tonight. Tomorrow might be too late.

As she rose to leave, a glint of reflected light caught Cotten's attention. Looking closer she saw links of a gold chain that disappeared beneath the neck of his gown. Cotten lifted the chain. The hospital staff had allowed John to continue wearing his gold cross. Being careful not to disturb the tubes and wires from the monitoring devices, she unhooked the clasp, removed the chain and cross, and slipped them into her pocket.

Cotten gave John a last look before leaving. As she went down in the elevator she kept her hand in her pocket palming his crucifix. Not until she was outside did she release it so she could make a call on her cell.

"Cotten, how's John?" Ted asked when he answered.

"No change," she said, working at holding back the tears.

"I'm really sorry."

"Ted, please don't ask any questions. I now know what I have to do to save John, and I need your help. I don't know how this will turn out for me, and that doesn't really matter. Please understand that. I'm going to tell you my plan and you have to promise to follow it through. No matter what I say or do later, you must do what I tell you now."

She fought to keep herself composed. What would she be like once she surrendered to the Darkness? Would she become evil? She had to make preparations now before that happened, and she had to be sure she could count on Ted. There was no one else. Taking a deep breath, she said, "Arrange for me to get clearance through the

State Department to travel to North Korea. Just say that the Communist leader has agreed to an exclusive SNN interview."

"I'll start the paperwork immediately." He sounded skeptical but didn't hesitate. "Anything else?"

"Yes, one more thing."

LAND OF LIES

THE AIR KORYO FLIGHT from Beijing approached Sunan International Airport from the north. Cotten watched the farmland and brown hills glide beneath as late afternoon turned to evening across the Democratic People's Republic of Korea. Only a third of the 198 seats in the Russian-built Ilyushin IL-62 were filled, and she occupied her own row. Whether it was because of the low number of passengers or it was pre-arranged so she would not have contact with the other passengers, she didn't know.

Cotten was dead tired. She had only slept in small segments on the fourteen-hour flight from New York to Beijing, tormented by John's deteriorating condition and the decision she made that would save him. The overnight stay at the Sino Swiss Airport Hotel was just as restless, for all the same reasons. Even with a high-level-approved visitor's visa, she was still made to sit in an isolated waiting room for most of the day in Beijing's Capital International Airport before the Korean flight took off for the five-hundred-mile trip to Pyongyang, an equally fatiguing experience. She dreaded seeing herself in a mirror, fearing she would resemble a character from a Tim Burton movie.

Cotten watched the modest terminal building roll into view, a three story, glass-front structure with a large portrait of the Communist Party General Secretary perched on top. Two bright red signs displaying the city name in Korean and English formed bookends on each side of the portrait. Once the jet had taxied to a stop, she prepared to deplane. Out her window she saw a dozen armed Korean soldiers forming a corridor between the plane and the building, keeping the passengers from straying. Cotten noticed a couple of military vehicles parked nearby. Mounted on the back of each were large caliber machine guns.

She was the last to disembark, and as she stepped off the stairway onto the tarmac, a man in a dark-green military uniform standing nearby said in a heavily accented voice, "This way please." He gestured toward a black Mercedes limousine parked a dozen yards away. Cotten had read in the State Department briefing papers supplied to SNN that North Korea had the largest fleet of state-owned Mercedes limos in the world. Stiff DPRK flags were mounted on both sides of the limo's front grill. A city police car, its emergency lights flashing, waited in front of the limo, another in the rear.

The officer held the door open for Cotten, and she slipped into the back seat. He joined her, taking the opposite, backward-facing seat. He was short and thin, perhaps only five feet five. His close-trimmed hair was dark, and he wore rimless glasses on a round face. He sat straight with his knees together and his arms crossed, gazing intently at Cotten. He had to be wondering why she was getting the star treatment in a country with only one star. There was no attempt at introductions or conversation.

A moment later, Cotten heard a thump as someone placed her bag into the trunk and closed the lid. Then the sirens wailed and the three-vehicle caravan accelerated off the concrete through a security checkpoint and onto the main highway for the fifteen-mile trip south into Pyongyang.

The traffic was almost non-existent. An occasional commercial or military vehicle passed in the other direction along the four-lane motorway. As the Mercedes entered the city, the traffic increased, but only slightly. In any other major city, Cotten thought, it would be considered extremely light. She was told in advance what to expect, yet it still amazed her. In what the State Department documents called the Land of Lies, Pyongyang was the City of Ghosts.

With few cars, buses, and taxis, Cotten thought the city was almost beautiful in an eerie sort of way. The limo passed tree-lined boulevards and sprawling public squares built around fountains and statues. Lovely but deserted parks, walkways, and plazas lined the Taedong River as it flowed through the center of the city. The buildings were dark, and the stores all appeared closed. She even caught a glimpse of the USS *Pueblo* and the *Pitcairn* moored bow to stern near the city's center. The limo drove past the 150,000-seat stadium constructed in a failed bid to capture a portion of the 1988 Olympics. Cotten watched the huge bowl-shape structure drift by, a gloomy monument as empty as the soul of this sad nation.

They pulled up to the front of the pyramid-shaped Sungyong Hotel, an impressive tower extending 106 stories, one story taller than the tallest building in South Korea.

Led by her military escort, Cotten exited the Mercedes and entered the hotel's grand atrium. Rather than approaching the front desk, he halted her in the middle of the athletic-field-sized lobby.

"You are not allowed to leave the hotel without official approval and a government chaperone," he said. "You are not to take any photographs. Do not speak to anyone but an official from the DPRK. Remember that you are from an aggressor nation and do not have the same privileges as our visiting friends from the former Soviet nations. Is that understood?"

"Yes."

"Do not test our hospitality."

Cotten watched as the limo driver carried her bag to a nearby bank of elevators.

The officer motioned, and the three entered the lift.

"How many rooms does the hotel have?" Cotten asked.

"Three thousand and one," the officer said after much hesitation as if he were revealing a state secret.

"But isn't it true that you only allow one thousand visitors into your country a year? What are the extra rooms for?"

His face reddened. With a huff, he said, "That is a matter of national security."

"Of course." Cotten shifted her gaze up to the floor indicator. They stopped on the fiftieth floor and exited.

The officer led her down a corridor to her room. He inserted a key—there were no magnetic cards used here. She stepped into a modestly furnished room with a single bed, dresser, and desk. A small TV sat on a corner stand. Thick black-out curtains covered the window. A large painting of the General Secretary poised atop a snow-clad mountain peak carrying the DPRK flag hung over the bed. He appeared to be leading a great army into battle.

Cotten turned to thank her escort just as the door clicked closed. The officer and driver were gone.

She wandered to the window and pulled open the drapes. The curtain rod slumped at one end, threatening to fall. What she saw was a sprinkling of street and traffic lights, a handful of vehicles, and a spotting of illumination from the windows of distant buildings. Night had enveloped Pyongyang like a cloak.

If she was about to make the journey into the Darkness, she had come to the right place.

SUPERNOVA

AFTER SHOWERING, COTTEN SLIPPED into bed and immediately fell asleep—the long trip finally catching up with her. Her dreams were filled with images of her father pulling the trigger of the gun he held to his head, her mother's face scored with lines of depression, and the spirit of her twin sister.

Suddenly, Cotten sat up wide awake. No light came through the window, the city slept in darkness. Feeling a presence in the room, she started to pull back the cover and search for the light switch.

"Stay," a voice said.

"Who's there?" she asked.

The voice had come from the direction of the window. The drapes were open but she saw nothing between her and the faint starlight beyond the glass.

"Daughter of Furmiel, I am pleased that you have come home to be with your family."

"I'm here to save the life of my friend. Being here has nothing to do with you." Her voice was shaky.

"You will soon come to understand that this is where you truly belong."

"Tell me your name so I know what to call you."

"I have many names."

Cotten pulled the covers to her shoulders. "Then give me one."

"Light bearer."

"I don't see a great deal of light here tonight."

Suddenly the room exploded with white light—a supernova flash that momentarily blinded her. She was certain that the heat had singed her hair. As the light diminished, she caught a glimpse of a form standing beside the window.

The image faded back to darkness. But she had seen enough to know it was her immortal enemy, the Son of the Dawn. The Beast. Lucifer. Satan.

The ice-cold hand of trepidation slithered down her spine.

"Do you need more light?" the voice asked.

Still reeling, her eyes stung and teared, her mouth and throat parched. "No," she managed to whisper. "That was quite enough."

"Good, then let's get on with our business."

TEMPTATION

"Why did you come here?" the Old Man asked.

"You already know the answer." Cotten now stood in the darkness of the hotel room, still shaken from the blast of blinding light. Once it had faded, his form appeared like a shadow against the starlight flowing from the window.

"*You* must say the words."

"I'm here to consummate an agreement between us to save the life of John Tyler."

"More specific," he said. "What does our agreement entail?"

His voice was surprisingly benevolent and velvety. Perhaps he knew that it would be difficult for her if he was forceful. The serenity did make the words come easier.

"In return for sparing John's life, I will succumb to my heritage and accept my true identity, which was passed on to me by my father."

"What is your heritage—your legacy and identity? And as you tell me, be at peace with it. Surrender to it as you speak the truth."

Cotten hesitated knowing that there would be no turning back. She choked as a lump of fear seemed to close off her throat. "In my veins flows the blood of the Nephilim. I am, and always have been, the daughter of a Fallen Angel. My soul belongs to the Darkness, to you."

"Very good. See, this is not so difficult. And do you agree to those terms?"

Cotten's eyes locked on his. "No," she whispered and swallowed hard. "Not yet."

The Old Man cocked his head and orange embers glowed behind his eyes.

"Why not? I have given my word, my promise. What is your hesitation?"

"I don't believe you have power over life and death. How am I to know for certain that you can save John's life?"

"Perhaps you are correct when you think of it in the traditional sense. But you make it too simplistic, too black and white. The power over life and death can take many forms. I do not need the kind of absolute authority for which you speak. My ego does not feast on supremacy. But I do have the powers of suggestion, persuasion, and temptation. With those powers I can halt, even reverse the ravaging attack of Black Needles on the human body and rid it of the disease. After all, I had a hand in creating it. However I accomplish it should not be your concern. The end result will be what you desire."

"How do I know you won't betray me?"

The Old Man moved against the background of the starlight and Cotten thought he became transparent.

303

"You, Daughter of Furmiel, are the centerpiece of my grand plan. Have you not figured that out? You are the last piece missing in my collection, the prodigal daughter finally come home. You will make our family complete."

He shifted again, and she was certain he was more mirage than solid form, like heat radiating off the desert highway. A wave of dizziness washed over Cotten, and she struggled for balance, concentrating on her task, looking past the Old Man and picturing John's deep blue eyes.

"I will need proof of life before I agree," she said. "I have to know that John is alive, that he is recovering."

"And how do I know that you will fulfill your end of the agreement?"

Cotten stiffened. Here was her stand, the chance she was going to have to take. "You don't."

"Then perhaps it is time that you see with new eyes so that you will not hesitate to consummate our contract."

Suddenly the room filled with a whirring roar, then a blustering hot wind and the crash of a violent thunderstorm.

Cotten stood naked atop a mountain. The gale blowing against her skin subsided to a warm and gentle breeze as if she were being wrapped in fur and satin, caressed by a million fingertips. She looked out over endless fields of gold and yellow flowers stretching from the base of the mountain to the horizon. Puffy clouds moved languidly across a sky so blue that it reminded her of tropical island waters. Birds soared among the clouds and butterflies darted from flower to flower. Total comfort, complete bliss, wanting nothing and needing only to enjoy the beauty and serenity of the scene.

"This place I will give to you, in all its perfectness, pleasure, and contentment," the Old Man said, standing beside her. "All your wants fulfilled, all desires come true, all needs satisfied, ecstasy beyond belief. Is that not the same as heaven?"

She said nothing and instantly found herself submerged in water. With no discomfort or panic, she breathed in the crystal clear liquid as it covered every inch, every pore, and every crevice of her body. Weightless, floating in a clear river of rapture, waves of pleasure undulated through her.

A voice inside her head said, "Daughter of Furmiel, this can be yours whenever you want it."

The water cascaded over her, draining away. Cotten opened her eyes to find herself sitting in a vast room filled with mountains of gold and jewels, more than what could possibly fill all the vaults and treasuries of the world. She reached down and ran her hand through a mound of diamonds. They ran between her fingers like ice crystals, the brilliance of their facets sparkling more than the stars of the night sky.

"You will never be in need of anything. All that you've seen will be yours by accepting who you are. Just say that you agree, Daughter of Furmiel, and you will have everything I have shown you."

"It's not enough," Cotten said. "You know what I want."

"And you shall have it. I give you my word. The priest will live."

Suddenly Cotten was ripped from the vision back to the darkness of the hotel room. The gathering dawn silhouetted the Old Man's form against the window.

With a frail voice, she whispered, "I agree."

IN MY NAME

COTTEN FELT A PART of her melting away as she stood in the dark hotel room. She couldn't pinpoint what was happening, but sensed a cavity open within, a cold empty space inside her that had not been there moments before. The instant she agreed to the contract with the Old Man, some part of her evaporated into the darkness. It wasn't that the sensation was unpleasant or even objectionable, just different. The only word she could think to describe what she felt was *hollow*.

"So what happens now?" Cotten asked.

"Nothing." The Old Man's voice seemed to come from far away.

She wondered if he was still in the room with her or if he was speaking through her thoughts as he had during the strange visions.

Cotten slowly turned in a circle, searching for him. She wanted a clear image of this ... this being to whom she had just given her soul. But he took no form that she could fix upon. "I still need proof of life," she said. "I have done what you asked. I want to be assured that you will do as you promised."

Almost imperceptibly, the voice whispered from behind her. "Understandable."

Cotten spun in the direction of the voice. "What do I do next?" she asked.

There was no reply.

For an instant the air in the room turned icy as if a window opened and allowed in a winter draft. She glanced toward the windowpane and found it still closed. Just as quickly as it had come, the chill dissipated.

Cotten looked out through the glass, laying her palms on the pane. The pale golden blush of daybreak brought the first tracings of the city below.

After a few moments, she returned to the bed and slid beneath the covers staring at the shadows on the ceiling, wondering how she would live her life now that she—

She what? she thought. Nothing magical had stricken her when she said yes to the Old Man. Nothing seemed different other than that feeling of hollowness, but perhaps that was only the relief of knowing her mission was complete. Hadn't the Old Man realized before that it would not be the promise of riches that would influence her decision? The reason she had made the journey to Korea was to save John's life, and that was beyond any other promise he could possibly make.

So what was this all about, this going into the Darkness? It wasn't what she anticipated, what she feared it might be. As a matter of fact, it felt good knowing she had the power to save the only man she had ever really loved … other than her father. She drifted off to sleep feeling a great contentment.

But the contentment was quickly interrupted. Her dreams spiraled around her in short and terrifying vignettes.

Falling.

Falling.

Falling through a black tunnel.

Demons' faces flashed and disappeared. Echoes of hideous laughter, screams of terror. Flares of unspeakable acts of murder and torture that satisfied some incommunicable hunger in her—shocking splashes of aberrant sexual acts and bestiality that unexpectedly excited her.

Falling.

Falling.

Falling.

Suddenly a blinding light snatched her up out of the tunnel until she ascended to wakefulness. She squinted into the bright sunlight that poured through the window.

"Bad dreams?" The voice came from near the window.

Cotten sat up, clutching the bed linens.

"Did I startle you?" the Old Man said, sitting in a chair by the window.

The glare of the sun made it hard for Cotten to look at him. She shaded her eyes with one hand and squinted. "I didn't expect to wake up and have someone in my room. Have I given up my privacy as well as my soul?"

He chuckled. "No. I was worried about you. So I stayed while you slept, to make sure you were all right. Your sleep did not seem restful. You tossed and even cried out once. But you see, nothing terrible has happened to you. You are safe."

The dreams flooded back in a series of quick bursts, mental explosions of still images. Cotten pressed two fingers to the space between her eyebrows. "My dreams were nightmarish. Demons and—"

"But as you see, they were only dreams. Just products of your imagination. Unfortunately, that is the result of the misinformation passed down through millennia. You have been programmed to expect what was in your dreams. It is what all mankind has been led to believe. God and His churches have essentially brainwashed generation after generation. And why? Because they fear you will see the light, the truth."

Cotten pushed up against the headboard, still trying to clearly see the Old Man's face. As in the night before, he appeared slightly luminescent and transparent.

He finally shifted so that half his face was visible, the other half still obscured by the glare. It was creased with age, his skin pale, and his ashen hair was neatly parted to the side. As was often said of older men who had a pleasing appearance, he was distinguished looking—an elderly Cary Grantish–type countenance.

"Did you expect red horns? A pointed tail and pitchfork?" He laughed.

"I don't know what I expected. Maybe."

"And a ritual with goat's blood and a pentagram." He leaned into the glare. "I let my legions play that game for their amusement. To be honest, I think it is so cliché."

"I suppose." Cotten found herself smiling, becoming more at ease.

"Do you realize that I am the one who single-handedly keeps God's churches, temples, and mosques in business? I am the best friend the religions of the world have. Without fear of me, they would collapse. Even though their notion of me is false. You see, I come to this world only by invitation—the proverbial Eve and the apple story. All that Eve and her children wanted was knowledge, then and now. Does that make someone evil? I think not."

"What kind of knowledge?"

"Simple truths. God wants you to be self-sacrificing, to believe it is better to give than to receive, to love your enemy, to turn the other cheek, to always be begging for Him to save you from despair. It pleases Him to always have you on your knees. In this way you remain subservient. I speak the truth. There is nothing evil about being productive, finding happiness, achieving success. Why should you not be self-loving and seek those things that bring you happiness? There is no need for groveling or believing yourself unworthy to eat the crumbs that fall from my table. That is how God wants you to be—helpless without him. I say be strong. Be efficient. Explore all the pleasures in life. Why spend a lifetime of self-imposed isolation from pure joy, depending on God for even the smallest fleck of happiness? That makes no sense." Again he revealed a portion of his face. "Even after all this time it remains astounding to me that mankind accepts such rubbish and continues to prefer self-inflicted suffering."

So this was all it meant? Cotten thought. Her heritage was simply the permission to allow herself to be happy? That didn't seem so frightful or evil.

"I do not expect you to accept all this instantly. You have spent a lifetime being programmed by God's religions. You do not even have to go to church for this to happen. It permeates and infiltrates your life every day. I realize it is a tremendous paradigm shift in your thinking."

"Yes, it is."

"Hear what is right and what is truth. It was *your* loving, forgiving Jehovah who sent his Angel of Death to murder all the innocent firstborns of Egypt on the night known as Passover. The wrath of a vengeful, spiteful, hateful God. That was done by *your* God's hand. Not mine. And let me leave you with something else to contemplate. Think of how many thousands have suffered and died in wars, all fought in the name of God. Never has there been a war fought in my name."

OUTBREAK

"AND IN MEDICAL NEWS," the SNN Headline News anchor said, "county health officials in Denver have reported over a dozen cases of extreme flu-like symptoms showing up in the emergency rooms of three major area hospitals. Those stricken with the yet-unidentified illness are complaining of high fever, vomiting, diarrhea, and some bleeding. Doctors are applying the usual antiviral drugs including neuraminidase inhibitors, but are reporting no success with the treatment so far. The mysterious outbreak has claimed the life of a five-year-old girl in Aurora, Colorado, and local health departments are investigating."

———

The roll-in voiceover said, "From Satellite News Network in New York, this is the Evening News with Charles Ross."

"Good evening," Ross said into camera one as he sat behind the anchor desk. "We start the broadcast tonight with reports of a suspicious flu-like outbreak showing up at clinics and emergency rooms throughout the country. What we first told you about yesterday as a number of cases in the Denver area is now spreading to other cities and communities. For the latest, we go to our chief medical correspondent, Robert Terrance, reporting from CDC headquarters in Atlanta, Georgia."

"Good evening, Charles," said Terrance as he held a microphone and stood with the sprawling CDC complex in the background. "In a news conference that ended just moments ago, Dr. Charlotte Swan, director of the Centers for Disease Control, stated that they are investigating a number of reported instances of advanced symptoms of a flu-like sickness in Baltimore, Los Angeles, Chicago, Birmingham, Denver, and Houston."

The image switched to a briefing room inside the CDC. Swan stood at a podium. "We are working with local and state medical authorities to isolate and identify this new strain of influenza. Most important is to gauge how many people are affected and determine the source of the virus. Because we are in the earliest stages of the investigation there is nothing concrete to report yet."

In a video clip, Terrance asked, "Dr. Swan, there are rumors that the flu-like symptoms you describe are actually more like those of Ebola or some other hemorrhagic virus. Is the CDC trying to downplay this in order to prevent panic? Doesn't the public have a right to know?"

Swan shuffled the papers on the podium, but didn't look down at them. "At this point, there is no confirmation that this outbreak is a hemorrhagic virus. The CDC operates on facts, not rumor, and until we have evidence that this is anything other than what I have described, we will continue to proceed according to protocol.

That's all the questions I'll take for now." Swan stepped away from the podium.

The video switched back to a live shot of Terrance. "Despite the downplaying of the threat by the CDC, we've learned that over six hundred cases have been reported so far, with at least thirty deaths occurring over the last twenty-four hours. All are attributed to the outbreak. The victims range in age from four years old to sixty-two. So far, conventional treatments have had no effect on stopping or slowing down the deadly epidemic."

A graphic showing the names of states and the number of fatalities appeared.

Terrance said, "Earlier today, I spoke with Dr. Richard Minor, Director of Infectious Diseases at the Broward Memorial Medical Center in Fort Lauderdale, Florida." The image changed to a man wearing a white physician's jacket with a stethoscope hanging around his neck. "Dr. Minor, your facility was one of the first to report a case of this virus outbreak we're seeing across the country. Now that you know there are others being stricken with it, what are your concerns?"

There was a slight delay before the physician spoke. "We are definitely concerned by the speed at which this event is taking place. Two days ago it was non-existent. Now we're admitting an average of one new patient every hour. We're working around the clock to isolate and treat what we believe is a deadly new strain of viral infection. We hope to have some progress made soon."

Terrance asked, "These rumors of it being a hemorrhagic virus—is there any truth to that? Can you tell us more about what you are seeing in the emergency room?"

"Patients are exhibiting numerous ailments from general malaise and fever to more specific flu-like symptoms, and yes, we have seen signs of hemorrhagic viruses, including bleeding and limited kidney and liver function. It's too early to tell if the hemorrhagic symptoms are a late phase in the illness or something entirely different."

"We've all had the flu at some point in our lives, and we know what that's like. Can you be more specific regarding the symptoms of a hemorrhagic virus?"

"Sure. Hemorrhagic comes, of course, from *hemorrhage*, which means bleeding. Generally, the bleeding occurs both internally, leaking through blood vessels, and externally, from orifices of the body. It is rare, however, for victims to die from blood loss."

A double screen of Dr. Minor and Robert Terrance appeared. "Thank you, Doctor. We appreciate your time."

Minor nodded, and the screen became devoted to Terrance. "As the number of reports of infections mount, experts like Doctor Minor and Director Swan seem increasingly perplexed. For now, we can only hope they find a quick solution to this deadly medical mystery. From Atlanta, this is Robert Terrance reporting for SNN."

"Rob?" Charles Ross said. "Before we let you go, it occurred to me that the symptoms of some of these victims in your report bear a striking resemblance to the unfortunate gentleman who died after collapsing here in our Manhattan studio lobby a few weeks ago. If you'll recall, he came into our building very ill and asking to see Cotten Stone."

"I thought of the same thing, Charles," Terrace said. "Perhaps there is a connection. We'll watch it closely."

"Thanks again, Rob." Ross turned to camera two. "And speaking of Cotten Stone—a programming note. As tension continues to mount over the threat of nuclear weapons development in North Korea, our senior investigative correspondent, Cotten Stone, will be conducting an exclusive interview with the head of the Communist government of North Korea on her primetime special, *Inside the Darkness*, airing next Tuesday at eight, seven central right here on SNN. You don't want to miss that one."

PROOF OF LIFE

EACH MORNING AT 7:00 AM, rousing, patriotic music blared from loudspeakers throughout Pyongyang. Cotten awoke to the tinny sound of a marching band and quickly rose, showered and dressed. Today was the day—she would be allowed to confirm that John was not only still alive but recovering from the Black Needles. She would receive proof of life.

By 7:30, she was waiting in the cavernous Sungyong Hotel lobby.

In the four days since arriving in North Korea, Cotten had only observed a handful of other hotel guests. When she was allowed to leave her room and go downstairs to eat, the restaurant was virtually empty, with only a spotting of Eastern European visitors and tourists. She saw few smiles from the hotel staff. They seemed to be obsessed with looking busy.

On the second day after her arrival, a guide had escorted her to a number of state museums and monuments around the city. The woman, a short, slim officer in the Korean army, never missed an opportunity to point out how wonderful it was living in North Korea and how her country had overcome the hardships of war crimes brought on by the imperialist aggressors.

In addition to the army guide, Cotten was always shadowed by a handful of security officers. It was hard for them to hide their presence. There was a small amount of foot traffic as she and her guide walked the immaculate streets and manicured parks. They would pass policewomen who directed a trickle of traffic and stores whose display windows were decorated with as many pictures of the General Secretary as merchandise.

Cotten learned that it was against the law for citizens to look foreigners in the eye or to speak to them, so she didn't bother to acknowledge or look at anyone on the street or in the museums they visited. The only eye contact was with those called *the selected*, trusted individuals who spoke multiple languages and often served as the guides and escorts.

Today, Cotten was met in the hotel lobby by her guide and four-man security detail.

"This way, please," the guide said, pointing to the front entrance. Outside, it was bitter cold under a cloudless blue sky. Cotten's eyes watered and stung at the bite of the icy air.

They walked briskly along An Sang Thaek Street for a quarter of a mile until they arrived at a park surrounding a bronze statue of Korea's great leader and father of the General Secretary. The guide motioned to a bench near the base of the statue. "Wait there."

Cotten obeyed and pulled the collar of her coat up about her neck as she sat waiting. She breathed into her gloved hands, the warmth and humidity of her breath taking the burn out of her lungs.

After ten minutes of cold and growing impatience, she saw a figure approaching. As he got closer, she recognized the Old Man.

He sat next to her, binding his scarf around his neck. She noticed the vapor of his breath in the air.

"I do not particularly care for the cold," he said.

"I'm not surprised."

He made a sound that might have been construed as a laugh. "Do you know what I especially admire about you, Daughter of Furmiel? You spit in the face of anything that strikes out at you. Plus, you have an engaging sense of humor. A special gift."

"A survival tool." Until now, she had only barely glanced at him. She looked to meet his gaze. "Are you ready to fulfill your promise? I've said I'll do what you ask. But I must have proof of life. I need to know that John is alive, that he's getting well. You said you could spare his life. Prove it. Right now, I have no idea what's happening in the rest of the world. I haven't been allowed any outside contact in this godforsaken place."

Again the Old Man chuckled. "I like your description. It is truly a godforsaken country." He wiped his nose with a handkerchief. "Cold air shrinks the nasal passages."

"You're avoiding my question."

"No, not at all." He pulled what appeared to be a satellite phone from a breast pocket inside his coat, flipped it open, and dialed a number. "I am calling your associate. He will confirm the condition of your friend that you worry so much about." He handed her the phone. "Keep it brief. The cost of these calls is exorbitant."

As she heard the digital processing of the call, she thought how absurd it was that the Old Man complained of phone costs. She could see her guide and security detail that waited at a discreet distance, shifting back and forth, blowing in their hands in reaction to the cold. It gave her a small sense of satisfaction that they were so uncomfortable.

After a few rings, Ted answered.

"I don't have much time," she said. "First, I'm fine. Second, I'm hoping that you've been able to keep up with things on your end. You know how much I'm counting on you."

The Old Man gave Cotten a suspicious look, and she tried to qualify her comment and make it seem more in line with what he expected to hear.

"I'm depending on you to tell me everything you know about John's condition. Don't hold anything back. It's imperative I know everything—good or bad."

"I have good news," Ted said, "maybe even a miracle. The doctors have tried a new experimental combination of drugs and it appears John is responding favorably. His fever has broken, he's conscious and alert, and his blood tests confirm that he has turned the corner, he's recovering. Other than being weak and tired, the symptoms seem to have reversed themselves and are receding. Very different from several days ago."

Cotten's eyes watered again, this time with tears of joy, not the sting of winter. "That's great news. Are you sure you aren't leaving anything out—any details that might upset me?"

"No. It's all good news. On all fronts."

Cotten glanced at the Old Man. "Thank you, Ted. You've made me feel much better. I have to go now and get ready for the interview. Everything is a go on this end." She snapped the phone closed.

"So, are you satisfied?" the Old Man asked.

She handed him the phone. "Very."

DETOUR

As evening approached, Moon sat alone in her office and watched the emails come into her inbox. Each of her satellite labs in Canada, the United Kingdom, Germany, France, Spain, Japan, and the two recently relocated in the United States reported the results of the first wave of the Black Needles bombers. Of the five hundred men and women who carried the deadly virus out to the public, 482 had reported reaching their targets—many to multiple targets. The remaining were presumed dead or incapacitated. The plan called for the bombers to release the trigger virus into large indoor gatherings such as metropolitan shopping malls, schools, grocery stores, sporting events, libraries, airports, subways—places where people gathered as they went about their lives. The first attacks had been three days ago. According to the news networks, the symptoms had already started showing up in cities around the world.

Tomorrow she would give the launch code for the next wave of attacks—these would be on basic services such as local governments and utilities, hospitals, police, first responders, and other law enforcement and emergency agencies. The bombers would simply walk into a police or fire station or city hall, ask a simple question, then cough or sneeze, and leave, touching door knobs, handrails, and any other obvious objects to contaminate.

The final assaults would come a day later. Those would strike government leaders in the United States Congress, the British Parliament, and the government centers of their allies. By the time the politicians and other leaders started showing the first symptoms of Black Needles, the general populace would already be in full panic mode as millions came down with the deadly disease. The media had already started covering it. Soon it would be a major disaster, bigger than 9/11. The entire world would freeze-frame with fear, terror, and paranoia. The threat of being exposed to the virus would paralyze every nation, making those not infected afraid to leave their homes. No one would risk going to work or sending their children to school. Commerce would shut down. Deliveries would not be made. Services would collapse. Emergency calls would go unanswered. Shock and terror would sweep through the imperialist aggressors as news of the deadly disease spread.

Moon smiled, knowing her time had finally come, her work was almost done.

She closed her laptop and rose, grabbed her overcoat and headed out of her office. She expected to sleep well tonight. Soon, there would be nothing left to do but watch those she hated most begin to fall to their knees in pain and suffering. Their deaths were inevitable.

She made her way through the winding halls, passing the different chemistry labs, cold storage systems, and surgical operating rooms until she emerged in the lobby of the facility. Moon nodded to the security guards and walked to the large glass doors leading out into the cold Korean night. One of the guards opened the door for her and walked a few steps ahead. In the twilight beyond she saw her limousine waiting as always with its dark-tinted windows and puffy clouds of condensation drifting from its exhaust pipes. The guard reached the vehicle first and opened the side door for her.

"Have a pleasant evening, Dr. Chung," he said.

Without acknowledging him, she slipped into the back seat. The bulky Mercedes pulled away from the facility parking lot and headed down a long road that passed a number of other government buildings. It was waved through the heavily guarded security gate and preceded onto the motorway toward the city. As the darkening countryside flowed by, Moon flipped on a small, personal spotlight overhead and made a few notes in her diary.

She thought of her parents and the many sacrifices they had made for her and their adopted country. Out of habit, she pulled the old photo from her pocket. *Soon, your deaths will be avenged.*

Moon continued making notes with the idea of someday writing a book on how she brought the world to its knees. She was convinced that historians would want to document how such a small, frail, elderly woman could have such an impact on the future of mankind. She tapped her pen on the pad and pictured the image of so many scientists reading her words and acknowledging her achievements. That's when she realized the car was slowing.

Although the smoked glass partition was in the up position, Moon could still make out the motorway ahead. A large box truck was stopped in the middle of the two lanes. Traffic was nonexistent this time of night, and it irritated her that she was being held up by such a trivial issue. Because of its cockeyed position across the highway, she assumed the truck had broken down. In the glow of the limo's headlights, Moon saw a man standing in the middle of the road waving his arms.

She pressed the intercom button on her armrest. "Go around him! No need to stop."

The driver held up his hand indicating that he heard her. He stopped the car and waved for the man to get out of the way.

She watched the stranger walk toward the car. There was something about him that disturbed her. His size. The long overcoat he wore. Something was wrong.

The stranger stood beside the driver's door and motioned for him to lower the window.

"This is holding me up," Moon said through the intercom. "Drive on." She heard the window go down.

The stranger's hand slipped under his coat. Something metallic emerged. A flash and muted thump. The driver's head slammed to the side. His body collapsed on the seat out of her sight. A spray of red coated the smoked glass.

"What is the meaning of this?" Moon screamed.

The man pulled the driver's body from the limo and dropped it onto the pavement. Then he slipped in behind the wheel and put the car in gear. The limo's tires squealed as the vehicle sped off.

Moon pushed the button on the intercom as if to shove it through the armrest. She was about to scream again when she heard the soft motor hum as the glass partition slid down. The driver glanced back at her. He had small, dark eyes, pasty white skin, a bulbous nose, and a bushy mustache. Obviously not Korean.

In English, she said, "Do you realize who I am?"

"You are big shot asshole doctor," the man said as he smiled and exposed a set of tobacco-stained teeth.

"Who the hell are you?" Moon sat up straight trying to appear as menacing as she could.

"Colonel Vladimir Ivanov, former KGB, now retired."

THE BRIDGE

COTTEN HAD ARRIVED ONLY ten minutes before the Korean television crew. She watched them set up the studio lights and video cameras cluttering the already cramped bridge of the *Pitcairn* with equipment, reflectors, and tripods. When they were finished, the crew stood by, waiting for the arrival of the Korean leader. DPRK soldiers were positioned at the port and starboard outside entrances to the ship's bridge, with a handful of others on the aft and forward decks.

Sitting in a chair facing a much larger one that the General Secretary would eventually occupy, she studied the notes given to her by the Department of Information. Each question led to a further glorification of the General Secretary's accomplishments and his powerful leadership of the fourth-largest military in the world, the 1.2 million-strong DPRK army.

Over the next few hours, the ship's bridge would be the backdrop for the scripted interview covering every major event in the Korean leader's life. Cotten had agreed to paint him as a visionary of the Asian world and his country as a growing global power to be reckoned with. Naturally, he had composed the questions himself. Her job would involve nothing more than reading each one and allowing him to answer.

Cotten rose and went to stand beside the helm of the 165-foot ship. She looked out over the bow toward the rusting USS *Pueblo* docked a short distance farther up the river—a long forgotten and deteriorating victim of the Cold War. On the other hand, the *Pitcairn* was still functional and well maintained. The General Secretary had chosen to keep it in proper working order to be used as part of the periodic military exercises along the Taedong River showcasing the power and might of the DPRK navy. It was also speculated that he wanted it kept in perfect condition in case he might decide to return it to Oceanautics as a gesture of his kindness and generosity.

As the hour of the interview approached, Cotten felt a fist in her chest. She wondered how much more stress her mind and body could take. What was about to happen here tonight would be her only chance to stop the global Black Needles threat. Failure meant the loss of thousands, if not millions, of lives. Her plan was thin and risky at best. At this point, she had no idea if it stood any chance at all. She hoped Ted was able to follow through with everything they had discussed, even though all she had been told was that the interview would take place on the *Pitcairn* in honor of the anniversary of its capture. There was no way of knowing if the plan had turned out to be feasible.

The approaching wail of a siren caused her to glance toward the shore. A small convoy of police vehicles approached along Pyong-chan Kangan Street and stopped at the entrance to *Pueblo* Monument Park. In the middle of the procession was a black limousine. After it parked curbside, the doors opened, and the General Secretary emerged from the limo. Accompanied by a handful of assistants that walked behind him, he made his way under the glow of the park's lights. A few military officers exited the other cars and followed.

Because of the cramped quarters on the *Pitcairn's* bridge, the assistants and officers remained behind in the park. The General Secretary, along with a woman dressed in a green army uniform, moved up the gangway and onto the ship. Cotten returned to stand beside her chair once she heard the approaching footsteps on the metal deck outside.

Showtime.

With a dramatic flair, a soldier opened the steel door to the bridge. He bowed at the waist and waited for his commander-in-chief to enter. Cotten had to admit that the General Secretary exhibited an impressive air of confidence about him as he stepped onto the bridge. He was shorter than she expected and wore a plain crisp uniform surprisingly void of any rank, medals, or decorations. His heavy-framed glasses looked old fashioned, and the thick lenses made his eyes appear to bulge.

After taking in his surroundings, he moved beside the overstuffed leather wingback chair in the middle of the circle of lights. Two photographers who came with the original TV crew moved around him with endless shutter clicks and camera flashes.

The General Secretary's interpreter stood beside him. She was shorter than Cotten—her uniform consisted of dark green pants and a lighter green shirt and tie under a green blazer with red epaulettes. She held a notepad and a small English dictionary tight against her chest. Once the photographers had finished document-ing the event from every angle, a silence fell over the bridge.

In what Cotten felt was a surprisingly thin voice, the General Secretary spoke for thirty seconds. When he finished, his inter-preter said, "Dear Leader wishes to welcome the honorable and noteworthy television journalist, Cotten Stone, to this most sig-nificant exclusive interview."

He raised his hand slightly in acknowledgment to Cotten.

The interpreter went on, "Tonight, on the one-year anniversary of the capture of the imperialist aggressor's spy ship, *Pitcairn*, we will discuss the important issues dealing with our glorious nation and the future plans to reveal to the whole world how the great Democratic Peoples Republic of Korea will play a primary part in tomorrow and beyond."

The General Secretary nodded before dropping down into the big chair. Cotten took this as a sign she could sit, too.

She heard the television crew confirm that they had camera speed and audio levels. When the interpreter indicated to her to begin, Cotten read the first question. "Dear Leader, please tell us about your birth at Baekdu Mountain and how it was heralded by the appearance of a double rainbow over the mountain and a new star in the heavens."

The interpreter did not bother to translate. Without hesitation, the General Secretary began an answer that took fifteen minutes to complete, interrupted often by the applause of the television crew and soldiers on the bridge who appeared on the verge of near rapture.

The next question dealt with his involvement in the Korean Children's Union and the Democratic Youth League. As before, the answer was lengthy. Number three covered his Marxist studies in college and his joining the Worker's Party of Korea after graduation. As he was finishing his reply, the door to the bridge opened. He paused and looked toward the sound, obvious irritation in his glare.

Cotten followed his gaze and saw a silver-haired woman enter, followed by a figure in a long overcoat who closed the door behind him. Cotten's eyes grew wide at the sight of Colonel Vladimir Ivanov.

The deck suddenly vibrated with a deep, throaty rumble as the *Pitcairn's* engines came to life.

The startled General Secretary shot a look at his soldiers, who appeared confused as if waiting for a command.

But before the soldiers could comprehend what was happening, Colonel Ivanov shoved Moon aside and swept an automatic pistol across the face of the interpreter with enough force to send her sprawling backward onto the floor, crashing into a cluster of lighting tripods. In one swift motion, the barrel of the gun came to rest against the North Korean leader's temple.

In almost the same instant, the door leading to the ship's aft compartments burst open. Victor, Krystof, and Alexei rushed onto the bridge, their silenced, automatic weapons flashing, looking to those on shore and deck no different from the camera flashes moments earlier.

The *Pitcairn's* bridge flashed with gunfire and the deck bloomed with scarlet ribbons of blood as one-by-one the soldiers were taken down before they had a chance to react and shoot back. In quick succession, muted thuds from the KGB agents' guns cut down the Korean TV crew scrambling to escape. Cotten heard bodies fall onto the steel floor, bringing with them the crash of stands and equipment. It took only seconds for the carnage to end and the ship's bridge to fall quiet.

UNDERWAY

"ARE YOU INSANE?" THE interpreter said, trying to lift herself up as blood dripped from her lip. She looked around at the dead bodies with fear in her eyes. "Do you realize what you have done?"

Colonel Ivanov kept his pistol pressed against the General Secretary's head as he glanced at her. "Speak again and we will need new translator." He looked at his friends. "Okay lazy bastards, must get ship underway." He grabbed the General Secretary by the arm and hoisted him up from his chair. "Bullshit interview over." He shoved the Korean leader up against the back wall of the bridge and forced him to sit on the floor.

Alexei and Krystof kicked bodies out of their way as they yanked cables from the lights and smashed cameras, leaving the bridge lit only by one remaining TV light and the glow from the ship's instruments.

Ivanov forced the interpreter through the door to the outside deck facing the park. "Tell soldiers Korean boss wants to go for boat ride. Tell them cast off lines." He emphasized his words by squeezing her arm.

"I will not!" She stood defiant until he pulled her wrist behind her and into an awkward position up her back. She groaned.

"Last chance to translate for Vladimir." He jerked her arm higher, causing the woman to bend over with a shriek.

"All right," she said, breathless, and shouted the orders in Korean.

Cotten watched the soldiers along the deck hesitate as if uncertain what to do. It also attracted the attention of the men in the park. They turned and stared toward the ship, obviously confused by the fact that black smoke poured from the exhaust funnels as the engines roared.

"Tell them get off ship," Ivanov said, shoving her arm upwards.

Cotten expected to hear the woman's bones breaking at any second.

The Korean called out the orders again, and the soldiers began making their way down the gangway to the shore. Others ran to pull the heavy cables off the dockside mooring posts and drop them into the water.

Ivanov heaved the woman back through the door to the bridge. "Clear," he called to Victor.

Cotten watched the former Russian destroyer captain jam the throttles forward and spin the wheel to port. She heard the sound of metal grinding and ripping as the gangway pulled free of the deck and fell with a huge splash into the river. The bow of the *Pitcairn* inched away from shore and moved past the stern of the *Pueblo*, missing the old ship by inches.

Through the window overlooking the park, Cotten saw the officials running around in panic as they must have finally understood what was happening—their Dear Leader was taken hostage. It was then that she realized something was wrong—someone was missing.

Cotten turned and scanned the bridge, counting heads and searching faces. "Where is Dr. Chung?"

Ivanov jerked up as he looked around the shadowy confines of the ship's bridge.

Cotten spun back to the window. In the glow of the spotty streetlamps beyond the park, she saw a black Mercedes limousine shoot away from the curb. In an instant she knew the Black Needles mastermind had escaped.

—

Moon's anger blazed as the accelerating car slammed her back into the leather seat. "Faster!" she screamed to the young soldier she had commandeered from the park. The Stone woman was about to ruin everything. All of Moon's plans, her years of work, teetered on the brink of collapse. She pounded her fist into the armrest. How could this have happened? How could Dear Leader have put so much trust in the mysterious Old Man and allowed him to bring that vile woman into their midst?

All Moon needed to do was get back to the lab and give the final attack commands. And that was what she intended to do. Two days premature should not make a difference at this point. The result would be the same—fear, panic, death. She did not need Dear Leader. She was the avenging angel about to strike. From her fingers, she would send the computer message and launch her terrible plague. She did it for her country. For her parents. The imperialist aggressors would pay for their crimes. She was judge and jury. And she had reached a verdict.

"Faster!" she ordered.

THE DECISION

THE REACTION OF THE Korean authorities was swift. The *Pitcairn* had not traveled more than a quarter of a mile before the emergency lights of police vehicles appeared on both sides of the broad Taedong River. Soon after that, a number of small police boats sped out of the darkness and began circling. As the ship slipped under the Chungsong Bridge and passed by Turu Island, larger naval gunboats roared at them from both directions, followed by combat helicopter gunships circling overhead. Searchlights lit up the research vessel, and shrill commands amplified from the speaker systems of the gunboats blasted the *Pitcairn* with what Cotten knew had to be orders to halt and shut down.

"They are demanding you stop immediately," the interpreter said. "Or they will fire upon us."

"And risk killing big-shot boss?" Ivanov said, tapping the pistol barrel on the top of the General Secretary's head. "No chance." He turned to Cotten. "We keep going, right?"

"We have no choice," she said, despondent over Dr. Chung's escape.

The General Secretary spoke, and his assistant interpreted. "Dear Leader informs you that you have failed. Dr. Chung is going to the lab to give the final Black Needles launch order. There is nothing you can do to stop her. He says that if you give up now he will see to it that your lives are spared."

Victor had pushed the throttles to their stops, causing the ship to pick up speed along the river. He turned to the others. "We stop, we die. Korean pricks are lying bastards."

The woman said something to the General Secretary and he replied. Then she said, "Dear Leader assures you that you will not be executed. Your mission has failed. Once Dr. Chung issues the final launch commands, there is nothing you or anyone can do to stop what will happen next. Give up now and you will be shown—"

Colonel Ivanov reared his hand back in a threat to strike her. She grimaced, but the blow never came. Instead, he said, "Shut mouth or I shut for you."

Feeling the weight of looming defeat pushing her down, Cotten dropped into her chair as her thoughts raced. She watched the searchlights sweep over the decks of the *Pitcairn* and flood the bridge with blinding light. The whooping of the helicopters overhead shook her dwindling courage, and the blast of the bullhorn commands kept her from concentrating. It had seemed like such a simple plan to kidnap the Korean leader and Dr. Chung, and escape on the ship. Now, with Chung gone, the General Secretary was right. Dr. Chung would issue the orders and there would be no stopping the virus from killing millions, and the world as she knew it from coming apart. Cotten felt she was resisting the inevitable. At some point, the military would storm the ship and rescue the General Secretary. She and her friends would wind up dead or spending the rest of their lives in a Korean prison. Either way, it was time to make a decision—surrender and cut her losses.

She stood, composing her words in her head to give Victor the order to shut the ship's engines down. At least she had saved John. She slipped her hand in her pocket and touched his crucifix, and suddenly she realized she had a solution.

The answer had been there all along, but somehow she hadn't seen it. Her hand closed around the cross. Cotten shook her head in dismay at her lack of faith, and she smiled at the simple clarity of what she had to do.

"I'm going to leave you for a while," she said.

Everyone's head turned in her direction. The interpreter whispered to the General Secretary, and he donned a confused expression.

"What?" Colonel Ivanov asked. "No place to go."

"It's something I must do," Cotten said. "Trust me. I have no choice. I should have done this before now, before I put your lives at risk."

"You have lost mind," Krystof said, standing beside the exit from the bridge to the deck. "Go outside and they fill you with bullets."

Cotten stood beside Krystof and placed her palm on his cheek. "Trust me like I trusted you." Then she opened the heavy metal door and stepped into the glare of the searchlights.

Remember ye implored
The assistance of your Lord,
And He answered you:
"I will assist you
With a thousand of the angels,
Ranks on ranks."
—Koran vs. viii. 9

STARDUST

COTTEN STOOD ON THE open deck of the *Pitcairn,* knowing she was an exposed target for the Korean snipers. But she had to trust, had to believe. She must force back the Darkness or it would win.

Trembling, Cotten lifted John's cross and chain from her pocket and raised it in her clenched fist toward the sky.

"I call upon the Almighty Creator of the Universe to send down His Heavenly Host. I call upon His legions of angels and archangels to bring His swift and just wrath upon this place. I call upon the armies of Heaven to stand beside me and strike out at the Darkness."

The ship picked up speed along the Taedong River, and she had to shield her eyes with her arm from the lights of the hundreds of military vehicles and circling aircraft that illuminated the vessel. Cotten closed her eyes, knowing that she had played her last card.

There was nothing more to be done. Either her gamble would work, or she was breathing her last breath.

"I pity you, Daughter of Furmiel," the Old Man said, coming to stand beside her on the ship's deck. "Why can't you just acquiesce to the fact that you have lost? There is no reason for you to stand here risking your life. Do you not understand that you have finally come home? Your real family welcomes you with open arms. Embrace your fate, your heritage, your true calling. Have I not given you what you wish? Do not be afraid. This is what you are, what you were meant to be."

Her anger grew as the Darkness inside her swelled. Hate festered inside. She wanted to reach out and rip open his flesh, spill his wicked blood on the steel plates at her feet.

Cotten pressed her fingers to her temples. She had to fight back. It was him putting the hate into her mind. It was his evil rankling inside her. The true meaning of the Darkness was showing itself.

"Embrace your family, Daughter of Furmiel," the Old Man said, his voice reminding her of a serpent's hiss.

Cotten had to still his voice, to rid herself of him. What had she learned along this journey of life? *Think, Cotten, think. Concentrate.* The thoughts came slow at first, deliberately constructed, then gained momentum until they tumbled like water over the falls. The blood that flowed through her was *not* only that of the Fallen.

She carried the bloodline of the angels.

Those who had chosen to fall from grace had done so of their own free will—their choosing. But their blood was still the same as all angels. And inside her flowed the heritage of those angels of Heaven as well as what God regarded as his most precious creation—man. The realization that she was the perfect mix of natural and supernatural made her quiver. Now, for the first time in her long, strange journey, she understood.

Perhaps the passage into the Darkness was the only way for her to be shown the truth and who she really was—to make her aware of the goodness inside her. The fact that she was standing there, resisting, fighting, rejecting the Darkness, was the real proof of life—her life.

Turning away from the Old Man, she raised her arm, letting the cross dangle from her hand. Tears flowed down her cheeks as the floodlights glimmered off the metal's surface.

But this time the light took on a strange, ethereal transformation. Instead of reflecting off the metal, it appeared to be emitting *from* the surface. Like golden waves on a glistening ocean, its brilliance grew to a blinding white that rushed across the surface of the river and up onto the shore. It swept through the air in a flash of blast-furnace intensity.

Then it transformed again, breaking apart into smaller fragments. Each fragment formed a star-shape that spun like a top. The sound of the spinning filled the air to a whirling roar as thousands, then millions of stars covered the surrounding river and enveloped the ship. As the stars spun, they showered down sparkling dust that settled upon the vessel, giving it the appearance of being coated with crushed diamonds.

"What is this?" the Old Man said, glancing around. He seemed to be taken aback by the transforming light. "A trick? Do you honestly believe you can trick me? There is no form of deceit that I did not invent."

"Maybe you missed one," Cotten said.

For he shall give his angels charge over you,
to keep you in all your ways.
They shall bear you up in their hands,
lest you dash your foot against a stone.
—Psalm 91:11-12

THUNDERCLAP

EVEN IN THE BLINDING glow of the stardust, Cotten saw the fiery hate filling the Old Man's eyes as his face contorted with rage.

"Did you think you could outwit me?" he said. "I gave you every chance I could to make you one of us. But you have denied the truth—down deep in your soul you are just like me."

Cotten met his glare with equal determination. "I am nothing like you."

"It no longer matters, Daughter of Furmiel. It is over—you have lost. For I am about to consume this place in the fires of hell."

In the next instant, Cotten saw them coming up the river. A few at first, then more and more. Tiny pinpoints of pale red light gathering and multiplying.

Fireflies. She immediately recognized them as demons taking the form of innocent-looking insects—Satan's legion summoned to do his bidding. Their deceiving glow reflected off the Taedong River like tiny rubies.

Cotten turned toward the stern of the ship and saw an equal number of fireflies coming from the direction of the city of Pyong-yang. Thousands, perhaps millions of tiny dots of light swarming toward her.

When the first wave of fireflies met the spinning stars, an ear-splitting thunderclap cracked across the water and shook the ship, sending Cotten crashing to the deck. The blinding glare of the stardust caused her to again shield her eyes.

Another thunderclap, like a supersonic jet breaking the sound barrier, slammed into the steel skin of the *Pitcairn*. For a second, Cotten believed the rivets holding the vessel together would pop from the metal and cause it to break apart.

Standing over her was the Old Man. He seemed frozen in place, staring straight ahead, fixated on the raging battle taking place around him. At times, he fell out of focus like the distortion of an image through heat rising.

Cotten felt the ship gaining speed, and she strained to see the shore in the blinding white light of the spinning stars. The *Pitcairn* was well beyond the city, passing forests and countryside, their details shooting by like raindrops on the window of a speeding car. Great foaming waves, caused by the momentum of the racing ship, folded from its bow and rushed toward the banks.

She tried to stand, but with each attempt she was thrown back to the deck as the concussion from another thunderclap slammed into the ship.

And with each blast, the stars spun faster, causing the fireflies' glow and numbers to diminish.

Cotten strained to see the Old Man, wondering just what he saw through his eyes. Could he see the angels themselves? Or his demons? His shape undulated, becoming a mirage as he watched the Host of Heaven and the Forces of Hell collide in a raging battle.

A scorching wind screamed across the deck like a gale over the crest of a desert dune. Stinging pinpricks blasted Cotten's skin, the sand-like particles spraying off the dissolving form of the Old Man as the wind eroded his body. His features disappeared until only his clothes whipped and snapped. Then they, too, rose up onto the blistering cyclone and disappeared into the stardust.

———

The ship trembled and quaked, shuddering all the way to its keel. The General Secretary cried out as he was thrown against a bulkhead of the bridge.

"Dear Leader!" the interpreter called.

He lay on the floor. "Where are my soldiers? My army? Why have they not come to rescue me?"

A moment later, parts of the ship's interior—the instruments, the helm, and the controls—flashed before falling back into the darkness that had engulfed the bridge since Cotten left.

"Am I dying?" he cried.

The lights flickered again, illuminating the bodies scattered around the deck. The cycle of deafening thunder and the flashes of light followed by darkness went on for what seemed like hours until the ship suddenly stopped rocking and shaking. A dead calm fell over the vessel.

The General Secretary sat up, working to move his limbs.

Beside him lay a haggard and weak-looking Colonel Ivanov.

Slowly, everyone struggled to their feet. Like dreamers awakening from a long sleep, they made their way to the windows. The water was as flat as slate, and the sky devoid of clouds. The sun had just emerged over the horizon, its golden orb ablaze on the surface of the sea.

Everyone turned at the sound of the metal latch clinking as the door to the bridge opened.

BLOCKADE

COTTEN ENTERED THE BRIDGE of the *Pitcairn,* followed by a number of men in military uniform. She scanned the control center of the research vessel, then gazed at each of the living and the dead. Her friends stood around with dazed and confused expressions. Victor, the white-haired grandfatherly man with thick glasses and crooked teeth, was still at the helm, but his white knuckles revealed that he held the wheel with a death grip. Krystof, the skinny little man with sad eyes and a perpetual growth of stubble, sat in the corner holding his head in his hands. The overweight Alexei leaned against the back wall, staring at the ceiling. And Colonel Ivanov still kept his pistol aimed at the Korean leader who was sitting beside the interpreter, her body prone on the floor.

As they all finally focused on Cotten, she said, "This is United States Navy Commander Walter J. Phillips, captain of the missile frigate, USS *Robert G. Bradley.*"

As her words seemed to bring them back to reality, everyone looked from Cotten to the officer and the other men who now entered the bridge. There was a mixture of naval personnel and armed U.S. Marines. Behind them came medics who went to each person, checking for injuries. All the survivors had been bumped around enough during the mysterious assault on the ship that they bore cuts and bruises.

Commander Phillips walked over to the interpreter and said, "Inform the General Secretary that he is in no danger. He is temporarily in my custody and under my protection."

She translated Phillips' words. The Korean leader rose to his feet and stood straight and proper, obviously trying to maintain his dignity.

"My God," Colonel Ivanov said. He had wandered over to the windows overlooking the port side of the ship.

"Sweet Jesus," Krystof said, joining him.

The interpreter, who was now standing, also went to the window and gasped, bringing her hand up to cover her mouth.

Stretching across the bright horizon were more than thirty warships, many bearing the flag of the United States, but others flying the colors of the United Kingdom, Australia, and Japan. The *Bradley* lay closest, perhaps a few hundred yards away. The others, ranging from destroyers, frigates, supply ships, and missile cruisers, lay scattered across the water beyond, with helicopters circling overhead. A number of motor launches shuttled between the *Pitcairn* and the other ships.

"Where are we?" Ivanov asked.

"Approximately one hundred kilometers off the west coast of North Korea," Phillips said.

"How could we have come so far?" Alexei asked. "And how did you find us?"

The interpreter translated their questions to the General Secretary.

"We came upon the *Pitcairn* just before dawn," Phillips said. "Your ship was powerless and adrift. How you got here we have no clue."

The Korean leader spoke and the woman translated, "Why are all these warships here?"

Phillips gave the General Secretary a stern look. "There are over 150 United States and allied warships off the east and west coasts of your country, about to put into place a total naval blockade. This is in response to the biological attack you have launched on our countries. Yesterday, President Brennan, the United States Congress, and the governments of our allies authorized the block-ade. I fully expect that the Congress will enact a declaration of war against North Korea within the next forty-eight hours. And before noon today, the Secretary of Defense and the Foreign Minister of the United Kingdom will be arriving here to inform you of the terms of surrender."

The woman translated the message. Cotten watched the General Secretary's face turn red. It was obvious he didn't like what he heard.

Through clenched teeth, he spoke in a rapid pace to his inter-preter. She said, "This is preposterous. I will not surrender to you or anyone. The charges you have made are unfounded and with-out merit. I demand to be released immediately."

Cotten stepped forward to give him even worse news, details Commander Phillips had told her a few moments earlier after he landed on the *Pitcairn*'s helo pad. "Tell your Dear Leader that Dr. Chung's attempt to send the final launch commands was intercepted and blocked. There will be no further Black Needles attacks. And the combination of medications that were used to halt the advance of the viral infection on Cardinal Tyler are now being adapted and used in hospitals throughout the world to stop and reverse the effects of the disease. Your grand plan to attack us and our friends is over. I would suggest you start to consider how quickly you will accept the unconditional terms of your surrender. Commander Phillips has assured me that the alternative will not be pleasant for you or the future of your country."

As the interpreter relayed Cotten's words, the Korean leader became noticeably deflated. Slowly, he moved to the big chair he had so recently filled with pomp and bluster, and dropped into it with the weight of dejection and gloom.

"Not taking news well," Colonel Ivanov said. "Big shot becomes little prick."

"That about sums it up," Cotten said as she turned and left the bridge of the *Pitcairn* for the last time.

FALLEN

As SHE DROVE FROM her hotel to the Georgetown University Medical Center, Cotten rehearsed what she would say to John. She knew she would have to tell him *everything*. But as much as she longed to see him, she dreaded revealing what she had done to save his life.

Now she waited beside the nurse's station for several minutes before having the courage to go down the hall and into John's room. Finally, gripping a handful of red carnations, she went to his door. After acknowledging the young Venatori agent nearby, Cotten knocked.

"Come in," John said. He stood by a window dressed in his robe, pajamas, and slippers. As he turned around, a smile spread across his face when he saw her standing in the doorway.

At first, she was shocked, fully expecting him to still be in bed hooked to tubes and monitoring devices. She finally smiled back, realizing that his rapid recovery was even more impressive than Ted had described.

A curious look came over him when she didn't move. "What's the matter?"

"Nothing." She went to him, slipped her arms around his waist, and held him tightly.

He hugged her back.

"It's truly a miracle seeing you like this. The last time I was here ... well, you look so much better now." She released him and placed the flowers on the narrow table stretching over his bed that still held the tray from breakfast.

"They're beautiful," John said. "I'll see if the nurse can find a vase."

"I thought red would be nice. Still too wintry for yellow. And red is appropriate for a cardinal, don't you think?"

"Absolutely."

Cotten glanced at a copy of the newspaper lying at the foot of his bed. The headlines read: *North Korean leader agrees to peace terms, turns over Black Needles mastermind to International Criminal Court.* A second story covered the death of the pope. "I'm sorry to hear about the pontiff."

"He's finally at rest. He put up a long courageous fight, but the cancer finally won."

"I'm sure the Vatican is anxious to get you back."

"They've requested I return as soon as the doctors release me."

"Have you heard anything more about what will happen to Dr. Chung?"

"Archbishop Montiagro was here earlier with the news about the Holy Father. He mentioned that Dr. Chung will be charged with crimes against humanity. No doubt she'll spend the rest of her life in prison. Given her deteriorating health, that might not be too long." John pointed to two chairs, and they both sat. "Okay, Cotten, what's on your mind? I can tell you want to say something, but can't quite get it out."

She scooted her chair close enough to reach out and take his hand in hers. "You know me so well."

"And you know that you can tell me anything."

She could tell him anything, but this was going to be the hardest of all. Every word she had rehearsed fled her mind. Leaning back in the chair, she took a deep breath. "The last time I was here, you weren't conscious. The doctors believed you were dying, and I blamed myself for that."

"Cotten—"

"No, it's true. Just listen. This is hard enough. Let me get through it."

"Okay."

"I was angry—angry with myself, with the world, with God. Right outside this hospital I cursed Him and everything around me. I cried out for help. Moments later, my cries were answered, but not from God. I had a visit from someone you know well, the Son of the Dawn. He reminded me of my legacy and who I am."

John sighed and shook his head.

"He told me that if I would give in to my heritage and embrace the person I really am, your life would be spared. John, that's all I wanted—just to have you live. I had brought you so much trouble and suffering over the years. I realized that it was finally enough. He was right about who I really am. And because of that, I had the power to save your life. So, I agreed."

She searched John's eyes for a reaction, for disgust or rejection. But she saw none of that, and her heart lifted.

"It was arranged for me to go to North Korea—to protect me from the risk of being infected by the Black Needles attacks. He also wanted to exploit my reputation as a journalist. I was to conduct an interview with the Communist leader. The interview was designed to glorify the General Secretary and help set him up in a place of power once his enemies started falling from the plague."

Once Cotten started, the rest of the story flowed out until she finally finished with the miraculous escape of the *Pitcairn* and how President Brennan had taken John's words to heart, admitted the possible threat, and called for a coalition of nations to form a naval blockade in preparation for a possible invasion. A multi-nation military exercise in the region helped get the warships into position within a few days of Cotten's arrival in North Korea.

"You've been—"

Cotten held her hand up. "There's more. Look at me. Look hard. You see before you a person who essentially sold her soul. And, John, here is the most frightening part of all. It was easy. So very easy. His argument made sense—all he asked was that I love myself. He told me that it isn't wrong to be strong, and happy, and prosperous. He said God wants us to always turn the other cheek, give and not receive, to depend on him for even our tiniest seconds of happiness."

"But—"

"I know, I know. You've told me before. He is a liar. I know that now. But I want you to understand why it could be so easy to give in. He said to me that his way doesn't mean I have to become a bad person. Simply love myself and enjoy the pleasures of the world. Such things are not here so that I can deny myself. Do you see how that could make someone feel?" She didn't expect John to answer. "It made me think about a lot of things I hadn't before. Like there is no hierarchy to the Ten Commandments. God doesn't separate *Thou shalt not bear false witness* from *Thou shalt not kill.* One is no more acceptable than the other. So how many times a day do we all slip over that line, say a tiny lie, covet something, or simply put ourselves first? In those moments, within some of those minute-by-minute decisions we make every day, are we surrendering to the Darkness like I did? Do we so easily slip in and out without thinking about it? And when we do cross that invisible line, do we become like him?"

"Fallen?"

ANOTHER TIME, ANOTHER PLACE

"NONE OF US ARE without sin." John paused while a nurse came in to take his vitals. Once she had left, he continued, "We are imperfect beings, Cotten. God doesn't expect us to be perfect."

She closed her eyes. "Sins of the father..." she whispered, then looked up. "What about me? I made a bargain knowing full well what it meant. It wasn't just telling a little white lie or stealing an apple from the fruit stand."

John shook his head. "Like you said, there is no hierarchy. And did you really go through with it? No, you fought it, drove the Darkness back. You couldn't do it."

"But I would have if I had to. I was willing to do anything to save your life. Anything."

"And for that and everything else you've done for me, I can never repay you." This time, it was John who reached to take her hand. "What you've just gone through is all behind you now. It's over. There's no need for us to talk about it ever again." He rubbed the top of her hand with his thumb. "It's part of the past. Okay?"

Cotten sandwiched his hand between hers. "Okay."

"So tell me more about how you got our old KGB buddies involved?"

"I didn't really know what it would be like or what would happen to me once I ..."

"Once you made the deal and agreed to his terms?"

"Right. So I realized I had to make all the arrangements I could before I left for North Korea. I discussed many ideas with Ted, none of which we could predict would be possible once I was there. I knew that if there was a chance of success, and you were safe, I would try to plan some way to turn the tables. But to do it, I would need a way to escape. I also knew I had to have help, and once inside that country, chances would be slim of getting any. The Fallen's first mistake was to tell me before leaving that I would be interviewing the Communist leader, and that it would take place aboard the *Pitcairn*. And the only reason anybody knew that was because the General Secretary was making such a big deal about the one-year anniversary of the *Pitcairn*'s capture, and he wanted to flaunt it. He's the one who insisted the interview take place on the ship. But who was going to help me? Certainly not anyone from the United States. We already knew that, for whatever reason, the President had downplayed the whole thing—something I still don't understand. Then it occurred to me that people from other countries, especially non-Western countries and those who still have ties with North Korea, are allowed to visit there as tourists. I told Ted to get in touch with the colonel to try to work out the details of a plan. After all, they had offered to help me anytime I needed. I knew that once I was over there, I'd be shut off from the rest of the world. As it turned out, Colonel Ivanov and his buddies easily entered the country as tourists. But until the moment the colonel walked onboard the ship with Dr. Chung, I was never 100 percent sure they could pull it off."

"You're amazing," John said.

Cotten smiled. "Thanks." She looked toward the window, deep in thought. The hard part was about to come, and she needed all the courage she could marshal.

Finally, she said, "I've made some decisions since getting back. This whole experience has had a profound impact on me. I have so many questions and very few answers. John, I need time to rethink my life." She breathed out a big sigh. "It's no secret how I feel about you. I tried to ignore the reality of what our relationship was, is, and could be. But I've come to terms with the fact that we can never be more than dear friends."

Cotten felt John's hand slip from between hers. At first she thought he was offended in some way, but then she felt his hand close around hers.

"There are many things," John said, "that would be worse than being dear friends. And you know how I feel. Everything you're saying is completely understandable, including the wanting to get away and rethink your future. We've been through a lot together. Despite our own personal feelings, we have chosen paths in life that are not destined to come together."

Reality settled into her heart and she felt profoundly sad. "How many times have we said that maybe in another time, another place, things might have been different? But not in this lifetime. There's nothing I can do to change that, nor can you. You are destined for great things, John. And what lies ahead for me is as much a mystery as ever. Even though I've been the cause of so much trouble for you, I haven't been able to let you go. That's not fair to you." Her face scrunched as she blinked back tears. "Talk about crossing that line on a daily basis and putting yourself first. I'm the poster child."

She choked up and had to wait a moment before she could get her voice back. "I have to stop. Enough is enough. And the only way I can get my head together is to take a break—a long break. I don't mean just from you, I mean from my job, my life, the rest of the world."

"If that's what you think it will take, Cotten," John said. "You've been through more than anyone I've ever known. Perhaps it will give you a chance to find yourself, but more importantly, find your relationship with God. Remember, he's always there waiting for you."

"I know that as soon as possible you'll be leaving for Rome. I wish we had a few days just to talk, to spend time together that was without a crisis and conflict. No battles to fight." Cotten rolled her tearing eyes. "There, you see, I'm doing it again. I know how important it is you get back to Rome quickly, and I'm wishing in my heart that you could stay."

"I would stay a little longer if it weren't for the funeral of the Holy Father. Will you be going to Rome to cover the story?"

"I can't imagine Ted assigning it to anyone else. But it would have to be my last assignment. I really do mean to get away for a while and get my life in order."

There was a moment of nervous silence, then Cotten cleared her throat to prevent whatever she said next from sounding strangled in tears. Cotten stood. "John, before I go, I have something for you." She reached for her purse. Removing a small, white box, she emptied the contents into her hand. Then she took his hand, turned it palm up, and dropped his gold cross and chain into it. She folded his fingers around it.

John rose from the chair and pulled her into his arms. "I so wish that it could be different for us. I want more than anything for you to find happiness, Cotten."

They held each other for a long time before letting go. She took a step back and looked into his eyes. A faint smile emerged on her lips. "Maybe in another time, another place."

WHITE SMOKE

COTTEN SAT IN THE network anchor booth inside St. Peter's Square and went over her notes from a Vatican expert in canon law and consultant to SNN. Early that morning the College of Cardinals had convened to elect the new pope. In tradition, after each round of voting, their ballots were counted and then burned in a small stove. Its famous chimney was clearly visible from St. Peter's Square. Custom held that if there was a failed ballot, wet straw was added to the ballots to make the smoke black. Upon a successful ballot, white smoke swirls into the sky.

Two hours ago a dramatic and unusual event took place. As millions watched on television, listened to the radio, or stood in St. Peter's Square, white smoke had curled into the sky after the first ballot. Now those same millions waited patiently to learn the identity of their new pontiff.

SNN was running regular programming, but stood ready to cut in with any breaking news from Rome.

"I'm taking a breather," Cotten said, removing her earpiece and unhooking the lapel mic.

A few moments later, she strolled through the cordoned-off press area, turning from time to time to gaze at St. Peter's Basilica and the rooftop of the Sistine Chapel just to its right. John was in there somewhere, surrounded by his fellow cardinals, probably congratulating the newly elected pope. She could imagine him assuring the new pontiff of his loyalty and devotion. As director of the Venatori, he might even be giving the pope a summary of the latest global situations he would face in the first few days of the new papacy.

How wonderful for him, she thought. He was immersed in his element, all that he loved and cherished. But as the thought came to her, she felt a door seem to close in her heart. A deep sadness rolled gently over her. John knew she was there covering the election, and he would probably try to get in touch with her before she left. But she thought it better not to see him. It would be too hard to say goodbye again.

Her thoughts were interrupted by a firm tap on her shoulder. "Cotten, get back to the booth." It was one of the production assistants. "They're about to make the announcement," he said.

The two hustled back to the SNN booth and Cotten took her seat next to the monsignor consultant. She gave a quick sound level and confirmed she could hear the director instructing her through the earpiece. They were about to go live.

A huge roar rose up from the throngs of people at the appearance of the Cardinal Deacon. He emerged on the balcony outside the central window of St. Peter's Basilica. Since the seventeenth century, this was the window from which the newly elected pope would appear and give his first papal blessing. The Cardinal Deacon's voice rang out through the Basilica's public address system. He spread his arms wide and said in Latin, "*Annuntio vobis gaudium magnum.*"

The crowd erupted in an even louder cheer.

"This is it," the monsignor said to Cotten. "We are about to receive the formal announcement."

"It's certainly an electrifying moment, Father." She watched her monitor as the camera zoomed in on the balcony.

From the speakers came the words, "*Habemus Papam!*"

"We have a pope," the monsignor said, translating the Latin.

Next came, "*Eminentissimum ac reverendissimum dominum. Dominum* John."

Cotten turned to the monsignor, a sense of trepidation trickling through her. She'd clearly heard the Deacon say *John.*

"The winning candidate's first name is John," said the monsignor. "Next will be the surname."

Cotten's eyes raced down the list of cardinal's names on her desk. Three were named John. There was John Tyler, of course ... As she stared at his name, the loud speakers came alive with the Deacon's next words.

HEAVEN ON EARTH

TED CASSELMAN PROPPED HIS glass of Stoli and cranberry juice on his thigh and leaned back in his living room recliner. The image of an unfurled ancient scroll rotated on his flat screen plasma while music that reminded him of "Chariots of Fire" pounded through his Bose surround-sound speakers. With a solid black backdrop and spotlights focused on the scroll, the inscribed gazelle skin appeared incredibly intact, considering it was at least 5,000 years old. The title of the *Relic*'s segment appeared: *Heaven on Earth*.

Ted took another sip.

The camera panned across rugged, mountainous terrain, until a figure could be seen in the distance. Zooming in, the image revealed Cotten as she stood beside the entrance to a cave opening at the base of a cliff. She looked better than Ted had seen her in a long time, a glowing happiness that, even on the screen, appeared to permeate her every cell.

"Just a year ago," Cotten said, "here in the rocky, inhospitable terrain, not far from where the Dead Sea Scrolls were discovered more than half a century ago, famed archaeologist John Tyler unearthed an ancient Essene repository of historical and religious documents, one of which is the fascinating scroll you just saw on your screen. The Essenes were a Jewish religious sect that flourished from the second century BC to the first century AD. This document however, unlike others found in the region, was not inscribed by the Essenes, but was protected and handed down by them through generations. And why would that be? Why would the Essenes believe this scroll to be so valuable that they guarded and preserved it along with their own most precious documents? That's what we'll try to answer as we follow the journey of the Essene Scroll and reveal its secret, coming up right after this."

During the commercial break, Ted smiled at how Cotten had introduced John—*famed archaeologist John Tyler*—not former priest John Tyler. He was sure that many viewers recognized John from the news accounts of the former Roman Catholic cardinal who gave up the priesthood to pursue his calling in the secular world. But what had never been made public was that as a cardinal, John had come to the threshold of the papacy. Just a year and a half ago, he stood before the College of Cardinals inside the secrecy of the Sistine Chapel conclave and declined to be considered a candidate. He stated that at last he understood God's plan for him, and the restrictions of the papacy were not part of it.

As the commercial ended and *Relics* returned, Ted's attention was drawn back to the rotating scroll.

Wide angle of Cotten with mountainous desert landscape behind.

"The inscription on the leather scroll appeared to be in pro-Elamite," she said, "the oldest known writing system of Iran. It was used briefly around three thousand years ago, and previous samples have never been deciphered. Dr. Tyler has been conservative regarding this discovery, not publicizing it or making speculations on the information in the text. That is until now. With the aid and cooperation of the National Security Agency and their highly sophisticated decryption tools, the script of this amazing artifact has finally been translated. And what it says may change all of us forever.

"Dr. Tyler tells us that even at first glance he thought he had something fantastic. And after a closer look, he was sure of it. So, what is it about this particular scroll, besides its age, that makes it such a treasure?"

Close-up on John coming to stand beside Cotten.

"Let's begin with the prophet Enoch," John said, "who lived around three thousand BC. Enoch is mentioned several times in Genesis, and his genealogy can also be found in the Old Testament. Enoch was the son of Jared, father of Methuselah, and great-grandfather of Noah. In the Qur'an, Enoch is called Idris, to the Greeks he is the same as Mercury, or Hermes Trismegistus who wrote the Emerald Tablets of Thoth. The Talmud tells of how when people on Earth went astray, Enoch lived a pious life, and by his sermons and speeches made the people give up idolatry and obey God's commands.

"Amazingly, Enoch is said to have lived for 365 years, a relatively short time compared to other patriarchs of the period before the Great Flood. But even that is not what makes Enoch so extraordinary. You see, God was so pleased with Enoch that he was taken up by God to Heaven, not once, but twice. The first time Enoch ascended to Heaven, he spent sixty days there and was shown all the secrets of Paradise. Before returning to Earth, it is said he wrote 366 books that he passed on to his sons. He was also made the guardian of the treasures of Heaven. A year later, God took him up again. Enoch never experienced death. Genesis five, verse twenty-four: *And Enoch walked with God: and he was not seen again, for God took him.*"

Close-up of the scroll with Cotten's voiceover.

"So again, we are asking what is so exceptional about this scroll, and what does it have to do with the prophet Enoch? Realizing the possible importance of this ancient document, Dr. Tyler worked with the NSA to have it deciphered. Though previous pro-Elamite texts had failed to be decoded, miraculously, this time there was success and the script was interpreted. Everyone was stunned by its staggering contents. You are now looking at a document scribed by Enoch on his return to Earth after his first ascension to Paradise."

Two-shot of John and Cotten.

John said, "The prophet Enoch writes that God permitted him to take three unique treasures of Heaven back to Earth. Once here, he hid the treasures away, and this scroll, scribed in Enoch's hand, tells the secret location of those treasures."

Close-up of John.

"Could it be that in the very near future we will be looking at undeniable proof of Heaven?"

Close-up of Cotten.

"Reporting for Satellite News Network from the remote banks of the Dead Sea, this is Cotten Stone Tyler."

THE END

Joe Moore (Florida) spent twenty-five years in the television post-production industry where he received two regional Emmy® awards for individual achievement in audio mixing. As a freelance writer, Joe reviewed fiction for the *Fort Lauderdale Sun-Sentinel*, the *Tampa Tribune*, and the *Jacksonville Florida Times Union*. He is a member of the International Thriller Writers, the Authors Guild, and Mystery Writers of America.

Lynn Sholes (Florida) is the writing coach for Citrus County Schools in South Florida. Writing as Lynn Armistead McKee, she penned six historical novels set in pre-Columbian Florida. As Lynn Sholes, she has changed genres and is writing mystery/thrillers. Lynn is a member of Mystery Writers of America, International Thriller Writers, Florida Writers Association, the Authors Guild, Sisters in Crime, and the National Council of Teachers of English.

WWW.MIDNIGHTINKBOOKS.COM

From the gritty streets of New York City to sacred tombs in the Middle East, it's always midnight somewhere. Join us online at any hour for fresh new voices in mystery fiction.

At midnightinkbooks.com you'll also find our author blog, new and upcoming books, events, book club questions, excerpts, mystery resources, and more.

MIDNIGHT INK ORDERING INFORMATION

Order Online:
• Visit our website www.midnightinkbooks.com, select your books, and order them on our secure server.

Order by Phone:
• Call toll-free within the U.S. and Canada at
  1-888-NITE-INK (1-888-648-3465)

• We accept VISA, MasterCard, and American Express

Order by Mail:
Send the full price of your order (MN residents add 6.5% sales tax) in U.S. funds, plus postage & handling to:

Midnight Ink
2143 Wooddale Drive, Dept 978-0-7387-1317-5
Woodbury, MN 55125-2989

Postage & Handling:
Standard (U.S., Mexico, & Canada). If your order is:
  $24.99 and under, add $3.00
  $25.00 and over, FREE STANDARD SHIPPING

AK, HI, PR: $15.00 for one book plus $1.00 for each additional book.

International Orders (airmail only):
  $16.00 for one book plus $3.00 for each additional book

Orders are processed within 2 business days. Please allow for normal shipping time. Postage and handling rates subject to change.